CORRADO

THE GUZZI
LEGACY BOOK 1

BETHANY-KRIS

www.bethanykris.com

Editor: Elizabeth Peters

Proofreaders: Tracy A., Mia B., Tori W. and Felicia F.

Cover Design © Under Cover Designs

Interior Design: Under Cover Designs

ISBN: 978-1-988197-93-7

For Tori and Sasha and London, who encouraged me to write these boys and their girl before anyone else ever knew they were going to be a thing.

CONTENTS

CHAPTER 1	1
CHAPTER 2	10
CHAPTER 3	21
CHAPTER 4	33
CHAPTER 5	41
CHAPTER 6	52
CHAPTER 7	63
CHAPTER 8	75
CHAPTER 9	90
CHAPTER 10	99
CHAPTER 11	117
CHAPTER 12	131
CHAPTER 13	142
CHAPTER 14	152
CHAPTER 15	170
CHAPTER 16	185
CHAPTER 17	195
CHAPTER 18	206
CHAPTER 19	216
CHAPTER 20	227
CHAPTER 21	237
CHAPTER 22	248
CHAPTER 23	260
CHAPTER 24	269
CHAPTER 25	282
CHAPTER 26	295
CHAPTER 27	303
CHAPTER 28	314
CHAPTER 29	321
CHAPTER 30	332
CHAPTER 31	340

ABOUT THE AUTHOR   349
BOOKS BY BETHANY-KRIS   351

PART ONE
BEFORE

CHAPTER 1
CORRADO

Koi no yokan.

Corrado read those words, inked in a script font and hidden on the inner elbow of his family priest's arm. It was the only time he ever noticed the tattoo, and that said something considering he attended this church since he was a newborn. They had christened him in this place. His first communion had been an interesting experience as a kid with a church of more than four hundred parishioners watching. Catholicism for the Guzzis was a second skin—the church, a second home. He recognized these walls inside and out.

But not that tattoo.

"What does that mean?" he asked.

The priest—Father Gene, they called him—looked up from the papers he'd been moving aside on his desk. The office, a mixture of dark woods, richly colored tapestries, smelled of old leather, and even older books. Compliments of the row of texts that looked like they had seen better days lining the shelves behind the priest's desk.

"What, Corrado?"

"That, there," Corrado said, pointing at the black script on the priest's inner elbow. "What do the words mean?"

Father Gene's hand came up to cover the small spot of ink as a smile curved his lips. "Something you wouldn't understand at seventeen, I assure you. And we're not here to talk about tattoos I had done before I joined the priesthood."

"How old were you, then?" Corrado tipped his head to the side. "When you joined?"

"I started the process at nineteen."

"So, you had the tattoo before then, but you won't tell me what it means because I won't understand because of my age?"

Father Gene stared at him from across the desk, silent. His father, Gian, would say this was one of *those* times. Out of all his siblings, including his identical twin, Corrado was the one who spoke when he should stay quiet.

He'd rather talk about other shit than what he came here for.

"Are we asking about my tattoo because you're attempting to avoid the conversation about your lack of confession for two years?"

Corrado stared at the cross over the window to his right rather than at the priest. "I don't need to do confession."

"But your father believes something is wrong ... he's the one who asked me to bring you in for a session of counsel, didn't he?"

He was smart, so he stayed quiet when he had nothing good to say. Like right now.

The priest didn't miss it.

"I'm worried about you," the man across the desk admitted. "You graduated high school three weeks ago, and according to your father, you have yet to decide on a *real* path of what you want to do. And without getting into the specifics of your father's business, because without me explaining that to *you,* he knows I don't approve, I'm concerned you will flounder with no stability to hold on to. No work, no college ... no *faith*."

Corrado's gaze snapped back to the priest. "I have faith."

He was sure of that. The problem? His faith and doctrine had taught him that certain parts of himself weren't *right*.

He found comfort in church, but he also found confusion, too.

"If you tell me why you stopped confession, and why you're struggling to move forward in your life, I will tell you what the tattoo means," Father Gene said, grinning. "And whatever you tell me, that will never go beyond these walls."

"Not even to my parents?"

"Not even to them, Corrado."

He stared down at where he'd clasped his hands in his lap. This way, he wouldn't fidget or distract himself. He didn't need his nerves on display. Another thing being a Guzzi had taught him—the appearance of calm and confidence was *most* important, but especially in their life.

Corrado was far from stupid, and he could tell what people assumed when they saw him. They assumed because he ran around with Guzzi blood in his veins, that like his older brother, Marcus, and even his twin, Chris, he would be the same and go into the family business.

La famiglia.

The mafia.

His last name said so. The legacy that came with it kept the demand alive. Tradition. Men in this life followed their father's footsteps, and even more so when one's father just happened to be *Gian* Guzzi—Cosa Nostra Don, controlling the largest and most powerful crime family in Canada. It was expected of Corrado; history said so.

Except his father. Gian never said a word about it. Not to Corrado.

"You're struggling," the priest said, his French clear. Maybe because he assumed it would comfort Corrado. The only person who spoke French to him now, besides associates of his father, *was* Gian. He didn't see his father's French-Italian side of the family enough to speak anything with them. "I can see."

"I'm not like them," Corrado said.

Father Gene raised a single eyebrow high as he leaned forward to rest his clasped hands on the desk. "Why would you say that?"

He'd been ready to spill his secret, to admit why he was, in fact, struggling between life and business. The reason for his lack of a decision, and his waffling.

"Corrado?"

He swallowed hard and stared down at his hands again. "I stopped coming to confession at fifteen because I had sex."

The priest sat back in his chair. "Oh." And then, the man added with a laugh, "That's not a reason to stop confessing, it's a reason *to* confess, Corrado."

"With another guy," he added lower.

That quieted Father Gene.

Corrado shifted in the high-back leather chair the longer the silence dragged on. "That's partly a lie. I had sex with a girl before that, but—"

"I understand," the priest murmured.

"This is not … our way." Corrado shrugged. "I hear what people say—inside this church, and outside, about people like me. In business, it's a weakness. Here, it's a sin. Except I can't be different, and so, I don't fit in."

He'd always been this way.

At first, Corrado didn't know what to label his sexuality. In high school, the only gay kid he was acquainted with—at the time—got treated like a second-class human. Because he liked girls, too, that helped to keep his attraction to guys under everyone else's radar. He kept it to himself because if that was how people behaved with someone at school, what would happen outside?

And then a new student came in—a guy that Corrado watched from afar as he navigated the terrain of private,

Catholic school. He wasn't sure what clued him in about the fact the guy was more like him than the other students, or even the one gay student in their school, but it happened.

Corrado learned a lot about himself from that. Bisexuality was fluid, and hard to explain to someone who wasn't like him. Being with a guy didn't change the fact he still liked the way the girl's legs looked in her skirt from the school down the road. Except to everyone else, it seemed like they didn't *get that*.

Gay was gay. Straight was straight. There was no in between. That's what people said.

Corrado was right in the fucking middle, trying to figure out what it meant, and what he should do. Stuck between a culture his family was deeply ingrained in that told him he would never *belong*—he couldn't *be*—and the choice of disappointing those around him when he didn't decide what they wanted for him.

He couldn't win.

Guzzis always won.

"Corrado, if you want me to say sex before marriage is not a sin, I can't do that," the priest said, dragging him from his thoughts.

"It's not the sex that worried me."

The man across the desk smiled softly. "No, I imagine you worried about the *other* bits."

He shrugged.

"If you want me to tell you homosexual attraction is not a sin, then I can't do that, either," the priest murmured.

Corrado let out a hard sigh, and readied to stand from the chair. The meeting was pointless. This wasn't news. He hadn't expected to get a different answer than the one he had.

He should have known better.

They all thought the same thing:

He was *wrong*.

He didn't belong.

He was different.

And because he was a Catholic, and the son of an Italian mafia boss, his problem was on a more prominent display for him about just how much he didn't fit in anywhere. He couldn't explain that to those around him without giving away his secret though.

"Sit down," Father Gene said.

Corrado passed the man a look. "I think we're good here, yeah?"

"If you didn't notice, allow me to point out to you what you missed about my statement," Father Gene replied, pointing a finger at the chair. Corrado sat his ass back down because he didn't have a choice, honestly. "I treated the sin of sex before marriage with the same tone and respect as I did homosexuality. Because sin is sin. And sin, no matter who is doing it, is all the same. The thing people seem to forget is that we do not get to weigh one sin against the other to bolster our own sanctity and pureness, Corrado. One sin does not trump another—sin is *sin*."

The man shrugged, adding, "And we are all sinners. That is what Christ teaches us. It is why Jesus died on the cross for *us*. Because He recognized we were all sinners, and we would all need forgiveness not once, but throughout our lifetime. People wrongly assume that their faith, and the way they live within the truth of their faith is the same way everyone else should, too, but they don't understand that isn't how it works."

Corrado chewed on his inner cheek. "How does it work, then?"

"Faith is a discipline for your own morality, Corrado, but it is not a right to dictate to others about *theirs*. And it would be ignorant for me to assume anything about someone else's relationship with God, or their right to faith. I know *my* relationship with God; it is strong, and I hear Him, drawing me to my path and calling. So, because of that, I share His words, and I celebrate them—I do not dictate His words like a tyrant from the pulpit. That defeats the purpose of the Bible, and of *Him*."

Corrado stared down at his lap, the gold Guzzi signet ring on his index finger glinting under the office light overheard. "So, what does that mean for me?"

"It means you are allowed to have faith, and your own relationship with God, and no one should expect to understand that relationship, or define it for themselves. They have their own faith to worry about before they need to even consider yours. It means you may be a sinner, and *no one* can or should tell you that your sins are worse than theirs because they don't sin like you do. It doesn't matter—sin is still *sin*. And yes, I believe you should aspire to live a life free of sin, but it's impossible. Even Jesus sinned, Corrado."

"Huh."

Out of the corner of his eye, he saw the priest smile again. "Not the answer you were expecting?"

"No."

"I'm sorry that people seem to interpret the Word in their own way without seeing the bigger picture. That's not your fault, Corrado. It is their own flaw."

He nodded. "It doesn't help me to make a choice, though."

Father Gene cleared his throat. "About your father, and business?"

"Yeah, all of that."

"Knowing Gian like I do, I think he will be happy as long as you are, young man. It is a matter of finding what makes *you* happy. Do you understand?"

Possibly.

"I think so," Corrado said.

"Good. Confession after the New Year. I expect to see you here. Also, I hear you're heading to Vegas this weekend —a trip for business with your father, yes?"

Yeah, a whole trip Corrado did not understand, if he were being honest. When Gian traveled for *la familiga*, he was quick to point out to his sons all the details of the organization they would be seeing. He liked for his boys to learn, so they never stepped out of line when it counted or caused a problem.

This time, his father said nothing.

Corrado wasn't sure what to expect.

"Safe travels," the priest told him, "I'll pray for it."

"Thank you, Father."

Corrado pushed up from the chair, moving to leave. It was only Father Gene's voice behind him that made his steps hesitate.

"Don't I owe you, now?"

Seemingly lighter on his feet, and like he could do something with what he learned here today, Corrado had no idea what he forgot. Giving the priest a glance over his shoulder, he asked, "And what's that?"

"*Koi no yokan*," the priest said, and Corrado's gaze darted to the tattoo on the man's inner elbow. "It's Japanese, and it doesn't have a meaning as much as *what* it is. A *feeling*, Corrado. It is the feeling upon meeting someone you know, eventually, you will fall in love with that person."

"Like love at first sight?"

"No. It's something else entirely."

"Is it a real thing?"

"It was for me," the man murmured.

He had a realization, then.

Like the priest said, they all sinned; their sins were simply different.

"You must tell me if it ever happens to you, too," Father Gene said. "Gian is waiting for you, isn't he? Have a blessed day."

CHAPTER 2
CORRADO

"What is this fucking place?"

Gian gave Christopher a look over his shoulder that quieted Corrado's twin *fast*. The oldest between the two of them, Chris, was far more likely to toe the line and behave. Corrado, on the other hand, seemed to find some sort of trouble wherever he went.

Life wasn't fun otherwise.

Today, both twins pushed their father's limits.

Chris side-eyed Corrado when their father's back was turned. If it were anyone else, he might have to ask what they were thinking in that moment. But it was his twin, and he never had to ask. When one shared the same face as someone else in the world, even their expressions could explain the things they didn't say.

The two took after their father in appearance—brown eyes flaked with gold, straight noses with a sharp slope, full lips that always seemed to be smirking, and dark brown hair that, when not cut into a shorter style, seemed to be fucking unmanageable. They took the angular shaped faces from their mother, Cara, though.

The rest?

All their dad.

Corrado shrugged to answer his brother's unspoken question about the building they were currently approaching. Deep in Nevada's rural, dry land, they might as well be in the middle of nowhere. There weren't even power lines out this far. It felt like they drove for hours after exiting their father's private jet only to turn off on a gravel road that still led to fucking *nowhere*. Until all of the sudden, a tan building—or rather, what seemed like several buildings, although it was hard to tell—started to form on the horizon.

A few trees towered around the building that, partly looked like a warehouse but also brought to mind the word *compound*, when Corrado thought about it. The plain cement walkway didn't give anything away about the place, but the very expensive cars parked any which way they wanted to stop next to the side of the building made him think something was happening here.

Out in the middle of the desert, apparently.

"Was that a fucking *tumbleweed?*" Corrado asked, his gaze drifting to the line of cars again and the dry item that skipped behind a black Hummer.

"If you two don't fix your mouths and questions," Gian murmured a few steps ahead. "Correct it before we go inside, *s'il vous plait.*"

"I'm just saying horror movies start like this, Papa."

Gian made a noise under his breath but said nothing else. At the front of the building, there were no windows. Just a wall of tan-colored brick and a black door. *Stark* black, really. One couldn't miss how it stood out blatantly compared to the rest of the yellow earth and walls surrounding it. Above the door rested a camera blinking with a red light.

Silently, Gian pulled a card from his pocket. Corrado glanced at it quickly, taking in the matte black cardstock, the wax seal on the back side with a cursive *L* stamped into it, and the white, classic lettering on the front.

What did it say?

The League, Corrado thought.

What in the hell was—

His thought process was interrupted by a buzzing noise that was loud enough to scare a scavenging bird sitting on top of the entrance door's eave. It squeaked before flying off to rest somewhere else. By the time Corrado glanced at his father, both Gian and Chris were already heading inside the dimmed corridor of the tan building.

Ha.

Just like how the fucking horror movies started.

"Are you coming?" Chris called back to him.

Corrado didn't think he had a choice, even if he didn't like the feeling this strange place left him with in his gut. Like a heavy weight had come to rest there, and he wasn't about to get rid of it anytime soon. He didn't pretend to understand all his father's business—being a criminal organization meant Gian did not dabble with just *one* thing. He had his hands in several pots, and Corrado was not aware of every single one of them.

Was this just another thing?

Why were *they* brought here?

Why not Marcus, their oldest brother?

He didn't consider Bene or Beni, his youngest brothers—another set of identical twins in their family; their mother's genes were strong, it seemed. Those two were wild, and there was no way they'd relax enough for something like this.

"Corrado!"

"I'm coming," he snapped.

Not that he wanted to. He had the distinct feeling that once he stepped inside this building, something was going to change. Maybe for him, or his brother or father, he didn't know. He just had that feeling, and Corrado wasn't the type to ignore his gut when it acted up.

Slipping inside the building, but not before shooting one last look over his shoulder at the outside world, his gaze took a second to adjust to the dim lighting just beyond the black door. A door, which, closed without prompting once Corrado was out of the way while doing that annoying buzzing sound again.

Gian slipped the black card he'd flashed at the camera back into his pocket before turning to his sons, his expression a mask of nothingness. He didn't give anything away before he said, "A couple of decades ago, I was approached by an old friend to ... invest in something. He had a plan—he wanted a League of people who could do many things, and who had many skills. Did someone need a robbery done? He had a person for it. A hit in another country on a political figure? There was someone for that. A retrieval of someone that had been missing? He could make it happen."

His father rubbed his hands together and glanced down a long hallway that led to yet another black door with a camera blinking red overhead. "The idea was interesting because imagine what someone could do with that kind of ability at their fingertips. I invested immediately. I invested *a lot*. And it has been incredibly beneficial for me in the long run. Here is where those people are trained."

Beside Corrado, his twin blinked. "Like mercenaries?"

Gian chuckled, and waved a finger at the older of the two twins. "Mercenaries are choosey—they *pick* what they want to do or who they want to work for, and often, their work is for the greater good even if they are doing bad things."

"Assassins," Corrado said. "They train assassins here."

"Smart boy," his father returned. "We call it The League. This is the new complex that was finished three months ago, but I haven't had time to make the trip to see how it turned out. I thought the two of you might enjoy getting a peek at another part of this business because you're ... at an age to come into the folds more than you already are."

Gian said that like he honestly meant what he said— directed at *both* his sons—but he really only looked at

Corrado. Was his father giving him another choice? Something other than what everyone else expected from him?

"This building is a living quarters, office, and training complex," Gian said. "Behave while we're here, *oui*, and try to stay out of trouble while I meet with my partner. Do you both understand me?"

Chris nodded first.

Corrado came second, but now, he didn't have that heavy feeling about this place like he did when he first stepped inside. He just wanted to know *more*.

~

Corrado was enthralled with the fact that the deeper they went into the complex, the more it seemed like a maze of living areas for *several* people. He saw those people, too, but they barely spoke as they moved from room to room, doing their business.

He stopped just outside of one room and peered in as his father headed further down the hall with a laugh.

"Dare," he heard Gian greet.

Corrado was busy staring at all the knives lining the wall inside the room in front of him. And when he meant a *wall* of knives, it was more like three walls. It wasn't all knives, he realized as he took one step inside to get a slightly better look. No, it was several different kinds of weapons, but all meant to be sharp and deadly.

At the far end of the room, which looked to be at least thirty feet long, if he were to guess, was a wall of targets. Wooden, mostly, with paper figures taped across them. One in particular still had an axe right through the head of the paper figure.

He swallowed hard as he neared the wall of black knives with sleek, shiny blades. He didn't know if his twin had continued to follow his father, or not. These knives were far more interesting to him than anything else at the moment.

Reaching up, he drifted his fingertips along the edge of a six-inch knife that he bet would be quite heavy in his hand. Wrapping his fingers around the hilt, he pulled the weapon down from its spot on the wall to get a better look at it. Eyeing the targets at the other end of the room, he wondered if he might be able to hit one—

"Careful with that. Rich hands aren't meant to throw those; they're meant to pay someone else to do it."

Corrado spun around so fast, the navy-blue walls of the room were nothing more than a blur to his eyes. He found the source of the voice standing in the doorway of the room. The man standing there took Corrado by surprise. Not because he was strikingly handsome—he was—but because he didn't look much older than Corrado's seventeen.

The guy arched a thick, dark eyebrow when Corrado stayed quiet. The action made his strong features and stormy blue eyes all the more intense. His thin lips pulled into a sly smirk, making his square jaw, covered with a few days' worth of stubble, tighten with the movement. A slight shake of his head made the shaggy hair that seemed a little too long around his ears fly in all directions. Corrado tried to shake off the strange hum buzzing over him the longer he stared at the guy. He wasn't the first good-looking person he'd run into, and he wouldn't be the last. He didn't need to feel stupid or speechless just *because* this guy looked half decent.

Except, that wasn't it at all.

It was the way the man *looked* at him. The way his gaze drifted over Corrado with the slowness that reminded him of a predator, maybe. Like this guy had just found prey, and he was considering whether the kill would be worth it.

It *irked* Corrado.

Irritated him like nothing fucking else.

He wasn't *prey*.

"What did you just say?" Corrado asked.

The guy laughed and tipped his head to the side as he pointed at the knife in Corrado's hands. "Be careful, we don't need you cutting yourself because you wouldn't know what to do with a knife unless you were paying someone else to do it for you. Clear enough?"

Okay.

Yeah.

Corrado wasn't even going to act like that was a comment he could brush off as though it hadn't been said at all. This guy wasn't even *trying* to be subtle about it; he was outright insulting Corrado, and with a fucking smile at the same time.

"Do I know you?" he asked.

The guy peeked over his shoulder, looking at something down the hall. "Not yet, but you will."

That humming sensation was back again. It kind of pissed Corrado off that the guy could be so dismissive and insulting to him, while at the same time, acting like he had better things to do than stand there and have a conversation with him. He remembered his father's warning about behaving, but he was *very* close to telling this guy to fuck off right before he busted his mouth for those comments while he was at it.

"How about," Corrado started to say, "you go find someone else to—"

"Alessio."

The guy's gaze drifted back to Corrado, his eyebrow still arched high like he didn't have a damn to give, as a new voice sounded right outside the doorway of the room. Almost as soon as the voice spoke, a new face came to the doorway, and clapped a hand on the guy's shoulder. Right behind him stood Corrado's father.

Gian stayed back a couple of steps, though.

He didn't intrude.

"Introducing yourself, Alessio?" the man asked.

Alessio.

Corrado decided right then that he hated that name. And the man it belonged to, as well. The problem was, when Alessio turned his gaze back on Corrado, the humming was back. He couldn't look away from the ocean of blue that stared back at him, or the way that as much as this guy rubbed him wrong … he wanted to know *why.*

Or anything about him at all.

"You're not causing trouble, are you, Corrado?" his father asked out in the hallway.

"Define trouble." Alessio chuckled. "Is he allowed to play with knives where someone can't keep an eye on him at the same time?"

The man next to Alessio smacked him in the back of the head, making him glower back at him.

"Fuck off, Dare," Alessio muttered.

"Play nice, Les."

He looked back to Corrado again.

"But why, though? This is way more fun."

Fuck him.

And the fact Corrado found he liked it.

Yeah, fuck that, too.

The other man, *Dare,* shook his head. "All right, Les, since you're feeling chatty today, you can take Corrado around and show him the rest of the complex while I talk business with Gian."

Alessio scowled. "I didn't volunteer to be some mafia *principe's* babysitter for the day."

Dare smirked. "I'm sorry. Did I preface that with, *if you feel up to it and it pleases your spoiled fucking ass to do it*? No, so do it."

"Fine."

"Did you introduce yourself properly?"

"No," Alessio said. "Because I didn't think there was a point."

Dare sighed and waved between the two boys. "Alessio, you already know Corrado Guzzi ... or you know what I told you about today. Corrado, meet the pain in my ass, also known as Alessio Sorrento."

"Thanks for that."

"But not a lie," Dare replied. "And now my good deed for the day is done. Gian, do you think these two will be fine alone?"

Corrado's father smiled a bit, amusement playing in his gaze as he nodded. "I think they'll be fine while we chat."

"Good, let's begin."

Alessio passed Corrado another look as Gian and Dare drifted away from the doorway, disappearing altogether. "Are you going to stand there all day, or what?"

Corrado didn't move. "I'm not doing anything with you."

"Yeah, that's not going to work. Dare said what he said."

"Fuck him, *and* you."

"Oh, he *swears*, too."

Corrado's jaw flexed with his annoyance. "What is your problem?"

Alessio looked him over again, his gaze slow and deliberate. All over again, Corrado felt that same flare of frustration and interest all rolled into one. It warred inside his mind, clashing together and making him want to punch this guy in the mouth just because.

"Do you like what you see, or ...?"

"Why, because I stare?" Alessio asked.

"Because your stare *lingers*. So, that means you either like what you see, or you're trying to decide if I'm a threat. I think you know who I am, and you think you know something about me."

Corrado replaced the knife on the wall, and headed for the door, only stopping directly in front of Alessio. He knew what this guy was doing—trying to size him up, but also make him feel out of place. Screw that noise. He didn't know his purpose for being here, but he wasn't going to run because of *Alessio*.

He leaned in close to Alessio, but the guy didn't move back an inch. If anything, he stayed firm in his spot, those blue eyes blazing with the same interest Corrado was sure reflected in his own gaze. "Let me be the first to fix that mistake of yours—you don't know fuck all about me, Alessio."

"I prefer Les."

Corrado tipped his chin up. "*And?*"

"And right now I'm wondering what your face might look like if I roughened it up a little. Do you box?"

He *blinked*.

"What?"

Alessio shrugged. "I didn't stutter."

He hadn't.

"Do you want to get your ass kicked?" Corrado asked. "Because that's what'll happen if we spar."

The man *laughed*.

And all Corrado could think was that he looked fucking amazing doing it. That smirk on his face? Entirely bad for him given the way his chest tightened at the sight of it.

Oh, yeah.

He was in a lot of trouble here.

It all started and ended with Alessio.

He knew it by the annoyance still trickling through his bloodstream, but also the humming that continued to buzz over his skin. A part of him wanted to tell his guy to fuck off somewhere, and another part wanted to find out all he could about him. He had a feeling the more he learned about Alessio, the less annoyed Corrado would feel, and the more interesting the man would become.

All it took were a few words, and blue eyes. Something about Alessio Sorrento drew Corrado in and made every single one of his nerves turn on in a good and bad way. He wanted to run away as much as he wanted to stay right there and do it all over again.

Was this what the priest meant?

Was this *koi no yokan*?

Because it felt like something.

It felt like change.

It felt important.

Well, fuck that noise.

Corrado didn't like it at all.

"Guess we'll see what you can do, *principe*," Alessio said, grinning just enough to show off his white teeth. "Or, I'll have a lot of fun watching you try."

CHAPTER 3
ALESSIO

By the age of ten, Alessio had learned the most important lesson he figured life had to teach him. It wasn't an easy one, or even *nice*. Very little about life was easy or nice, though. That lesson was simple, too.

Blood didn't always make family.

When he was two, his father died from a heart attack. A man he never really remembered, and only vaguely knew from the stories of others. Maximo Sorrento—mafia Don to a Cosa Nostra faction controlling Vegas, who also seemed to have a taste for women who were a fraction of his age. Like Alessio's mother, Elizabeth.

His father dying wasn't the memory that stood out to him the most, but rather how everyone else treated his mother, the man's mistress, after the fact. She'd lived comfortably, Alessio had been told, cared for and kept because she was a favorite of Maximo's, and she had given him a son, even if the boy was illegitimate.

Then, he was no more.

No, Alessio didn't remember his father dying, and he didn't have many feelings about it, but he vividly recalled the years that followed the death. Like how his mother spiraled, her young life wasted with every pill she popped, and every needle she put into her veins. Empty bottles littering the floor and the faint smell of old cigarette smoke accompanied Alessio's dreams every time he closed his eyes.

That was how he remembered his mother.

And that he never mattered to her.

Whether it was because she was so entirely heartbroken that she had lost Maximo, despite the fact he was three times her age, or because she had lost her status and importance without him there to give it to her ... she forgot about Alessio in the process.

He was ten when his mother overdosed.

Ten when he buried her.

Yet, it felt like he'd been in the process of burying her for years before that. Life had a funny way of reminding the forgotten and the neglected at the worst of times that they weren't worth very much to the people who weren't faced with their struggle every single day. That had never been more apparent to Alessio than after his mother's death.

That was when Dare came in.

And Cree, another high-ranking member of The League.

Alessio was never sure *when* they found him after his mother's death, because the days passed by in a confusing blur that he'd rather not revisit, but they were a saving grace for him if there ever was one. Dare, having known Alessio's mother *before* Maximo, took him in.

For all purposes, Dare was his family.

The League, his home.

Here, he struggled *more*. Here, he learned to be something and someone. Behind these walls, he was given a purpose and stability. He was not the forgotten bastard son of a man who he didn't remember, or the child of an addict who died not knowing her son would be the one to find her cold on the floor the next morning.

Here, he was better.

At seventeen, almost eighteen now, Alessio spent much of his life feeling as though he didn't belong to any one person or place. Until Dare, Cree, and The League. He held this place so close to that thing in his chest that people called a heart, no one would ever understand. If someone thought to fuck with it, he was going to *rip them apart*.

And so, it pissed Alessio off to see some privileged prick like Corrado Guzzi walking around the place with a curious eye like he had any business being there in the first place. Sure, Dare was smart enough to explain to Alessio the week before the Guzzis arrival that Gian would be visiting to check out the new complex, with two of his five sons, but it hadn't bothered him until he saw one of those sons in that training room.

One of many training rooms here, really.

People didn't get an *inside* look at The League. If someone was brought in, it was because they were a client using one of the assassins for a job, or it was a prospect who had signed on to be trained.

No one was allowed here.

It was *his* home.

Except, there came the fucking Guzzis like they owned the place, and that just rubbed him all kinds of wrong. But especially Corrado—who thought to speak to Alessio like the two were on equal footing in some kind of way. Like he wasn't any different from him.

They were not at all the same.

He doubted a rich, spoiled mafia *principe* like Corrado had ever understood struggle, and The League certainly wasn't a place made for someone like him. They weren't here to *coddle* men and women—they were here to break them.

So yeah, the guy just rubbed him wrong.

The other thing pissing him off currently?

The fact he found Corrado attractive, and that he might like the guy even more if he could shut him the fuck up by either kissing him, or stuffing something in his mouth. Like maybe his cock …

"Are we even supposed to be in here doing this?" Corrado asked from inside the boxing ring.

Alessio made a harsh noise under his breath—the only sign of his irritation, really. He suspected Corrado believed it was because he questioned Alessio's choice to have them spar for fun in the gym section of the complex, but that wasn't it at all.

It was that he'd interrupted a nice picture.

He wasn't about to admit that out loud, though. Thing was, just because *he* felt attraction to someone didn't mean they felt the same way. Sometimes, it was obvious, and he could tell when a guy liked one thing or the other—or *both*. Maybe it was the way a guy would look him over, or when a hand on his shoulder lingered a beat longer than a straight guy would when it came to friendly actions. But with Corrado, he didn't know.

It was fucked up.

He hated him on sight.

And he didn't hate him at the same time.

It didn't help that Corrado *was* attractive in a way most men weren't. Something that Alessio recognized about him straight away—an air of confidence and cockiness followed him around whether he knew it or not. Like he'd been *born* with it. Most people had to learn that shit. And that was before Alessio got too detailed in Corrado's physical features, from the strong lines of his face that made up an angular jaw line, to the dark brown eyes that didn't seem to give anything away, not even when he *smirked*.

Classically handsome.

Disgustingly so, really.

Add that to the whole confidence shit and Alessio had a big problem here. Mostly, the fact that he noticed *at all*.

Dare was always clear when it came to Alessio and relationships or sex. As long as it didn't fuck up The League and the shit they were doing here, he was free to explore and do what he wanted. He couldn't remember how old he was when he figured out he liked boys as much as he liked girls—nine, maybe?

He was lucky that he didn't find confusion or pain in his sexuality swinging both ways like he knew some did when they realized they were bisexual. Here, he had been free to explore and find out what it meant to be a sexual being with varied interests. No one ever stepped in to shame him as long as it was consensual, and he was being safe. That was all Dare ever cared about when it came to Alessio.

"Are you listening to me?" Corrado asked.

Alessio clenched his teeth to stay quiet as he finished wrapping up his fists before slipping the leather, fingerless gloves overtop. Turning to find Corrado lingering in the far corner of the ring, ready to go, he used his teeth to tighten the wrist straps on the gloves.

"Are you used to just saying something, and people *jumping* to give you what you want?" Alessio asked back.

Corrado's brow dipped before he scowled.

Fuck.

Why'd he look good doing that, too?

Alessio ignored the clenching of his gut as he stepped up into the ring and dipped under the ropes to get into position. He figured this sparring match probably wouldn't end well for Corrado, all things considered. He doubted the guy knew he'd been training with The League from the time he was twelve.

Weapons.

Fighting.

Recon.

Killing.

All of it, he could do.

And he was only seventeen.

He doubted Corrado could say the same.

"What is it that gets under your skin the most?" Corrado asked back. "The fact that I have money, or the fact you don't?"

Alessio sucked air through his teeth.

Damn.

That was a good one.

Pretty boy mafia prince could cut with words, and Alessio liked that way more than he was willing to admit. His respect notched up a bit—this would have been incredibly boring for him if after everything, Corrado just laid down and took the shit Alessio threw at him. When someone became uninteresting to him, Alessio was quick to move the fuck on.

Not right now, though.

"You assume I don't have money," Alessio returned.

He did.

Probably not as much as Corrado, but he had enough to be more than comfortable. The longer he stayed with The League, the more money he would have, too. Not that money had ever been a motivating factor for his choice to train here. He'd gone for years without money—it was just paper to get someone by, nothing more.

He'd be fine either way.

Corrado shrugged before he tugged his T-shirt up over his head, and then tossed it to the side of the ring. Even from all the way across the ring, Alessio couldn't help but admire the hard lines that made up Corrado's body—or how those muscles shifted as he moved from one foot to the other.

Shit.

Yeah, he needed to move away from that thought.

Now.

"I say it," Corrado returned, "because you keep needling

at me like something about me pisses you off. Maybe it's my money, privilege … my last name. Which one is it?"

Nope.

He wasn't falling down that rabbit hole.

Alessio grinned, removing his own shirt and enjoying the way Corrado's gaze drifted over the ink on his arms, and the Bible passage written in script down his rib cage. His stare lingered a beat too long, but he wasn't going to point it out to the man, not when he still wasn't *sure*. He waved two fingers at Corrado as if to tell him *let's go*. "Don't worry, I'll go easy on you."

"No need. I have four brothers. If you think you're the first person who thought they could kick my ass because you had a problem with me, you're not even the *fourth*."

"Do you annoy your brothers just by *being* there as much as you do me?"

Corrado smirked and cocked his head to the side. "Do I annoy you, or unsettle you?"

That irked Alessio like nothing else.

Because the asshole wasn't wrong.

Back to the sparring, he figured. It was better than where his mind was trying to go, not to mention the way he was sure Corrado was looking at him. Like maybe he didn't need to wonder if the guy swung both ways like Alessio did …

"No cheap shots," Alessio warned.

"But your face is fair game, right?"

"Just like yours, Corrado."

Corrado nodded. "Fair enough."

Alessio intended for this little sparring match to be a quick thing for him—a way for him to knock Corrado down a few pegs, and nothing more. Yet, when the two young men met at the middle of the ring and tapped fingerless gloves together, he knew this wasn't going to be easy or clean between them at all.

They'd barely even moved their hands apart before Corrado came in with a jab to Alessio's right kidney. Who the fuck knew, but maybe he thought Corrado wouldn't know how to throw a half decent punch to save his life.

Ha.

He'd been so wrong.

That knocked the wind out of him.

"*Shit*," he grunted, backing up a quick step.

Corrado laughed, his tongue coming up in his sneer to touch his upper lip as he stepped back and forth from foot to foot.

He just looked *too* arrogant.

Too confident.

Too good.

It all looked *too damn good* to Alessio.

A challenge, even.

And fuck him, he liked those.

"Just one cheap shot," Corrado said, "don't fault me for doing it. You deserved it."

Alessio nodded and pointed his fist at his opponent. "You're going to regret that when I fuck up your face, asshole."

"But then what would you stare at when you think I'm not looking, Alessio?"

Yep.

So entirely fucked.

"I told you, it's *Les.*"

Corrado nodded. "That's nice."

All right, Alessio was done fucking around now. He wasn't wrong—Corrado didn't give up easily. And yeah, he didn't have the sharply honed skills with hand-to-hand combat like Alessio did, but he could still hold his own. He wasn't so stupid that he didn't know to protect his face, and he was quick on his feet, moving from one side of the mat to the other when he really wanted to get Alessio pissed off.

They were supposed to keep it clean, and Alessio fully intended on doing that until he realized *this* wasn't going to teach Corrado shit. So, when he had the chance and was close enough after tossing hits back and forth for a few minutes, he made his move. Spinning a bit on his left heel, he raised his right foot from the mat, and came back around with a roundhouse that landed flat to the middle of Corrado's chest.

The force of the kick sent him hitting the mat, all the air rushing out of his chest in a loud *whoosh* at the same time. Alessio might have enjoyed the sight of the other man on the mat, blinking like he was trying to gain his bearings and figure out how this happened to him, but he didn't get the chance.

Corrado swung his leg out, and swept Alessio's feet right out from under him. In the next breath, he found *himself* on the mat, too. A rookie mistake, really. He never should have gotten close to a man on the ground unless he was willing to get down there with him.

Lesson number *one*.

Not that Alessio had the time to reflect on his mistake. Corrado had rolled over just as fast to pin him to the mat as fists rained down on his face—one after the other; *smack, smack, smack, smack*. The guy was fucking relentless, never letting up for even a second. Through his gloved hands, Alessio was struck by the intensity that sharpened Corrado's features as he focused on his goal.

Alessio, that was.

And beating the hell out of him.

He'd be a damned liar if he said that hardness roughening the strong lines of Corrado's face as he clenched his teeth—blood dripping down his full lips from an earlier punch compliments of Alessio—and the muscles of his arms and shoulders flexing with every punch didn't *do something* for him.

Because it did.

Wicked things.

Sinful fucking things.

Godly things.

Alessio used a common maneuver that he'd been taught to flip the two of them over by wrapping his legs around Corrado's back. Now, with him on top, he focused his efforts on getting the image of Corrado on top of him out of his mind and replacing it with the sight of him beating the hell out of him, instead.

Not that it worked.

Of course, it didn't fucking work.

And unlike Alessio, Corrado didn't use a move to try and right himself again, or to get the upper hand. Because he wasn't trained, and he didn't know *how* to get out of this. Instead, his body arched upward, all of his weight pressing against Alessio as he tried to force the man off. It didn't work. Just like when he used his knees to push against Alessio's stomach, it too was a dead effort.

All it served to do was get their bodies closer.

His fists rained down.

Corrado protected his face and tried harder to get away.

Still, hard lines met hard lines. Alessio was hyper aware of the way Corrado felt moving under him, never mind the fact that *something* felt hard against the curve of the backside of his thigh.

Alessio pushed his fingerless gloves hard against Corrado's chest, his breaths coming out hard and fast because *fuck* … why was his body this tense—this *hot*? Beneath him, Corrado panted, too, his bloodstained teeth still clenched as he glared up at Alessio.

Corrado shifted again.

Alessio felt *that* again.

Time slowed, or that's what it felt like. There was no hiding the erection he was sitting on, or the fact that his own cock was pressing against the seam of his jeans. He swore if he moved again—or Corrado, for that matter—he was going to explode.

What in the hell just happened?

"I fucking *knew* it," Alessio whispered as Corrado tried to force him off again, but it only served to have the ridge of his erection pressing against his body again. "*I knew it.*"

Corrado's gaze darted away. "Get off me."

He would have.

But he leaned in close, instead.

A bloody sneer answered him back.

"Do you really want me to?" Alessio asked.

Corrado let out a hard breath. "*Fuck you.*"

He kissed him, then.

Brutal, and fast.

Unforgiving.

He didn't know what made him do it. God knew Alessio had more control than this, but here he was, and he couldn't really complain when Corrado answered him back with a kiss of his own that had his whole body feeling like it was on *fire*.

Corrado tasted like blood and *heat*. His tongue lashed against Alessio's without shame, his fingers coming up to drag against the muscles of his chest like he wanted more. He understood that need—it was currently driving him insane, too.

There was nothing easy about the kiss.

Nothing *soft*.

No sweetness.

It felt like war.

Teeth biting his lower lip, and stubble dragging across his

skin. It all felt like a fight he wasn't going to win but fuck him if he didn't *try*. Kissing never felt like war before—it didn't feel like his body was going to rip itself in half if he didn't *get what he wanted right now*.

Until this moment. With *Corrado*.

It was then that Alessio should have known what was going to happen here between him, and Corrado when this was all said and done. Corrado Guzzi was a fucking problem. One he was never going to escape.

Then, someone cleared their throat.

Ah, fuck.

CHAPTER 4
CORRADO

A throat clearing would have made Corrado jump back from the man he was kissing *fast*. But not Alessio. No, he didn't jump to get off Corrado, or even act like whoever had interrupted them bothered him in the slightest.

Before he did climb off Corrado on the mat, he pushed his gloved fists one more time against his chest and cocked a brow like he was daring him to *do something*. More than anything, Corrado wanted to do exactly that, but given the fact he was still hard under his jeans, and his mouth now tasted like *Alessio* and blood, he didn't think it would work out very well for him.

Corrado drew in another sharp breath, because even as Alessio left him alone on the mat to go to the other side of the ring, it didn't matter. His body still felt the man—his weight keeping him down, hard lines pressing into his, and those lips working savagely against his own. His tongue snaked out to run along his lower lip, and he *willed* his raging erection to go down just a little bit before he moved.

Pride was a bitch.

Corrado had too much of it.

It was only the sound of footsteps approaching the ring that finally made Corrado roll over to his knees and stand up from the mat. He shot a look over his shoulder to find Alessio at the other side of the ring, slipping on a T-shirt like he didn't have a care in the world. That irked Corrado a bit, too. How could he be so flippant about what just happened?

His fucking heart was *still* racing.

Christopher came up to the side of the ring and rested his arms along the ropes. His brother arched one eyebrow at him, a mirror of his own reflection right there staring back at him. He didn't need his brother to ask the question to *know* what Chris was asking him. *What in the hell was that?*

Corrado could count on two fingers the amount of people who knew he was bi. His brother was one of them because one day, Chris outright asked, and Corrado had never been able to lie to his twin for some fucking reason. The two weren't very much alike despite their identical features—Chris was more reserved, and Corrado wasn't; his brother tended to think things through, and Corrado went in full steam on something if he wanted to do it.

But lying?

Nope.

He never could.

If Chris didn't know he was lying right away, then Corrado felt like shit and eventually just spilled the truth to his twin, anyway. Because wasn't life just fucking grand like that?

Chris cleared his throat when Corrado stayed silent as he reached for his shirt hanging off the ropes of the ring. "Was that supposed to happen?"

"Mind your business."

"I am—you're my business."

Corrado shifted from foot to foot, punching his arms through the shirt before yanking it down over his head. All the while, he avoided his twin's stare like the plague. "Just … forget about it, Chris."

"All right, whatever. Papa's down the hall talking with that Dare guy."

"What were you doing?"

"Trailing behind you and …" Chris tipped his head in Alessio's direction, but Corrado refused to look that way. Not when he was still attempting to calm the semi hard-on he sported. "That one there. Did you forget I was here, too, or …?"

"*Vaffanculo*," Corrado muttered.

Chris smirked. "No judgement, if you're doing what you wanna do and all, I'm just saying you're not usually that obvious about it, you know?"

"Would you fucking knock it off?"

Laughter echoed from his brother.

Chris was enjoying this too much.

Heat flooded Corrado's face. He didn't even know it was possible for him to blush, but he was pretty sure his face was red. It wasn't *what* he had been doing that embarrassed him, but rather, that someone was there to see it. His *twin*, for that matter.

Not that Chris ever cared.

A part of Corrado knew his family didn't give a shit because his twin was a good indicator of how the rest of them would react if he outed the fact he was bi. It wasn't so much *them* as it was the people around them that concerned him at the end of the day.

Being the son of a criminal boss meant Corrado had to factor other people into their lives, as well. People who didn't share their blood or live in their home but would still think they had some right to speak about his sexuality either way. And it was those people who he didn't care to let in on his business.

Because they wouldn't shut the fuck up about it. Or, they wouldn't leave his father alone, or worse, blame him for something that no one could help. Which just pissed

Corrado off more because *he didn't need help*. He wasn't sick, and something wasn't wired differently inside his head.

To them, he would be wrong.

To them, he would be broken.

That's what they had taught him.

Except he couldn't be any of those things when he was just born this way. And so, he adopted his simple strategy about it all. If nobody thought to ask, then he didn't have fuck all to tell them. His family included. They could assume, and he was fine with that, but he wasn't offering the information up willingly.

"Round two another day, Guzzi?"

Corrado couldn't even hide the way Alessio's voice from across the ring affected him as it reached his spot. His back tensed, and all over again, he could feel the man's mouth coming down on his, and the way his fingers had dug into his chest as those fingerless leather gloves came down against his body. His jaw clenched, and outside the ring, Chris raised an eyebrow again, clearly not missing Corrado's odd behavior.

"Don't," he warned his twin.

His brother just laughed, hit the ropes of the ring with his hand, and stepped back like he was done with the conversation.

"Round two another day," came a new, deep voice.

Corrado spun around fast to find where the voice had come from. Parts of the gym were shrouded in darkness, the different lines of machines barely visible in the shadows as Alessio had only flicked on two light switches instead of the other fifteen. At the very far right end of the gym, a man leaning against the side of a treadmill watched Corrado.

His hair, a sleek black and braided, fell over broad shoulders. He'd hooked one leg over the other lazily as he used the machine to keep him upright, arms folded over his chest.

Corrado couldn't see the man's eye color until he moved closer—a dark russet brown. It complimented the golden brown of his skin, too.

"Fuck, *Cree*," Alessio said, giving the man a look as he neared the ring. "You could have let me know you were in here when I first came in."

Cree didn't bother to give Alessio his attention. "But why, so I could miss the show?"

That time, it was Alessio's turn to flush with a reddish color. Corrado would have laughed except he realized while he had also been on the mat, in a very compromising position. So, that *show* included him.

He chose to shut his mouth.

Cree pointed at Corrado. "*You.*"

He stiffened. "What about me?"

"You have a lot of anger, no?"

"What?"

The man used a closed fist to hit the middle of his chest, coming to a stop right outside the ropes of the ring. "Here, you have a lot of anger. And no place to do anything with it."

Corrado quieted.

Cree wasn't wrong.

Chris cleared his throat on the other side of the ring, but Corrado wasn't paying any attention to his brother because now, something else had his attention.

"How do you know that just by watching me?" Corrado asked.

Cree grinned a bit. "A talent."

"That's a non-answer."

"Smart, too," he said, finally directing a comment at Alessio. "And someone willing to put up with your shit. Congratulations on finding *that*, Les. I never thought you would."

Alessio opened his mouth, but Cree was quick to put up

a hand to shut the other man up before he could start. He snapped his jaw shut with an audible click, which made Cree smirk before he turned back to Corrado.

What just happened?

He felt like he missed something.

"Do you know, Corrado," he said, tipping his head in Alessio's direction, "that this one has a tendency to ... pick fights when he wants attention? Oh, he won't *say that*. He doesn't admit that's what he does." Cree pointed at his temple and narrowed his eyes with a suspicious smile as he added, "But I know because I watch him a lot. I watch *everyone* a lot. It's how I know what someone needs to break and make them."

"Would you fuck off some—"

"Quite enough from you," Cree told Alessio without even looking away from Corrado. "And *you*, Corrado, you have a lot of anger and nowhere to do something with it. I think you would learn a lot here."

Corrado blinked. "What?"

"I thought what I said was quite clear."

"Cree, you can't be fucking serious."

"I am," he returned to Alessio, "but it's not about you, so shut up."

"*Cree.*"

The native man didn't turn away from Corrado even as Alessio fumed at the other side of the ring. Corrado felt stupid—shocked, really.

"You mean here, at The League?"

Cree shrugged. "Why not?"

Alessio made a harsh noise under his breath, taking Cree's attention away from Corrado for a second. "If you think some privileged fuck from—"

The man waved a hand at Alessio like he was dismissing

him as he said, "Yes, I can see you have some issues you need to handle, too, Les. I'll come back to you."

That shut Alessio up *fast*.

It almost made Corrado want to ask what it was about Cree that clearly put Alessio on edge, but really, he figured he already knew. The man just seemed to know what everyone's bullshit was before they could even open their mouth and try to lie about it.

Cree came back to Corrado. "Well, what do you think?"

"Corrado," Chris said from behind him.

He stayed silent.

Considering ...

"And what's happening in here?"

Corrado didn't need to turn around to know his father had stepped into the gym. He continued staring at Cree, all the while, thinking about the man's offer. Cree answered for him.

"Actually," Cree said, looking to the side of Corrado's legs from his position on the floor below the ring to speak to Gian from across the room, "I was making an offer to your son."

Gian didn't miss a beat. "What kind of offer?"

"To join The League."

"Cree," came another voice.

Dare.

The guy his father had been talking to earlier.

Dare's simple statement of Cree's name sounded like a warning, but clearly not one Cree intended to heed as he only stared between Gian and Corrado.

"Corrado?"

At his father's call of his name, he glanced over his shoulder. For some reason, he was worried then that he might find disappointment in his father's eyes. Even though Gian never outright told Corrado what he had to do—be a made man like him, or anything else he wanted to be—a part of him still wondered what his father *really* felt about it all.

"Yeah, Papa?"

Gian smiled, though it was faint and barely there at all. "It's your choice. It's always been, *fils.*"

Cree clapped his hands loudly. "Great. And what do you say, Corrado?"

It was only his twin speaking up from behind Corrado that broke his stretch of silence after the question

"If he does this, I do it," Chris said.

"Chris," Corrado muttered, not bothering to turn around to face his twin, "you don't have—"

"I said what I said."

He sighed.

Stubborn.

That's what Chris was.

Yes, they were different.

They were still the same, too.

Chris would *never* let his twin go into something without being there to do it, too. Even if the idea of that thing wasn't something that interested him at all.

Cree leaned to the side, just enough to get Chris in his sights before he straightened again to stare up at Corrado in the ring. The man nodded once. "All right, I've never trained twins before. This could be … interesting."

"*Cree,*" Dare said again.

"Yeah, yeah." Cree didn't move, still *waiting*. "Corrado?"

"All right," Corrado said quietly.

Cree smiled widely and wagged a finger at him. "Remember this was what you wanted, okay?"

What did that mean?

CHAPTER 5
ALESSIO

"Gian, I don't think you understand—"

"I understand very well what it means for them, Dare."

Silence echoed from within the office. Alessio, standing where the two men inside couldn't see him, used the wall as a prop for his shoulder to rest against as he waited for the conversation to continue on.

Dare sighed heavily, and hands smacked on something solid. "The training is intensive, and—"

"We've gone over the training. I know what happens."

"If you would stop interrupting me, that would be great."

"By all means ..."

Dare grumbled under his breath. "The training—it's going to break them at *every* level, Gian. Mentally, physically ... that's the purpose of it, for us to find their limits, shatter them, and then teach them there is no limit. They're seventeen."

"Nearly eighteen, but all right. And how old is the one Corrado followed around today?"

"That is not the point."

"How old?"

"Alessio will be eighteen soon, but—"

"Mmm, I know you're going to say he's been with you and Cree from the time he was ten, but you're not going to lie right to my face and say you've been training him since then, will you? I didn't take you to be an ignorant man, Dare."

"He started the intensive training at fifteen, but he watched others and participated in different things from the time he was about twelve, yes."

"And is he out on assignments yet?"

"No," Dare replied.

"Why?"

"My choice. Cree thinks he's ready either way."

"But again, *why*?" Gian asked again, his tone sharpening the word. "Because I am sure the fifty percent that I fronted on this venture of yours allows me the right to ask a question and *promises* you will give me a truthful answer. Unless I missed something in that paperwork, and if so, by all means … correct me, Dare."

"Gian, this isn't about Alessio."

"I think it is about Alessio in the way that you are looking at him the way I look at my boys. And as I understand your relationship with Cree—"

"Could we not? *No one* gets the right to discuss my personal business. You included, regardless of how much money you have in this company."

Gian cleared his throat. "You know that's not an issue for me. I meant to say, I know that with *that*, and the fact you both have had Alessio for so long, he feels like a son to you. I understand *why*. *You* have chosen to keep him here for as long as you can—yes?"

The sound of Dare swallowing was audible. "Well, you're not *wrong*."

A chuckle echoed.

"I didn't think so," Gian replied quietly. "When will he be put out on assignments?"

"Cree decided eighteen."

Gian made a noise under his breath. "*Cree* decided?"

"I don't want to talk about it."

"And what about the auction, then? What will happen to him with that?"

"Another fight—I settled that one. He'll make the choice for himself after he's done a few independent jobs. If he wants to go up on the auction for a term of four years to do jobs for a specific client, then he can."

"Yet, the other assassins you've trained here don't get that choice at all. Or did I miss something from the last time we talked about the process here? Because I am positive *every* prospect you and Cree begin training sign the same contract —they *will* go up for a term of four years in the auctions the company holds, and then it's renegotiated after, yes?"

"How did this fucking conversation turn around on me? Because I am sure that's not what we were discussing two minutes ago, Gian."

"Ah, so now you understand."

"I beg your pardon?"

"Now you understand, Dare." Gian laughed under his breath. "See, you became defensive as soon as I pointed out the emotional side of your attachment here—to a specific person, sure, but it's still there nonetheless. Because *that's* how you feel about your boy, blood or not. And you expect me to have the same reaction about mine, but you're wrong."

"I—"

"I'm not finished. You seem to think," Gian said, his tone remaining level, "that I would pull rank on my sons simply *because* they are my sons. While I don't actually expect their mother to be happy about this decision, if only because that means at least a year she'll be without them, I don't have an opinion one way or another. If this is what Chris and Corrado want to do, then this is what they'll do. They have independent minds, I made sure of that. I wanted all my boys to be able to think for themselves. I love them, but they have to make themselves into something. I can't do it for them."

"Well …"

"Hmm?"

Dare grunted under his breath. "Cree says Corrado is the best fit here. Because of his temperament, and the fact he seems willing to learn."

"And Chris?"

A laugh answered that back.

"What?" Gian asked. "Just say it."

"He says Chris's reasons are clearly self—"

"Don't call Chris selfish. He is *a lot* of things, but out of all of them, selfish is not one of them. He is the most *selfless* of all my children, although I never understood why."

"Okay, then I will rephrase. He thinks he is only doing this because of his twin, and not because he actually wants to. Rather, because he wants to do what his twin does, if you get what I am saying."

"So again, selfless."

"I will let Cree know that *selfish* is the wrong choice of word for Christopher."

"*Merci.*"

"I won't ask again, but I want to be sure you understand what will happen after you leave tonight."

"I understand. It's what they want, Dare."

"Or is it—"

"Barring Christopher, let me point out something about Corrado I am sure you and *Cree* don't know—since he's the one who feeds you information, and you get in your feelings about it. Corrado has never fit in anywhere with the rest of us. He's been under my feet, and men like me, for his entire life, and yet … he's not found the space where he belongs. He's not a normal boy, and he won't live a normal life. He can't when he has just a little too much of me and my blood in him, if you understand."

"So, what does that mean?"

"He might find where he belongs here, and if he has to sacrifice to do it, then so be it."

"And the other one—Chris?"

Gian made a dismissive sound. "Selfless. It's his path to choose, Dare."

"I see."

"Have we said all we need to say, then?"

A chair squeaked before Dare replied, "It seems so. They've already signed the contracts, but I haven't yet. I will now. It'll begin tonight once you're gone."

"I expect the same for them that you have given to Alessio," Gian added. "Put in as an addendum to their contracts for me—I *will* look for it."

"Which is what?"

"Independent contractors for The League—they only choose the auction route if they want when training is finished. If they decline the auctions when it is all said and done, I will pay the training fees to recoup the costs."

"Cree does want to make a team that he can use for his contacts."

"So, that's a yes, then?"

"That's a yes, Gian. I will add it in."

Gian hummed before adding lower, "He's scared of water."

"Which one?"

"Christopher. He almost drowned when he was two— slipped off the side of the dock at the small lake at his uncle's vacation home. A relative jumped in after him, but it was touch and go. The tank and the dark room are phase one for training, correct?"

"You expect him to react badly."

"I'm explaining why he might, yes."

"And yet you're still willing to allow him—"

"It's what he wants."

"But without knowing what will happen, Gian."

"He's not stupid, like Corrado isn't, as well. He has to know *anything* is a possibility here. I think … it might help him to control that fear of his because I know it's overwhelming to him at times."

"All right. I'll be in touch, Gian."

"I expect it—regular updates, *oui*?"

"Absolutely."

Alessio didn't have time to move away from the doorway so that the men inside wouldn't find him eavesdropping on their conversation in the hallway. Gian's footsteps came toward the door far too fast for Alessio to figure out something, or somewhere, to hide.

So, he just stayed there leaning against the wall.

Like an idiot.

Gian looked him over as he stepped out of the office, the lack of surprise in his features telling Alessio that the man expected *someone* to be out here. And he wasn't all that shocked about who it was, either.

Silence accompanied Gian's presence. Alessio didn't have anything to say to the man when he was still digesting parts of the conversation he'd just overheard. He hadn't realized how much the romantic aspect of Dare and Cree's relationship affected their business together. Not that *anyone* knew a whole hell of a lot about the two men, and what went on between them behind closed doors.

Alessio had never been privy to that, despite living with them for the last seven, almost eight, years. For all purposes,

Cree and Dare kept the private parts of their life *private*. Even to Alessio. He only knew about it because someone made a comment once. He put two and two together about their relationship because of things he'd seen but overlooked, and at the time, he'd also been too young to really understand the complexities of a relationship like the one Dare and Cree shared. Eventually, he did outright ask Dare who confirmed that Cree was his partner in more than just the business.

That was the extent of the conversation.

Nothing else was on the table.

It had taught him that love was coveted here.

It was *protected*.

In their life, love was weakness. Love was a fucking *target*. It was something people could use to hurt you, and when you loved someone *that much* ... you did everything you could to keep it and safeguard it from whoever might try to take it from you. Even if that meant hurting the person you loved in the process, too. Because sometimes, one had to do what one had to do.

"I am sure I'll be seeing you again, Alessio," Gian said, dragging him from his thoughts.

Alessio frowned. "I doubt it."

Gian grinned, and something shined in his gaze that Alessio didn't recognize as the man looked him over again—a *fondness*, maybe? "I'm not so sure."

"What does that mean?"

Did he know what happened between Alessio and his son in the gym? Had Cree run his fucking mouth about it? It wouldn't be like Cree to do something like that, but Alessio couldn't be sure, either.

Gian didn't say one way or another, simply murmuring, "I guess we'll see."

And then the man was gone, heading down the hallway

with his hands stuffed in the pockets of his three-piece Armani suit like he didn't have a care in the world. Or, that's what one might think by watching him, but Alessio saw something different. The way Gian kept his head tilted down, how his hands had been clenched a bit before he hid them away, and now, the fact that his shoulders seemed tense beneath his suit.

He was worried.

He should be.

This place broke men.

Repeatedly.

"Alessio!" Dare's bark had Alessio jumping in place before he glared at the doorway. "Get in here, I know you're out there spying like a little shit."

"I was—"

"Don't lie."

Alessio scowled and turned to enter the office. He didn't move further than inside the doorway, but he didn't have to, either. Across the office, Dare sat behind his large desk. With his fingers steepled in front of him, he leaned back in the leather office chair, and watched Alessio with a pensive eye.

Like he was *considering* him.

God, he hated when Cree and Dare did that.

It meant they thought they knew something that he was hiding. And usually, they weren't wrong.

"What?" he asked.

"Nothing. Do you have anything you want to ask me?"

Alessio's cheek twitched, because *yes*. Between Cree and Dare … he didn't get away with shit. Cree was the person who knew when Alessio was up to something, and constantly kept him on his toes because it felt like the man had insight to his mind that even he didn't know. Dare, though?

Well, he was something else.

For all purposes, they were both family to Alessio. One

might consider them his adoptive fathers, but he never called them that, and they never asked, either. Still ... in a way, Dare felt more like a father figure to him than anyone else ever had.

Cree, more like a brother.

He didn't want to disappoint either of them.

"You're the reason I can't go out on an assignment until I turn eighteen?" Alessio asked quietly.

"Apparently so. I told you spying was a bad thing."

"Cree says I'm ready."

"And I want you here. Guess who gets the final say?"

"That's unfair," he pointed out.

He tried not to sound like a whiney fuck.

And probably failed.

Dare arched a brow, not bothering to indulge Alessio further because that's also how this worked between them. If he said something, it was done. "And why were you spying?"

"I wasn't—"

"You did."

"I was coming to tell you that they're not good choices for prospects here," Alessio returned, "but Gian was in here, so I thought it would be rude to interrupt."

"Or you took your chance to *spy*."

Alessio gritted his teeth. "I don't want to talk about it."

Dare smiled a little. "Is it that you don't think they're the right fit—because you follow Cree around too much and assume you can think the way he does—or because you like one of them? Corrado, I believe. I heard about how the gym was put into use this afternoon, yeah?"

Fuck.

So, Cree *had* told someone.

"It's not about *that*," Alessio muttered, annoyed.

Although, part of it was. Alessio had never felt such a strong attraction to another person who he would need to be around almost twenty-four-seven before. Not to mention, the fact that same person also managed to get under his skin in the worst of ways.

It was going to be a mess.

"Are you worried *for* him, Les?" Dare asked.

"Could you not do that?"

"Cree isn't the only one who can see your shit for what it is."

"Well, *don't.*"

"Mmm," Dare said, standing from his chair. "Them being here … the contracts for them to begin training … none of it is your choice, Les. If you want to help the young man be his best here, then do that, but don't do it by attempting to sabotage him. Now, if you'll excuse me, I have to call in the team to begin the training tonight. I assume you don't want to be a part of this one, right?"

"I …" He struggled to refuse, but knew it was for the best if he did exactly that. If he said he agreed to help the team, then he would need to take part in some of the training that would be *most* difficult for Corrado and his twin. He helped to train others; this one couldn't be the same because Dare wasn't wrong, and he did have *some* interest in Corrado. His feelings might come into play. Lamely, he muttered, "I don't think I should."

"That's what I thought."

Alessio glowered, but Dare couldn't see it because he had already turned to leave the room. Clearly, this was going to get him nowhere and he didn't want to sit here and bother with it any more than he already had.

He hated wasting time.

"Oh, and Les?"

Alessio tensed in the doorway of the office. "What now?"

"If you're interested in Corrado Guzzi, my suggestion is

instead of trying to pick a fight with him to get his attention, you might want to ... oh, I don't know, *talk* to him?"

"Fuck you."

Dare's laughter chased him out of the office.

Asshole.

CHAPTER 6
CORRADO

"How are they running power to this place?" Chris asked.

Gian tapped a finger to his ear. "Listen for it, *fils*."

Corrado heard the humming in the distance—somewhere behind them, he thought. Maybe in the middle of the complex? When they'd first come up on it, in the light, he thought it was several buildings close together. After walking around a bit, he realized it was actually one building, but in varied sizes depending on location.

"Generators," Corrado said.

"Oh," Chris said.

At the driver's side of the black Mercedes they'd arrived in, Gian turned to face his sons. Corrado stayed close to Chris, their equal six-foot-two height putting them pretty close to eye-level with their father. He couldn't remember when that happened, really. A growth spurt came along, and suddenly, he was no longer looking up at his dad.

He was staring him straight in the face.

"Corrado," Gian murmured.

His gaze lifted to meet his father's. "Yeah?"

"I know you're looking for something here."

"You think?"

Gian smiled faintly. "I hope you find it."

A thickness tightened his throat, but he nodded and said, "Yeah, me too."

Then, their father turned on Chris. "And *you*."

Chris grinned. "What about me?"

"I hope you know what you just signed up for."

"Not really."

Gian released a slow breath. "This is not ... easy, Christopher."

"I'm here until he isn't."

"You don't have to look out for your twin every day of your life. That's not why you were put on this earth. You understand that, don't you?"

Chris only shrugged.

Corrado knew there was no point in his father trying to explain to Chris that he didn't really have to be here with his brother if he didn't want to be. Once they made up their minds, it was done—a Guzzi trait they took from their father, whether he wanted to admit it or not.

"All right," Gian murmured, pulling the key fob for the car from his pocket. "You know the deal—very little contact for the first year of training, but we'll see if the rules are bent. Believe it or not, but this wasn't my intention when I brought you both here."

Corrado smirked. "Not *at all.*"

Gian shook his head. "I thought it might give *you* a chance to see that there were other options in the business, if you were determined to stay in the life, but no, I did not assume it would be here. And now, I get to return home without both of you ... your mother will be pleased, I'm sure."

Next to him, Chris made a noise under his breath. He didn't even have to say anything for that one sound to speak volumes. *Yes*, their father was in for hell when he got back to their ma. *Yes*, they were going to miss their mother like no one would ever understand. It was just how they were raised —Cara Guzzi made their worlds go around, and now, where would she be?

Corrado stuffed his hands in his pockets, and eyed their surroundings now that it was dark. A lot of the cars from earlier were gone—the people had drifted out of the complex throughout the day, without much of a word to him. There were still a few scattered vehicles, but he didn't know who they belonged to.

"Enough of this," Gian said roughly, "I should get going. *I love you*. Both of you, huh? Be *smart*, Corrado." Then, to Chris, their father said, "Don't panic when it starts, okay? It only seems like you won't get out, but I promise it'll never go as far as you think it will."

Chris's brow furrowed. "What does that mean?"

Gian's shoulders lifted with his stress. "Just remember what I said, son."

"All right."

Corrado figured his father would get in the car, and drive off after that, but Gian surprised them. Then again, their father had always been different than the other men around him—more in tune to his children, and he actually gave a fuck about what they wanted or needed at any given time. He also wasn't sure when the physical affection started to lessen with his father, but as they grew older, the hugs and kisses slowed.

A part of him knew it was because of them—he didn't need that shit to know his father gave a damn, and so, he stopped *asking* for it. Right then, though, Gian stepped forward, and embraced each of his sons one at a time, used his hand to pat the backs of their heads, and pressed a quick kiss to their foreheads before moving back just as fast.

Like it hadn't happened at all.

"Wish me luck with your mother, hmm?"

"Good luck," the twins echoed.

He was going to need it.

No doubt about that.

Gian was careful not to look over his shoulder as he slipped into the car, and turned the engine over. It wasn't until Chris and Corrado could only see a very faint outline of the car's taillights in the distance did they finally turn away from their disappearing father.

"What happens now?" Chris asked.

Corrado had no idea. "Something, I guess."

"I don't like *not knowing* things."

"Yeah, you're probably going to have to work on that, Chris."

His twin made a disgusted noise, but Corrado didn't reply because he wasn't lying. Neither of them knew *anything* about what was going to happen to them now. Other than the small bag with a couple of changes of clothes, he didn't even know where that shit would be coming from. No one thought to tell them because apparently, they didn't need to know.

That's what they had been told.

Next to going over a contract—that in all honesty, didn't give them much to go on—which basically explained the next year of their lives would be essentially owned by The League, and what the company wanted to do with them ... that was all Corrado knew. *Training*, the contract said over and over again. Except nothing in the damn paperwork explained what exactly this training would include.

"You know," Corrado said as the two of them headed back toward the black door with the camera overhead, "Papa was right."

"That I don't have to be here for you?"

"Yeah."

Chris shook his head. "No, he wasn't."

Well, all right.

Who was Corrado to argue with what was basically his reflection?

He knew better.

~

Not that anything at The League's complex made sense to him—something he thought was intentional on their part— but for whatever reason, the sleeping quarters that had been designated to Corrado were an entire wing away from the one that had been given to Chris. The two had broken off as they realized the hallway lights were starting to shut off or dim significantly, and headed to their own rooms.

Trailing his finger over a simple three-drawer dresser that looked like he could probably put his fist through the thin, pressed wood if he wanted to, Corrado eyed the rest of the space. It wasn't much—fifteen feet by fifteen feet or so. A double bed rested along one wall with a stand beside it, and a very small window overtop.

Given his room was on the third floor of a certain area deep within the large complex, no one would even be able to see inside because they couldn't possibly reach the window. There were no pieces of artwork on the bare, tan-colored walls to give it a comfortable feeling, and other than a small desk with nothing on top ... the room was basically empty. Clean, gleaming hardwood floors, white sheets on the bed, and very little else.

Welcome home for the next year, Corrado.

His mind was a special breed of hell when it wanted to be. This might have been made easier for him had he under-stood what was going to come next, but no. He had to be left in fucking suspense, which only made everything far worse.

The building itself, he'd realized as he walked through its hallways and sections earlier, was a fucking maze. It looked huge from the outside, but that didn't *begin* to touch how large and confusing it truly was once you were inside the damn place.

"Bored?"

Corrado spun fast to find a familiar—and *annoying*—man leaning in his doorway. "What do you want, Alessio?"

"I still prefer Les."

"Yeah, and how's that mood of yours, anyway?"

Alessio grinned. "How's that mouth of yours, huh?"

"Fair."

He nodded, and then inched a bit into the room. Corrado thought to tell him to get the fuck out, but he didn't bother. Besides, Alessio might be able to answer some of his questions, and he couldn't pry information from the guy when he chased him off, right?

"How big is this complex?"

"In total?"

"Yeah."

Alessio rocked back on his heels. "Around a hundred thousand square feet, give or take a few thousand. The main floorplan, back when they first planned to build it, covered a full acre of land. Some things changed as they moved forward, third floors were added, like *here*. What about it?"

"Curious."

"You know, the less questions you ask here, the better it'll be for you."

Corrado passed him a look. "*You know*, humans are curious by nature, don't you? It's how we learn new things."

Throwing those words back at Alessio didn't seem to bother him in the slightest. If anything, that grin he sported simply grew a little deeper. Corrado might think it was *sexy*, even, if it didn't fucking infuriate him so much. A part of him hated how Alessio could treat everything so flippantly—like it was a damn joke to him, and nothing more.

Even *him*.

Corrado didn't want to be a joke to anybody.

"Don't worry," Alessio said quietly, "they'll beat the curiosity, and almost everything else, right out of you by the time they're done."

He stilled on the spot, tension tightening his shoulders. "Is that what happens next?"

"Partly. You have to break before they can make you into something better. Some parts of you take longer to break than others, you know? That's the hard part, though. Once you get through that, it's mostly smooth sailing. It's what they have to take from you first that just about kills you. Oh, and how they do it, I guess."

"How do they do it?"

Alessio didn't reply.

Corrado wasn't one to accept a non-answer, so he moved a little closer to Alessio until the two of them were only a few inches apart. He fully intended to get an answer out of him, but it slipped his mind when he noticed the way Alessio's gaze darted down to his lips, and then quickly back up to his eyes.

Like he was *remembering*.

That memory flooded Corrado's mind, too.

Fuck.

Not what he needed right now.

"Was Cree right?" Corrado asked. "About you, I mean."

"I don't—"

"That you pick a fight to get attention."

Alessio's eyes blazed. "*No.*"

"Really? So, you didn't try to cause a problem with me today because you didn't want to just come up and say *hello*? I don't know, like a normal person might."

"Cree says a lot of shit."

"I noticed a lot of it was right, though."

Alessio's throat jumped when he swallowed hard. "Possibly. Doesn't mean all of it is."

"Sure."

"I don't know whether I like you or not," Alessio muttered.

"Same."

This time, it was Corrado that found his gaze drifted down from the shaggy hair covering Alessio's eyes to where his lips rested in what almost seemed like a smirk. Not quite, but *almost*. Like the guy just had a natural arrogance about him. That was something Corrado found *most* annoying in others, but with Alessio, it drew him in.

Another problem?

Probably.

It had been Alessio that kissed him earlier, and Corrado wasn't entirely sure why he felt the strangest urge to see if the man tasted the same *now*, but he made the move this time. It didn't seem to come as any kind of shock to Alessio when Corrado's mouth came down on his, and he backed him into the wall.

Alessio's fingers found the waistband of his pants, his fingers digging into the hard muscles there as his tongue swept the seam of Corrado's lips. Just like that first kiss, this still felt like a fight to Corrado … like neither of them were willing to yield to the other. No softness; no careful exploration. It was just *war*. Tongues clashing against each other as he realized, *yes*, Alessio tasted exactly the same.

Like fucking *sin*.

His teeth caught Alessio's bottom lip, and then the man's fingers pressed harder into his skin *just because*. If anything, it only made Corrado lurch forward, so he didn't just have Alessio backed against the wall. No, he had his body *pinning* him there. Just like when the man had him pinned to the fucking mat of the ring earlier. He wanted him to know what that felt like—to be under someone else's control, and to *like* it at the same time.

And yes, he could feel just how much Alessio liked it.

Corrado let out a harsh exhale, his lips grazing down Alessio's jaw as he tipped his head back to the wall. "*Fuck*, so that's a yes on the whole picking a fight thing, then?"

"Fuck you, Guzzi."

He just laughed.

What else could he do?

A noisy buzz echoed throughout the room, sending Corrado and Alessio's gaze flying upward to find the sound. Above the doorway, a light turned from green to red, making Corrado even more confused than he already was. It was Alessio who seemed to understand what was going on as he cursed under his breath.

"Shit, I gotta go," Alessio muttered.

"Wait," Corrado said, refusing to move to let him get past, "what does that mean?"

"It's starting."

"*What's* starting?"

Alessio wet his lips, his gaze meeting Corrado's. "*Training*. I hope you fucking make it through what they're about to do to you and your brother."

Ice slipped through Corrado's blood stream.

What had they signed up for?

"Why that hope?"

Alessio flashed a grin, as small as it was. "Because maybe I want to know what happens next with us."

Corrado jerked fast away from the wall at those words. Alessio wasted no time slipping out of the room, leaving him alone to his racing heart, and his thoughts. Out in the hallway, he heard footsteps—Alessio leaving, maybe?

And *doors* shutting.

He stared up at that red light again.

No one—or very few people—were left inside the complex. Why did it sound like all the doors were closing one by *one*? Hadn't Alessio said it was all electronic? Someone could control the doors without physically needing to shut them by hand?

The footsteps got louder, though.

And closer.

Definitely not Alessio.

Not anymore.

Corrado looked down to stare out his still opened doorway. Except now, the hallway outside of it wasn't empty. Black-clothed figures stood there, their faces covered with masks, and their hands steady on the weapons they held.

"It's time to get started, Corrado," the one in front of the group said.

He recognized that voice.

Cree.

"Doing what?" Corrado asked.

"You don't get to ask questions. Make this easy."

Right.

That probably wasn't going to work for him. Not when he didn't know what in the hell was going on, and he didn't know what might come next. His heart ached from beating so hard, but he was positive there was no way out of here.

Was that what they wanted, though?

For him to *fight*?

Because he could do that.

"Where's my brother?" he demanded.

"Walk outside the room, Corrado."

"No."

"You do understand that this *will* happen one way or another."

"That doesn't tell me—"

"Easy or hard," Cree said behind the black mask.

"Tell me where my brother is."

"Hard it is."

They came in on him, then.

All of them.

Corrado couldn't ever remember being taken to the ground so fast or hard before. His bones *shook* when they put him to the floor, an ache radiating throughout his whole body. He let out a shout, and tried to fight back. It was fucking pointless, though. There were too many, and only one of him.

His gaze darted from one mask-covered face to the other, but they didn't speak. Five of them, he thought, but maybe six. It was hard to tell when they moved so fast, and he still didn't know what in the hell was going on. His arms were tied at his back, but hell, he hadn't even seen the zip ties come out for them to do it.

Someone dragged him up from the floor while someone else leaned in beside him, their eyes being the only thing he could see behind the mask as they said, "Don't make this worse for yourself, kid. You're already *in*, and there's no way out. Just let it happen."

Right.

Okay.

Damn.

"W-what happens now?" Corrado asked as he was pulled from the room.

"It's gonna hurt before it gets better."

Who said that?

He didn't even know.

CHAPTER 7
ALESSIO

Hidden in the shadows of the hallway, Alessio watched from a safe distance as Corrado was pulled from his room by the team. The *team* being a small group of men and women hand-picked by Cree to help him train whoever had signed the contract. They were never easy about it—they didn't go in easy, either.

All or nothing.

Corrado's shout echoed down the corridor, his voice thick with panic and uncertainty. Not fear, though. *Not yet.* That would come soon enough, Alessio knew. The fear would come when he was either locked in total darkness, rounds of beatings marking the passing hours he spent in isolation to fuck his mind entirely up, or when they put him in the *tank.*

Fuck.

That fucking *tank.*

Alessio felt the pressure building in his chest simply remembering his own time in that cold, dark water. It never got any better in the tank, or the darkness. Long stretches of time where your mind was too awake—fear saturating your entire body because you never knew what was going to happen next.

And when it did happen …

"Where the fuck is my bro—"

Corrado's question cut off abruptly when the first hit

came. The sound of flesh meeting flesh was sickening, and *unforgiving*. A grunt followed the hit before a second one came, and then another and another. Alessio tipped his head back so all he could see was the white ceiling of the corridor, and then he closed his eyes altogether when the beating continued.

They didn't want him to ask questions.

He wasn't *allowed*.

Orders were given.

He was to follow.

Alessio knew how this *worked*, but the problem was, he couldn't tell Corrado that. Maybe back in his room, but even then ... it wouldn't have helped. This was something *all* The League's prospects had to learn on their own, in their time. It was the very purpose of the training—to take a man who was already set in his ways, break him, and then change him into a better version of himself.

Even if that better version was created from violence, darkness, isolation, fear, and *pain*. Alessio didn't make the rules here; he only knew how to follow them.

"*Stand up*," he heard ordered.

That was the thing that made him open his eyes again, although he didn't try to peek around the corner to look down the hallway. Part of him knew it wasn't a good idea. Cree would be pissed off like nothing else if someone interrupted his training team, but especially at the very beginning. He needed to stay out of sight as much as possible.

Coming to this end of the complex to get a couple of minutes with Corrado before the training began was a fucking risk anyway. A stupid one, probably, but he wasn't going to admit that to himself. Alessio wasn't very good at denying himself something he wanted, as it was, and he kept being drawn back to Corrado when he shouldn't want anything to do with him at all.

And it's only been a day.

Fuck.

The beating down the hall continued on like Alessio wasn't having a whole fucking moment at the other end, just around the corner. Not that the rest of them could know that he was in the midst of his own goddamn issues.

Alessio had to give credit where it was due, though.

Corrado didn't beg.

He fought back, by the sounds of it.

He didn't take *shit*.

Some cried. That wasn't unusual, and no one said a thing when it was all said and done. Some puked. Fear had a funny way of making the body do things no one could possibly understand unless it was them in the situation. Others begged and pleaded, realizing their mistake in signing a contract for something they didn't truly comprehend. It was too late by then, though.

They were *in*.

There was no out until it was done, or you were dead.

But for now, Corrado wasn't like the others. Very little was said to him from the team—orders like *stand* or *move* or *stop asking questions*. But nothing deep, nothing that answered the questions he kept demanding be answered about his brother.

Even Alessio didn't know the answer to that.

Usually, one person was trained at a time because it *was* so intensive. Maybe Cree was going to try a new way of training the twins because it would happen side by side in time, essentially, but Alessio didn't think he could stomach it to ask the details.

Part of him just didn't want to *know*.

"You're going to *learn*," Alessio heard a muffled voice say down the hall.

"*Fuck you.*"

Corrado's words were mumbled now—like he couldn't speak right, or he had to make a great effort to do it.

That was enough for Alessio.

He knew what came next.

Instead of standing there to listen to it, he slipped down the corridor to go in the opposite direction from the rest of the team. They were taking Corrado to the west side of the complex, deep into the basement where even the people who milled about the building wouldn't be able to hear the fucking *screams*.

Alessio went east, to *Dare*.

He suspected he would find Dare in his office, sitting at his desk and handling the paperwork of the day. People who *thought* they knew the inner workings of The League thought Dare was untouchable in a lot of ways because he never directly handled the assassins, for the most part. That was usually Cree, and his team of people.

They also assumed Dare was ... the very top.

In a way, he was.

It was the same way people assumed Cree—his choice— was just another assassin with a bit more leg room to move in the organization than usual. They were cautious about keeping Cree's *real* hand in controlling part of The League quiet. Instead, a carefully constructed story and persona for Cree was spoon-fed to the prospects and clients of The League where Cree was concerned, making them think he was less of a *boss* and more like them. They were far more likely to trust him in that case.

Dare, though, also had people like Gian Guzzi who fronted a lot of money for this organization to become something no one could possibly ruin, which meant things never stopped around here. If it wasn't a new prospect being trained, it was the auctions selling off the assassins to people with deep enough pockets all around the world who might be in need of someone with a particular set of skills. And if wasn't *those* things, then they were working.

Instead of finding Dare in his office, Alessio wandered the halls until he came to the control room. Or, that's what they liked to refer to it as. Inside, standing in front of a wall of screens, Dare used a sleek, thin remote with a touchscreen pad to separate what was actually *one* giant screen—that looked broken into several different screens—to bring up specific cameras. Just as quickly, he switched to a separate screen on the wall of moving pictures that brought up something else entirely.

A wall of doors, it looked like.

His thumb raced across the touchscreen, and Alessio watched on the screen as the opened doors in the hallway began to close one by one. Then, just as fast, Corrado was brought into view by the team … close to the tank room, now.

Well, the dark room *and* the tank room.

They were right across from one another. The walls inside were so thick, one couldn't even *blow* them out with dynamite. The floors, a cold cement that constantly seemed to stay wet from one thing or another.

"Did you watch mine, too?" Alessio asked.

His chest *ached*.

He wasn't sure why.

Maybe it was the memories racing past his eyes—the idea that a couple of years ago, this had been *him*. He'd been dragged through those halls, had the shit beat out of him, and was then thrown into hell for a month or more to break him beyond recognition. He'd thought he was ready; he'd watched from afar for other trainings before his time.

He had not been anywhere near ready.

Dare turned slowly, realizing he wasn't alone as his gaze fell on Alessio in the doorway. "I'm sorry?"

"Did you watch my training, too?"

"I did not."

"Why?"

"I don't have ... a good answer for that, Les," Dare murmured.

"Or you don't want to sound like a coward."

"Maybe I was wrong."

"What?"

Dare shrugged, and looked back at the screens. "I said earlier you only *thought* you could think like Cree does, but I might have been wrong about that."

It took Alessio a second to understand.

Then, two.

"Because you *couldn't* watch me go through the first phase, right?" he asked.

Dare let out a heavy exhale. "If you asked for it to stop even once ... *and they all ask* ... I would have dragged you out of there myself. Because I was weak—love does that to you, Alessio, and I want you to remember that. It makes you *weak.* And so, when something is for the greater good when it comes to someone you love, even if it means hurting them, you have to take a step back and let it happen. Or in my case, be forced to do it."

"What does that mean?"

Across the room, Dare waved the remote at the screens, saying, "Cree had the team go in on you for phase one, then he locked me in the office and wouldn't let me out for that first night. It ... was not a good moment for me."

Alessio frowned. "What?"

"You heard what I said."

"Cree wasn't in on my—"

"Not for phase one. He was too close to it, too."

Alessio hadn't known that, mostly because the team had been very careful not to speak to him during the first phase of his training. Other than a barked word here to there to give him an order, which he knew better than to defy them.

It only made shit worse.

"Did you ask for it to stop?" Dare asked.

Alessio watched the screens, another hallway ... the rooms were coming faster now. Soon, Corrado wouldn't know what daylight was for a long fucking time.

"Not until the third round in the tank room," Alessio said, scratching at the side of his arm because *that* memory made him anxious as fuck, and he knew better than to show it. That's what training had taught him—he didn't deal with any of that in the same way anymore. Fear, panic ... it was all secondary to everything else, now. "I couldn't find the pocket to breathe, the water kept coming in my mouth, and—"

Dare made a dark noise.

"Sorry," Alessio muttered.

"It's what you wanted, no?"

"It was."

Ten feet away, he watched Dare nod at the screens.

"And it's what they want, too, Les. You'll have to remember that for the next little while."

"Where is the other one—Chris?"

"In his room, *fine*. That's why we put them on opposite ends of the complex for living quarters. If we put them in the same corridor, it was likely one would panic and do something outlandish when the other was removed from their room. A risk Cree didn't want to take, of course. It'll be only once Corrado is situated—we knew he would be the more difficult one at first—that we'll begin phase one for the other twin. Rotational trips between the rooms for them, of course. Instead of long spreads in each like we typically do. The one, he's going to need a break in-between the tank."

"Christopher, you mean."

"Scared of water, yeah."

"But even if he asks for it to stop—"

"We can't stop it once it begins, that isn't how training works."

"What if he reacts *really* badly to the tank?" Alessio asked.

Dare chuckled dryly. "The best way to deal with a fear is head-on."

"Except it's more than a *fear*. Everybody is scared of things like the dark when it's been too long, or of the unknown for something like the tank. But that might not be the same."

"Then, he will break sooner than his twin because of it, won't he? A healthy mind processes things like anxiety and fear, or pain and discomfort in a completely different way than a broken one does, Les. And so, we need them broken before we can begin to rebuild. You know this."

"I guess."

"You don't like it, though," Dare replied.

"Not this time."

"Hmm."

On the screens, a battered Corrado had finally made it to the basement. The team stood outside of the two large, metal doors on either side of them that would lead into the dark room, or the tank room.

"They're about to begin," Dare said. "You should probably leave."

Alessio didn't move.

"I think I better stay, actually."

"Don't say I didn't warn you."

～

Safely behind one-way glass, Alessio watched the scene that seemed surreal happening beyond cement walls. The light from the hallway in the complex's basement allowed *him* the ability to see inside the tank room, but no one in there could see him.

Well, the *one* person in there.

The straightjacket attached to a chain and cable keeping Corrado suspended over a square tank of water that was *just* big enough to drown a man when he was dropped into it—if he didn't figure out how to save himself the first couple of dunks—was tight to his body. His eyes drifted closed, tiredness from the last few days of being rotated between the tank and the dark room finally getting to him.

It happened to everyone.

That was when this became *most* dangerous.

Alessio's gaze darted to the chain as it jerked. At the same time, Corrado's eyes flew wide open, and for a brief second, he swore the man was looking right at him though the small window he was able to watch through.

He knew it wasn't possible, though.

It lasted all of a half of a second before Corrado was *dropped.* Like a sack of dead weight, really. Right into the tank, where freezing cold water awaited him, and a top attached to an automatic arm slammed closed right after.

Alessio dragged in a sharp breath and stared upward, knowing what was happening inside the tank room now. He didn't have to watch it happen to *know.* Fuck, he knew it all too well as it was, honestly.

Corrado would struggle.

Under water.

Straight jacket on.

The top wouldn't budge.

More water pumped in.

His body remained constantly cold, wet, and *aching.*

From the rotational beatings, and the lack of food and water. His mind would be spinning and out of control —fear and panic welling and rushing like the waves of the water inside that tank, making sure he thought at all times, this was it. *This* was the moment he would die.

Every dunk became longer.

A second here.

Two there.

Until he was under water for up to three and half minutes, or so. Until his vision began to blacken, and he swallowed water because the body's natural reaction was to *try* to breathe at that point, even if it meant no air would be waiting for him.

He'd fight against all of it—his own panic, the water, the need to breathe, and even the walls of the tank surrounding him.

And then the top would flip up, the chain would drag him out, and he would hang again … waiting to be dropped into the water for another round of hell.

Over.

And over.

And over again.

Until the dark room.

Currently, that's where Corrado's twin was being held. He was about due for a beating, too, come to think of it, which meant he probably shouldn't be down here. The rotational beatings and the occasional bit of food and water were the only markers of time passing down in these fucking rooms.

It seemed cruel.

Pointless, even.

Alessio, and every other person who had gone through this training, would be the first to say they came out better for it—physically, and mentally. They were the last to panic, and the first to face everything without fear.

When you'd been so close to death time and time again … everything that came after was nothing compared to it, really. Everything else was just a *bonus*, he figured.

"What are you doing down here?"

Alessio didn't turn at the sound of Cree's voice, but he did look back through the one-way glass to see Corrado being pulled out of the water, almost entirely unconscious, but not quite. Just *almost*.

"Watching," Alessio murmured.

"You shouldn't be down here."

"I know."

Cree came to stand next to him and crossed his arms over his broad chest. "He's going to be difficult … to break, I mean. His pride holds him back. All of that has to go … the pride, dignity … the harder it is to take those things from him, the longer this process goes on."

Yeah.

He knew that, too.

"What about the other one?" Alessio asked, glancing over his shoulder at the dark room where Chris was having his rotation. "How did that go in the tank?"

"He about broke the fucking top trying to get out, one of the jacket's arms came undone … I have never seen someone fight *that* hard against it, and I have seen some things happen down in these rooms."

"Adrenaline?"

"Likely," Cree returned. "His second rotation in the tank starts tomorrow. We'll see how it goes, or if we get a different result."

Of course.

Alessio knew how this went.

Break the body; break the mind.

"As for *you*," the man said next to him, "you don't need to be down here reliving your own time in these rooms because you feel something for one of the two currently experiencing theirs. You realize that, don't you?"

He did.

All Alessio could think to reply was, "But shouldn't I?"

CHAPTER 8
CORRADO

"*Stay down.*"

Corrado didn't.

His knees ached, and his legs shook so badly he was sure they were going to give out the second he put all of his weight back onto them, but he still forced his body back up. Back to his feet, he didn't stand quite as straight as he did the last ten times, not when he couldn't breathe doing it.

The straighter his spine, the worse the pain became. He trembled from the top of his head to his toes pressing against cold, damp cement. The amount of effort it took to pull his body up from the ground that time was clearly more than he realized.

Would he be able to do it again?

Corrado didn't know.

Fuck him if he wouldn't *try*.

Keeping his hands resting against his knees to give him a bit more support so he didn't topple over entirely—*that* was not happening—he took a few quick inhales to try and soothe the pain flaring in his side.

Was that his fucking kidney?

His ribs?

A collapsed lung?

All of the above?

Likely.

"You're a stubborn fuck, you know that?"

Corrado didn't reply to the voice in the darkness because that was the thing … he barely saw a flicker of them in the blackened room before they struck out at him again with those goddamn bamboo rods. Flexible, and *painful*, the rods didn't do serious damage to his body. Typically no blood, and nothing that was going to force them to pull him out of these fucking rooms, but they still hurt. They bruised, and they *broke*.

It didn't matter.

He'd learned early on during these rotational beatings when he was in the dark room—a far better place than the tank, as far as he was concerned—that they were looking for something from him. And maybe it was his stubbornness or his damn pride, but he refused to give it to them.

Today, they wanted him to stay on the floor.

Just *stay down*, they kept saying.

Corrado got back up. Every single time they put him to his knees, or on his back, he forced his body back up to his feet. If they wanted him down there on the ground like a *dog*, then they were going to have to make sure he *couldn't* get back up.

Simple as that.

It was stupid.

Part of him knew that.

The beating—their *lesson*—would end as soon as he continued to follow their directions. As soon as he lost himself in the darkness of the room where he wasn't sure where the blackness ended and he began, it would end because they broke him.

Corrado didn't want to be broken.

Not like *that*.

"*Stay down*," the order came again.

This voice was new—it didn't belong to Cree, or some of the others he'd become accustomed to joining him in the tank or the dark room. Then again, they barely spoke at all so he couldn't honestly say it was a new person. They very well might have been involved in this phase of his training for the entire time, but tonight was the first time they chose to spoke.

He preferred it when they didn't speak.

It pissed him off more.

Corrado dragged in a painful breath, one that hurt right down to the marrow in his bones—old blood made his tongue have a rusty flavor that seemed thick; the smell of piss lingered in the room, but he wasn't even sure if that was from him, or not; the stench of vomit clung to the walls, wherever the fuck they were.

This place was *hell*.

Dignity?

What was that?

Probably in that bucket in the corner where he was expected to use the bathroom, for fuck's sake. He still had his fucking pride. The pride was what was going to kill him here. Of that, he was most sure. If he could just give it up, right along with his dignity and everything else they had ripped away from him in these goddamn rooms, then this would *end*.

Corrado knew it.

He'd figured out the *trick*.

Pride was a bitch, though. The one thing he wouldn't give up to anyone for *anything*. Ever. He didn't know if that was the Guzzi in him—although, he wouldn't blame his twin a bit if Chris had already given up and given in to this process—or if it was simply the way his brain was wired.

It was pride that made him drag in one more quick breath, settle into the pain of what was going to come next when he made the move, and then he focused all his efforts into making his muscles do what he needed and wanted them to do. Which was stand—entirely straight again, not bent at the knees to give him support and rest from the ache radiating throughout his entire body.

No, straight.

All the way up again.

In the darkness, one's eyes might eventually become accustomed to it. Not so much so that they would be able to see everything like they could in the daytime, but just enough that where it only seemed like black space before, now there were shadows.

Corrado watched one of the shadows move. It came fast, the strike *hard*. Right against his chest was where it landed, the second coming right after to crack him against his knees. That one probably hurt the worst.

If he *never* saw bamboo again, it would be a great day for him. He'd decided. Not that he had time to think on that for too long.

He was on the floor again, blinking up at darkness and choking on the laughter that crawled its way out of his throat. The sound of his own distress and sardonic amusement echoed in the space, reverberating back to his spot on the cold, damp floor to taunt him.

Except he liked that sound.

It was better than the hell he usually found here.

"*Stay down*," he was told again.

Fuck that.

Corrado rolled over to his knees despite the way his entire body protested at the action. There was pain, and then there was agony. Some people liked to use those words interchangeably like they were the same things.

Here, he learned they were not.

He wished he felt simple pain, now.

Only pain.

Instead, he felt agony—straight, *pure* agony everywhere.

And not just from the beatings ... not just from the way his body felt broken, and ready to be done with this. No, because inside his mind, and in his heart, it was as though he were being torn in *two*.

The part that wanted to stop.

The part that needed to *continue*.

They would not break him.

He would not beg.

But *fuck* ... were they going to kill him trying?

He didn't know.

"*God*, stay down," he heard somewhere behind him.

Corrado couldn't.

That wasn't how he was made.

They could take the rest of it from him—a lot of it, they already had. Should they want his dignity so he wouldn't understand what shame felt like? *Fine*, take it. If they needed his body to learn to enjoy pain and discomfort so it could never be used against him? *Great*, they had that now. Did they need to take his emotions and twist them like his dark thoughts, lost to blackened walls and the water that rushed into his lungs every time they put him in the tank? *Okay*, he no longer cared.

But not his pride.

That was his.

There were times when the darkness of the rooms seemed like an old friend to Corrado. He found comfort in the rooms when he was totally alone—when the time bled together because he no longer knew what day it was.

Ha.

That was funny.

He had no clue how long he'd been doing this.

Days?

Weeks?

Months?

It could be any or all of those things, he understood. There was no real thing for him to use to mark the time in these rooms. Not when the people came just enough to give him food, as little as that was, or to beat the hell out of him again.

Never mind when they switched rooms.

Hood over his head.

Rough hands.

Harsh orders in his ears.

Still, he found comfort in the silence and the darkness. Oh, it played tricks on him, sure. The darkness chased away his ability to sleep, making him wired and staring into black space until he was sure he fell asleep just like that.

Sitting there.

With his eyes open.

Some people couldn't take darkness.

Corrado found he liked it.

He'd started measuring his breaths to combat the pain he constantly battled, but even that wasn't helping *now*. Nothing helped.

A buzz speared through the silence of the room, but unlike before when Corrado was new to these rooms, he no longer froze in fear and panic at the sound. That buzzer meant one of three things, and none of them made him afraid anymore.

One, a room switch.

Two, a beating.

Three, food and water.

There was no fourth option, and he had become so used to it being either a room switch or a beating far more often than food that he no longer gave a damn. He wasn't going to start in fear every time they came into the room for him—maybe they wanted that, or perhaps they liked it too much.

Whatever it was, he wouldn't be doing it.

The door opening was the only bit of light he got to see now. Just a slate of bright yellow color that seemed so blinding when the door moved that he had to look away from it so that his eyes didn't sting. Although, the one thing that never changed regardless if they were bringing him food or there to deliver a beating was the fact that the whole team entered the room.

All five of them.

Or was it six?

Corrado wasn't sure.

It didn't matter.

All of them contributed to his *training*. In one way or another.

Except this time, only one person was haloed by the light of the door. His shadow stretched along the cement floor with the stream of color, dragging through wet spots and cracks only to stop right before Corrado's feet.

A part of him just *knew* who it was. Maybe by the body shape, or the shaggy hair that the figure pushed back with one hand.

"Les," he mumbled.

It was easier than saying Alessio's full name.

His mouth *hurt*.

It all fucking hurt.

Alessio crossed the floor with quick steps, and never once did the door close behind him. Something else that was entirely unusual. When the team stepped into the rooms, the door *always* closed behind them. Like they were worried he might try to bolt, and they decided to take the option away altogether.

Not this time.

Corrado blinked as Alessio kneeled down beside him, and set a couple of items to the floor. He tried to take in his features, but he was pretty sure one of his eyes were swollen shut, and he couldn't see all that well in the darkness anyway. Not with that added bit of light shadowing Alessio's face as he put together something he'd set on the floor.

"You called me Les this time."

Corrado chuckled, but that hurt, too. "Don't get used to it, okay?"

"Mmm, here," Alessio said quietly, "*drink*."

Corrado didn't even bother to ask what it was that the man offered him—but it was cool, had a fruity flavor, if not a bit *chalky*, too. Still, he drank it down, eventually taking the bottle directly from Alessio to hold it up himself with shaking hands that clenched too tightly around the plastic, so much so that he spilled a bit.

Alessio didn't seem to mind.

"It has vitamins, and … other things," Alessio explained, even though Corrado hadn't asked. "It'll help; you've been down here too long, and you need *something*."

"How long?"

"A month."

That long?

Corrado tried to settle that, but he couldn't. Not that it mattered, as his mind wasn't working that well, anyway. Even there, it seemed like all he could think about was darkness and silence. Was that a part of the plan, too?

"Chris?"

Alessio, seemingly understanding his question even though he hadn't given much detail, said, "He started phase two last week."

But he was out of the rooms.

Out of the *tank*.

Corrado could breathe easier for that.

He hadn't startled when the door was open, or when he realized it was Alessio that came into the room, but he did jump a bit when something warm pressed against the side of his face in the darkness. Alessio's hand, he quickly knew. His palm curved against Corrado's jaw, and then his thumb drifted over the swell of his bottom lip.

Gentle.

Slow.

Kind.

All things he was not given in these rooms.

"You have to give them what they want," Alessio murmured, "do you hear me?"

"They want too much."

"You *have to.*"

He didn't reply because he didn't feel like repeating himself.

Alessio's sigh echoed beside him, his thumb sweeping Corrado's mouth again. "*Stubborn.* That's what you are. It's a process, Corrado, you have to trust it."

"I gave them everything."

All that he could give, anyway.

"The rest, I'm keeping," he mumbled.

Silently, Alessio leaned in, and pressed his forehead to the side of Corrado's cheek. He didn't linger there for very long. Just quick enough for Corrado to feel his warmth, and know his presence was *real.* This hadn't been something that the darkness did to his mind—it wasn't another trick.

"I gotta go," Alessio quietly, his words whispering along Corrado's bruised skin.

"I know."

"*Trust the process.*"

He did.

Just not the way they wanted him to.

~

Another round in the fucking tank.

Another round in the dark room.

Corrado wanted it to *end*.

It was a mantra in his mind now—one that wouldn't leave him alone during his waking hours. Which was damn near constantly. He found it hard to sleep in the darkness now. Impossible, really. He was sure humans weren't made to go days and days and days without sleep, but somehow, he was doing it.

Or … he was falling asleep and waking up without realizing it. He closed his eyes to darkness and opened them to the same thing. Time was irrelevant, and he didn't even comprehend when it was passing him by.

The first time they put him in the dark room, he *hated* the floor. Sure, he liked it more than being dunked into the tank for several minutes at a time without being allowed to breathe, but he still fucking hated it. Cold, wet, and cracked … there was no way to get comfortable, and he was convinced that coldness soaked into his bones *constantly*. And the wetness? He was never going to get dry.

Now, though?

Now, he didn't care at all. The discomfort he used to feel at being on the floor of the dark room was a moot point to everything else. He didn't get chilled from the cold, and the wetness making his dirty clothes irritate his bruised skin further was a background thought.

He simply didn't feel it at all.

Even the tank didn't bother him so much now. That had been the worst—trying to overcome the realization that, yes, he was probably going to die in that fucking water if they kept the top on him for another ten seconds. His vision would blacken, and his lungs protested so much when he was under the water that he was sure death was imminent.

Now, he just wished it would happen.

If it was going to kill him, then *do it*.

Resting on his stomach in the dark room, Corrado's head rested on his arms, and he faced what he suspected was the door. He couldn't be sure because they still brought him in here with a hood over his head to confuse the hell out of him.

It worked, too.

Every damn time.

Still, he laid there and waited.

For a beating.

For food.

For *light*.

Drumming his fingers to the floor, a sharp thought sliced through his mind—something he'd not really considered before right *now*. He was bored.

The beatings wouldn't kill him.

The food would be fine.

The light didn't last.

And he was just … bored.

Corrado blinked, but what else could he do?

He stayed on the floor.

Bored.

He wasn't sure how long he was down there like that, waiting for something that wouldn't come. Long enough that he realized, *somehow* without a sense of time, that they were incredibly late bringing him food. And it had been a span of time since the team came in to try and beat the pride out of him, too.

He was on the floor for long enough that he was sure he would die there, wasted and broken, but it seemed like The League had one more surprise for him. Once again, when the buzz rang out in the room to signal the door opening, he didn't move an inch.

A beating?

Food?

Les?

He doubted it would be Alessio.

It was actually ... no one.

The door stayed open, light spilling in to streak across the floor from the corridor. No one came to stand there. Nothing happened at all.

Corrado kept waiting.

Still, nothing changed.

The door stayed open.

Maybe it was because his body had been put through hell, and his mind was currently shattered into a thousand tiny pieces, but he didn't move, either. He stayed right there on the floor, watching the light spill in and waiting for something to happen.

Anything.

It was the not knowing that bothered him the most. He'd become accustomed to their routine down here, and what he could expect to happen to him. He found comfort in that—in the *knowing*. And right now, he didn't know a fucking thing.

Minutes passed.

Then, maybe an hour.

It took Corrado entirely too long to get up from the floor when he realized no one was coming, and the door had been purposefully opened. Or, he suspected that was the case. They didn't open it if they didn't mean to.

Stumbling, weak, and nauseous with every step he took, Corrado left the dark room. He couldn't properly process things in the light, but he forced himself to walk down the corridor. How long did that take?

Too long.

And then another corridor.

Stairs that made his bones ache.

At the top of those, he found a black door with a camera overhead. He stared up at it because the door didn't actually have a handle on it for him to open it. Tipping his head to the side, he waited for a second before a buzz echoed, and *that* door opened, too.

In the next corridor, he realized all the other doors stayed firmly shut. He was being *guided* through The League's complex. Only allowed to walk where they allowed him to, and granted entry to the corridors and stairwells where they wanted him to be.

The dark room taught him something else.

Trust them.

They could and would do a lot to him—everything and anything to break him, or take from him, but they wouldn't kill him. They wanted him to understand that. They *needed* him to trust their process, and *listen.*

Orders were not always verbal.

Requests, not always obvious.

Lessons, found between the *lines.*

They got their point across.

But he still had his pride.

Corrado followed whoever was controlling the doors, and guiding him. His steps were far too slow, and *painful.* But he pushed through it because if anything, those rooms downstairs taught him he could handle a hell of a lot more than a little bit of pain.

Pain would pass.

Or he would get used to it.

One or the other.

Soon, he started to recognize the corridors, even though the doors to the rooms were still tightly shut as he passed them. Only one—the first room he'd spent any amount of time in when he first arrived at The League—was open.

The knife room.

Corrado stood in the doorway, and watched the man standing about twenty feet from the target blocks. He either didn't care that Corrado was behind him, or he hadn't noticed his arrival. Flicking his wrist back, Alessio tossed a knife that spun through the air so fast, it was nothing more than a blur before it embedded itself directly into the middle of the red circle on the target.

"Good shot," Corrado mumbled.

Alessio didn't startle at his words, simply glanced over his shoulder with a kind gaze that drifted over him like he was taking him in without judgement or comment. "Takes practice—you'll learn, too, if you excel in it."

Huh.

Corrado swallowed the thickness in his throat, managing to ask, "Is letting me out to wander the halls part of the process, too?"

Alessio picked up another knife from the table beside him, but instead of throwing that one, he flipped it over and over in his palm. "Possibly. It all depends on the prospect, and what they need, I think."

Ah.

Corrado understood.

He didn't need to be explicitly told.

They were going to kill him down there trying to take from him what he wouldn't give, and so, someone decided that it was better to compromise. And here he was, *out.*

"Want to try?" Alessio asked, holding out the knife for Corrado to take.

He didn't move.

His body hurt too much.

"What happens now?"

Alessio arched a brow. "Phase two."

"What is—"

"Recovery for a short bit, then the tests begin to find where you excel the most, so they can focus, and hone your skills."

"Well, all right."

What could he say to that?

"Corrado."

He looked up, meeting Alessio's gaze across the room. "Yeah?"

"You did well."

"I feel like death."

Alessio grinned. "You look like it, too."

He cleared his throat. "I spent my eighteenth birthday in those rooms."

Silence coated the space between the two of them. Not for long, though.

"I spent mine watching you," Alessio returned.

"Oh."

Alessio offered the knife again. "You're probably too weak, but you can try, if you want."

"I thought rich hands weren't meant to touch those, only pay someone else to do it."

"I can be wrong sometimes."

"Can you?"

Alessio gave him a look.

"Can you *really*?" Corrado pressed.

"Don't get used to it," Alessio told him.

Corrado smiled. "Good to know."

CHAPTER 9
ALESSIO

"I know what you said. *Eighteen*, Dare."

The current source of Alessio's irritation—although if he were being an honest man, he had a lot of those annoyances lately—didn't turn away from the electronic map that covered the touchscreen on his office wall. He waved a hand over his shoulder, like Alessio was a fly he was trying to bat away.

"Are you even listening to me?"

"Annoying, isn't it?" Dare returned. "You do the same thing to literally everyone else, Les. If you don't like when people ignore *you*, perhaps you should attempt to stop doing it to us. You're beyond the annoying stage where I can use your age as an excuse for your bad fucking attitude. Besides, what I need more than you out on an assignment is for you to listen."

"Yeah, well, we don't all get what we want."

"Keep thinking that way, and see where it gets you."

Alessio glared at the back of Dare's head, willing the man to combust right on the spot. Sometimes, it was the little things that inspired the worst kinds of reactions in him. This was certainly one of those things.

Again, if he were being honest, there were many.

This was a big one, though.

"I went through all that training for you to keep me—"

"I have several job offers on the table right now," Dare

interjected, still seemingly unwilling to turn around and face Alessio in the doorway. "And while *some* will go to others, because they have the specific skills for those assignments, I am deciding which one might be best for you. I don't take every job that comes in from clients who don't have a contract with a specific League member, and a lot of these are exactly that."

"So, I'll have an assignment soon, then?"

"I didn't say that."

Fuck.

Frustration slipped through Alessio's bloodstream, heavy and thick. Like every other conversation he tried to have with Dare, he suspected this one was going to end the same exact way as it always did. Dare talking him in circles, Alessio getting pissed, and after he'd walked away, he would realize he didn't get shit that he wanted.

"I want an assignment," Alessio said.

"And you will get one when you are ready for one."

"I'm ready now!"

Dare pointed at the map he'd been surveying since the moment Alessio came to his office. "That's a mountain range there—do you think a complex *within* a mountain would be a possibility? A back up, we'll call it. Just in case something happened, and I needed to move out the main area of operation for safety reasons."

"I ... *what?*"

"A complex *inside* a mountain range."

"What does that have anything to do with the fact I want to go out on an assignment?" Alessio demanded.

Dare glanced over his shoulder, his brow furrowing. "Oh, I thought you realized I was done with that conversation. So, if you don't want to indulge these new plans of mine, you don't need to keep standing there."

Alessio *balked.*

It took him entirely too long to come up with a suitable response to that, and it wasn't nearly as insulting as he wanted it to be. Shame, really.

"You're impossible," he snapped at Dare.

"But am I really, though?"

"*Yes.*"

"And you wonder where you get it from, no?"

The two of them stared at one another for a spread of time, neither of them moving an inch or giving a damn inch. Finally, Alessio's irritation spilled over as he made a disgusted noise under his breath and turned to leave the office.

At his back, Dare called, "And don't bother the trainees today, Les, they need to *focus.*"

"I want an assignment!"

"Soon."

Yeah, *right.*

To Dare, that could mean months.

Fuck it.

He'd go to Cree.

⌇

Prospects for The League were given one week to recover after phase one before phase two began in full force. A single week with whatever medical care they needed, all the rest that would put them mostly back on their feet again, and then it was back to business as normal.

If intensive, seven-day-a-week training was normal.

The prospects were shoved from one thing to the next— tested on every skill The League could throw at them within a few weeks, and once they figured out where someone *really* excelled, then that's where they started to focus.

For himself, it had been weapons.

Knives, guns, and more.

Any weapon they put in his hands, he could use. And he could probably use it in several different ways to kill someone, if that was the need. He could also *make* a weapon out of just about anything because to him, everything *was* dangerous enough to kill. He just needed to figure out he wanted to do it.

Corrado and Chris were still in their second week of skill testing. Which was why he wasn't very surprised to find Cree hanging a few steps back from the mats set out on the gym floor where the twins were currently working with a League member who excelled in weapons, and specifically, fighting *with* weapons.

"What do you need?" Cree asked before Alessio had even spoke behind him.

He sighed. "I hate when you do that."

"Do what?"

"*Know* where I am."

"Yes, it's a *terrible* thing that I concern myself with your whereabouts so that I can make sure you're not finding some trouble when I'm not looking."

Just like Dare.

Alessio decided he wasn't falling down *this* rabbit hole again today. He'd done that already with Dare, and he wasn't doing it with Cree. It would end *worse* than the first time, that was a fucking guarantee. Cree was even less likely to take his shit.

"So, what do you want?" Cree asked.

Alessio's gaze cut to the mat when a *smack* echoed. The stick of bamboo Oliver was using as a stand-in for a weapon —it still hurt like a motherfucker, but it was *safer*—cracked against the back of Corrado's legs, and sent him sprawling to the mat with a hissed *shit* falling from his cringing lips.

He flinched, too.

That one *hurt*.

On the other side of the mat, watching from a safe distance because it probably wasn't his turn yet, Chris clicked his tongue, and looked like he was ready to back away altogether. That was the thing about The League.

No one said the training was *stupid*.

The same shit they used to break them with were the same tools they used to train them later. No doubt, the twins had more than enough of bamboo sticks being used to leave bruises on their body after the rooms downstairs. So, that meant they were either going to learn *fast* how to avoid those fucking strikes, or they were going to get knocked down time and time again.

It was a mind fuck, really.

"Les," Cree said again.

Yeah, yeah.

The whole reason he was here, right.

He kept one gaze on Corrado who pushed up from the mat with a snarl under his breath to face Oliver once again. Only this time, Oliver was smirking a little too much for Alessio's liking. It was one thing to be trained, but it was quite another when someone took it a little too far, and began taunting you at the same time when you failed.

"Dare," Alessio said, "you need to talk to him."

Cree raised a single black eyebrow, but didn't look away from the mats. "Why would I need to do that?"

"I want an assignment."

"And he won't give you one?"

"Exactly that."

Thud.

Alessio turned in just enough time to see Corrado crash to the mat, only this time, on his back. His arms flew out wide, and his eyes squeezed shut as the air rushed from his lips with a heavy *whoosh*. Oliver's laughter echoed in the gym as he pointed the stick of bamboo in Corrado's direction on the mat, his sneer wicked and amused.

"Come on, now, get up," Oliver said, his hand tightening further around the middle of the stick as he rounded the mats to come slightly closer to Corrado's prone form. "I heard you kept doing that in the dark room, yeah? You kept getting up, didn't you? Even when you were supposed to stay the fuck down, so don't disappoint me now, shithead. *Get up.*"

Alessio scowled, ready to tell Oliver where he could shove his fucking taunts. After all, Corrado wasn't the only one who spent time in those rooms downstairs, and Alessio had been in the complex two years ago when Oliver was trained, too.

He remembered how the man begged.

How he *cried*.

"It's possible," Cree said, dragging his attention away from the situation a few feet away, "that Dare thinks you might be more useful here for a little while."

"Why in the hell would he think that?"

Cree's gaze drifted from the people on the mats to Alessio, and then back again. *Very* pointedly. "Do you think Dare would have allowed you down in that room when someone was actively in phase one—when you *weren't* part of the training team, mind you—if he didn't think you would help? Or when he was released from the rooms, the path he was allowed to take led him to someone he would immediately trust when he would need it the most?"

"I—"

"Not everything is about you, Les," Cree murmured, his attention going back to the training. "And that is something you should remember. If you are better *here* for a time, then here is where Dare is going to keep you. You think it's about you, and Dare's feelings, which means you're selfish because you automatically dismiss the needs of *others*. The League is about more than just you—something we have always made clear."

Well …

Damn.

"All right," he muttered.

He wasn't happy about it, though.

Another loud smack drew Alessio's attention back to the fight happening on the mat. Or rather, the ass-whooping Oliver was currently inflicting on Corrado. Not to mention, the taunts that followed every single crack of the bamboo against another part of Corrado's form.

He was going too far.

Alessio knew it.

No one was expected to pick up one specific part of training right away. It took time, and muscle memory for some of it. Other parts of it was all in someone's mind. Except, Oliver was acting as though Corrado should be on his feet, and able to duck and dodge that fucking bamboo like the rest of them could when he was wielding it.

"*Get*." Smack. "*Up*." Smack. "Now."

"Cree," Alessio said under his breath, "tell him to knock it *off*."

Cree said nothing, only tipped his head to the side like he was considering the scene in front of him. His gaze drifted from the twin at the other side of the mats watching, to the one currently on his knees with his arm raised to protect his face in case that stick came back down again, and then to the asshole with a God complex.

"*Cree*."

"Is that what it is, Corrado?" Oliver asked. "You *like* getting knocked on your ass like a fucking idiot?"

Corrado said nothing.

He didn't even react.

Not a blink.

Not a word.

Not a scowl.

Nothing.

He simply tried to stand again because *that's* what he was supposed to do—Alessio knew it. He was supposed to keep getting back up, and trying again until he could dodge the attack, and then they would switch places for his twin to do the same. Except, Oliver didn't even let him stand before he hit him *again.*

Knocking him back again.

And then, Oliver pulled the rod back to swing before Corrado even had time to adjust to the fact that he was on the mat again. He was going to hit him *because* he was down; something he wanted to do, not because it would teach a lesson, or was part of the training.

Alessio moved before he could think better of it. Darting forward fast, out of Cree's reach who likely would have pulled him back had he understood what Alessio was going to do, he stepped onto the mats, grabbed the smooth end of the bamboo rod where Oliver had it extended, and yanked *hard.*

The surprise move—Oliver was only thinking about what was in front of him, not behind—allowed Alessio to snatch the weapon right out of the man's hand. He flicked his wrist, flipping the rod over to his dominant hand, where he caught it right in the middle. Flexing his arm once to swing it back, he let the rod fly, cracking Oliver right in the middle of the throat with enough force to send him to his back on the mats, and *without* the ability to breathe, too.

Then, he took one more step, the weapon already poised to strike again as he pointed it at Oliver's chest. The assassin on the floor stared up at him with fury, his fists balling against the mats as he tried to gain his bearings.

"Remember where *you* started," Alessio murmured, "and how you got *here*."

That said, he dropped the bamboo to Oliver's chest. He turned to step off the mat, done with putting Oliver in his place, and willing to see how the man treated his prospect *now*. It was the sharp edge in Corrado's voice when he called his name that made his steps hesitate.

"*Alessio.*"

Over his shoulder, he found Corrado glaring at him.

Scowl in place.

Fists clenched.

Body tense.

Angry all over.

"Don't do that again," Corrado uttered, teeth clenched.

Alessio said nothing because he didn't need to. There was one thing the rooms downstairs didn't take from Corrado, and while it may not seem important in the grand scheme of things, it might be the only thing that would get him through the training.

If only because he couldn't give up.

His *pride*.

Not bothering to respond—Corrado wouldn't want him to—he turned to leave the gym altogether. Dare had been right; he didn't need to bother the prospects when they were being trained. He *was* a distraction.

At least, for this particular one.

"Les," Cree said quietly as he passed, "you know better."

He shrugged, saying nothing.

Cree only nodded back.

CHAPTER 10
CORRADO

"Tomorrow, six AM, *sharp*," Oliver said to the twins, "make sure you are both down here, and ready to go again."

Corrado felt like telling the man to stick his early morning training session right up his fucking ass, but he didn't think that would do him any good. Except to maybe have Oliver riding *his* ass worse than he already did.

"Got it," Chris muttered, taking it slow as he bent down to pick up the shirt he'd discarded earlier. "Ass crack of dawn to get the shit beat out of me again—*perfect*."

"I can hear the sarcasm."

"I wanted you to."

Corrado might have enjoyed the rare sight of his twin being a smartass—Chris was far more likely to fall back and stay in line—but he was too sore and *way* too pissed for that. If his entire body wasn't a canvas of newly formed bruises, then he was going to be very shocked. He fucking hated bamboo now.

Hated it.

"And you, did you hear me?"

Corrado's back tensed, knowing Oliver was talking to him. The only thing he really wanted to do to that prick was bust his mouth, but he had other things to handle first. Eventually, he would get his chance to put Oliver in his place, but today was *not* that day.

Unfortunately.

Soon.

"*Corrado.* Did you hear me?"

"Yeah, I heard you," Corrado said, waving a hand over his shoulder.

Stepping off the mats, he didn't even bother to turn around to directly speak to Oliver—he was a background thought, now. This session was done for the day, the asshole would get to leave the complex, and Corrado wouldn't have to deal with him until tomorrow. That was fine with him.

"Cree."

"What, Oliver?"

"Next week … I want Alessio down here to spar with them both. He's close to their height, give or take an inch, and build. We both know he's good with a weapon in his hands."

"That's fine."

"Good—"

"For Christopher," Cree added, keeping that same bored tenor as he spoke. "We'll have to find someone else for Corrado."

"Why? They're the same fucking *people.*"

Their conversation wasn't all that important to Corrado. His thoughts were somewhere else entirely as he stepped behind the half partition wall in front of a line of showers that gave them *some* privacy from the rest of the gym. Not that it gave them any privacy when someone else was under the showers, too.

But that was the thing.

Here, there was no privacy. And if one *thought* they were having a private moment, then they were foolish. There was also no sense of a man—or woman, although Corrado had only seen a handful of those since his arrival—holding onto any shred of dignity, either.

After the *rooms*, what was the point?

Dignity was gone.

Corrado wondered if he might get his dignity back or even his sense of *shame* ... but he didn't think so. At least, not while he was at The League. They made sure to remind them whenever it was needed that here, things like that were nothing more than a distraction. Lose it, get rid of it, hand it over, tuck it away ... whatever someone needed to do to forget about it, that's what The League expected. They were here to mold them into what they wanted them to be, not to hold someone's hand because they were worried someone might see their cock when they showered.

Not that he was concerned about *that*.

If people wanted to look, they could look.

Fuck 'em.

Corrado *tried* to follow along with Cree and Oliver's conversation as he dropped his shorts, and slung them over the wall. He still wasn't even sure what the problem was, or why Cree was giving Oliver a hard time over his request that Alessio be in the gym next week to spar with both twins, but whatever.

"I just don't understand why we have to bring in a whole second member to train with the other—"

"Because I said so," Cree replied dryly.

"What's he on about?" Chris asked, slipping behind the wall.

Corrado shrugged, stepping under the spray of hot water after turning the dial almost as hot as it would go. There was nothing better on sore, aching muscles than hot water. Later, he might see if he could find a bathtub in this maze of *hell*.

"I mean, didn't you spar with Alessio the first day we were here?"

Water sluiced down Corrado's face, and he closed his eyes as he scrubbed his hands down his jaw to relieve some of the tension there, too. He wasn't even listening to his twin, not when the hot water was making him feel ten times better than he had just a few minutes ago.

Chris didn't seem to care. "Oliver is right. That doesn't make sense."

"Cree—"

"You cannot teach *affection* with your fists," Cree said, "and that is not a lesson either of them need to learn between one another, sparring or not. If it is okay one time, it becomes okay at other times. My decision is made—find someone else."

Corrado's eyes popped open.

Chris made a noise under his breath. "*Well*, all right … he ain't wrong."

He might have told his twin to shut the fuck up, but he was more interested in the fact that Oliver looked like a gaping fish, and Cree had turned away from the man now. Briefly, Cree looked his way, met Corrado's gaze, and then just as quickly, left the gym altogether without as much as a glance back.

He was done.

Said what he said.

Cree never offered more than what he gave, Corrado found, but it was usually *important* things when he did speak. A man of few words because he watched more than he talked, Cree noticed far more than people gave him credit for, and he considered *everything* because of it.

Corrado cranked the latch to stop the water, wanting to get the hell out of the gym and back to the other thing that was currently on his mind. He barely bothered to use one of the towels waiting on hooks to dry off, instead haphazardly running it through his hair before throwing on his shirt and shorts.

"Hey," Chris said.

He didn't look back at his twin. "I'll catch you later, okay?"

"*Corrado.*"

"*What*, Chris?"

Chris's shower was turned off then, too. Corrado turned to face his brother—who was still naked, and didn't seem to give a damn, much like he hadn't earlier—without a shred of emotion on his face. He didn't *want* people to know that it bothered him that his interest in Alessio was clear, or vice versa. Those were things he always kept to himself, and he wasn't interested in sharing them now.

"It's okay," Chris said, lifting one shoulder like it didn't matter, "you know that, right? It's *fine*, Corrado."

He was *so* fucking grateful that there was another person in this world who not only shared his face, but also his mind. Because apparently Chris could just tell what his twin was thinking without needing to be told.

Yeah, just *great*.

Perfect.

Except it wasn't.

"Leave it alone," he told his brother.

Chris sighed. "It's not a big deal that other people *notice* there's something going on. He didn't say something to make it a *thing*. He said it because he's looking out for both of you —he had a point, too. Don't get in your fucking feelings about it."

"Leave it alone, Chris."

Corrado *got it*.

He understood why his twin thought he was making a big deal out of nothing, but Chris didn't understand. It wasn't *just* about his sexuality for Corrado—it went beyond that, too. And it seemed just like with everything else in his life lately, the issue started and ended with Alessio. This problem was no different.

It wasn't only about his sexuality.

It was more than that.

Like the fact Corrado walked into The League, and people—Alessio, for one, but he suspected there were more —looked at him with an opinion already formed. About who he was, what he came from, and the things he was capable of. It wasn't *just* Alessio, although he had been the first to verbally make his opinion known to Corrado. It didn't matter; he'd heard *other* members make the same kind of comments when they thought his back was turned.

He was *spoiled*.

He'd been pampered.

He didn't know how to *work*.

As it was, Corrado already had *that* shit he was dealing with here. It showed him he would need to work twice as hard to prove himself here, and make a spot that was his which said he, too, was *worthy*.

Now, there was this, too.

This.

If the members of The League who milled about, or those who were actively taking part in training the twins, didn't already believe something was happening between Corrado and Alessio—they wouldn't be wrong—they probably had a good idea *now*. For one, because of Alessio's show earlier in the gym, and now because of Cree, too.

It was yet another thing.

Something else for someone to use and say, *he's only where he is because of this.* Or, *he'll always need someone watching his back because he wasn't treated the same as the rest of us.* Corrado knew how this garbage went, and he didn't want to be put in the same trash pile.

Once again … his pride was still a bitch.

That was why Corrado found himself standing in the doorway of Alessio's private rooms instead of his own, where he should have been to change clothes before going to find something to eat. No, he had to deal with *this* first.

"What you did today—don't *ever* fucking do it again. You got me?"

Resting on the bed with his right ankle propped over his bent, left knee, Alessio slowly looked over the edge of the thriller in his hands. His stormy blue gaze drifted to the side as though he was considering what Corrado said, before coming back to the angry man standing his doorway.

"Sure, come in," Alessio muttered. "Why not?"

"Cut the shit."

An arched brow answered Corrado back. Alessio and his attitude was fucking *infamous* around this place. One could tell if the guy was going to be easy to deal with simply by the way he walked out of his rooms first thing in the morning. Head down, he was ready to *fight*. Head up, he'd be mildly pleasant. That attitude of his never went away.

The book in Alessio's hands pissed Corrado off more, though.

Alessio didn't move it, or set it aside. In fact, he went back to reading like he had better things to do than bother with Corrado. "All right, come back when you're in a better mood."

"*Les.*"

"Hmm?"

"What you did earlier in the gym … that can't happen again. It's bad enough that I already have people who think I shouldn't be here to begin with. *You* were one of those fucking people, remember? I don't need you—"

"I was trying to help."

"It doesn't help. It makes shit worse."

"Corrado—"

"Don't step in for me again," Corrado said, his jaw tensing with every word. "The last thing I need is that kind of help around here, and you know it."

His piece said—because he was sure he didn't need to say more now—he turned to leave. It was only Alessio's next words that made him hesitate to leave.

"Sorry I fucking gave a shit, then."

Corrado spun back around so fast, the room was a blur. The thing was, by the time he turned around to respond, Alessio had already tossed his book aside so he could stand from the bed. The two of them met toe-to-toe in the middle of the room, never once breaking eye contact, either. He didn't know what bothered him more ... the fact Alessio didn't *get it*, or that it felt like he didn't fucking care either way.

"What did you just say?"

Alessio cocked his head to the side. "I didn't stutter. If you want to make an issue out of nothing, then do that, but do it *somewhere else*, Corrado."

He moved closer one inch.

Alessio didn't back away.

That probably wasn't the best idea, if only because *now* Corrado was close enough to Alessio that their chests grazed when he breathed a little too deeply. He could feel the other man's *heat*—smell the woodsy aroma that always accompanied the leather undertones of his scent. Like this, so fucking close, he could see the flakes of dark navy that made his blue eyes rage like a storm, and the small scar that ran right through the cupid's bow on his upper lip. He could count the few scattered freckles that dotted the bridge of his nose, nearly the same tanned color of his skin, so they would be missed if one was too far away. Except, right then, Corrado wasn't too far away. He was *too* close.

And he noticed everything.

Things that made Alessio uniquely *him*.

Things Corrado liked.

He wanted to be *pissed*. It was easier for him to deal with Alessio and the shit he felt when the other man was around when his anger was present because that took over everything else first, and nothing else mattered.

Things weren't so confusing.

But it was.

Alessio made it confusing.

"That kind of help doesn't *help*," Corrado said.

"Or you got in your feelings because it was me."

"No—"

"I think that's exactly what happened."

"I think you don't listen as well as you *talk*."

Alessio blinked.

Corrado stood firm.

"If you want to help, that isn't the way you do it," Corrado said, reaching up to poke Alessio right in the middle of his chest hard enough that it moved him a bit. Slightly, and not much, but it still did. "Do you hear me?"

Alessio's gaze blazed with fury ... and something else entirely. "Don't put your hands on me unless you plan to use them in a way I'll like. Do you hear *me*?"

He hesitated, then, his mind snapping back to earlier. To important words, and a lesson he hadn't thought about, really.

Fists cannot teach affection.

Here, at The League, fists taught *a lot*. Violence kept them in line, and made sure they understood exactly what was expected of them. And yet, it had been made explicitly clear, even if the words hadn't been told to him directly, that between Corrado and Alessio ... violence should never be the first default.

Ever.

He didn't understand this *thing* happening between him and Alessio. Sometimes, it made him infuriated. Sometimes, he was drawn in again just because. It left him a mess, and that wasn't something he was accustomed to.

It didn't matter, though.

Something *was* happening.

He had to be mindful.

Corrado dropped his hand instantly. "Sorry."

"Good. And don't do it again."

"Same for you, then."

"Is that really a fucking problem for you?"

Corrado let out a hard breath, and it ached the whole way out. "Yeah, man, it *is*. It doesn't help me here, and if you gave a shit, you'd realize that."

It took a second.

Then, two.

Alessio's stance softened. "I do ... know that, I mean. I didn't think."

"*Try.*"

In a blink, Alessio's defensiveness was back. His gaze narrowed. "Is that what you want to do right now—*fight* because you've got a problem with your fucking pride? Didn't you get enough of that with Oliver beating the hell out of you all day?"

Corrado's fists flexed, but not because he wanted to hit Alessio. More because he was still quite aware of just how close the two were together, and *no* ... he didn't want to fight at all.

"No, I don't."

"Don't, *what?*"

"Want to fight."

He didn't mean for his voice to *roughen* like that—to

come out husky, and thick, but it still did. There was no mistaking what that meant.

Alessio swallowed hard, his gaze darting to Corrado's mouth before coming back up to meet his stare. "All you gotta do is *say*, Corrado. If you want something, then you say it."

Yeah, okay.

"I don't want to fi—"

He didn't even get to finish. Alessio caught that hand of his, and curled it in his own before his other came up to grab Corrado by his jaw. Fingers dug into his skin in the best way a split second before Alessio's mouth collided with his. The force of the kiss pushed him back against the wall, but not once did Alessio let him go.

Not once did he *back off*.

Corrado didn't want him to, anyway. Not when Alessio's hand let his go so that he could shove his under the waistband of his shorts to find his cock. Tight, fast strokes had his dick hardening quickly as Alessio's teeth dragged across his lower lip. And then that hand was gone from his shorts, replaced instead by Alessio's body pressing into his—the hard ridge of *his* erection grinding against Corrado's while the wall kept him steady when he felt like he might fucking *fall*.

He couldn't think to stand right then.

He didn't trust himself.

"The door," Corrado heard himself mutter when that kiss drifted down to the line of his jaw, and then lower still to where his pulse raced in his throat. "*The fucking door*."

"Close it."

The words were grunted against his skin—hard, and *hot*. The sound alone hit a spot inside that he didn't fucking know existed until that moment. A place that felt raw, and primal. Sex had always been fulfilling a need for Corrado, something he *did* because it felt good, and he wanted to. This right here, with Alessio …

Well, it felt like that first kiss had.

Like *war*.

With hands pulling roughly at clothes to get them *off*. Mouths that said very little, but couldn't stop seeking the other's out. Couldn't stop tasting and biting and *learning*. Skin rough from two-day stubble.

And then, when clothes were gone, and Alessio was on his knees, reaching for Corrado's cock, he tipped his head back and let out a hard groan. He felt the warm air hit the head of his dick a second before Alessio had him in his mouth, taking him down to the base, and coming up tight around his head with each suck.

He'd blow his load like that.

Just like that.

Seeing him on his knees like that?

Taking him like that?

Yeah.

And then Alessio had to go and fucking stun him— letting him go altogether, and standing fast to crash his mouth against Corrado's. He had to know, then, how fucking hard was he for him? Did his cock feel like it was aching as badly as his was?

Corrado stared down between them, reaching for the man's cock. Alessio's lips drifted over the side of his cheek as he watched while he stroked him in his hand. Hard, tight strokes that had Alessio cursing against his cheek in heavy exhales.

Tight against the head.

Looser at the base.

"Gonna make me come if you—"

"*Nah*," Corrado replied, letting Alessio go altogether, and pushing a hand against his chest to move him back a step.

"Not like *that*—not yet." One step turned into two, and then three. Alessio didn't drop his stare, hands shaking at his sides. Corrado got that; he understood why when his own body *vibrated* too. With need—for whatever *this* was. "Is this what you—"

"Yeah, I want that," Alessio murmured. "*You.*"

"I need—"

Alessio tipped his head to the side. "Nightstand."

He didn't even have to get the words out entirely, Alessio just knew, and for some reason ... the fact that the man wanted it that bad, that he wanted to be the one *fucked*, made the anticipation thrum deeper inside of Corrado. Until all he could feel was the bass of his heart thrumming right along with it.

Fuck.

Yet, Alessio didn't move as Corrado crossed the space to open the small drawer attached to the nightstand. He stayed standing even as Corrado pulled the items—condom, lube— out before dropping them to the sheets.

He met Alessio's stare as he stood straight again, inching in closer until their chests touched. It was in his eyes that he found the truth reflecting back to him—the truth that *yes*, what he wanted was to be the one beneath the other, he still had *fight* there. A battle that said he wanted to win, to control, to *fuck*. That same war Corrado found in their kiss, and their touches.

The roughness that spoke of a man, and who *liked* that, too.

Because that was the difference between men and women. In sex, women *could* be rough, and they could make it *hurt*, but those were far and few between. Sex, with women, he always found was soft, no matter how rough. Something that fulfilled an entirely different need for sex with him.

Men were not the same—that attraction, for Corrado, were two entirely different things. He wouldn't be so arrogant to say *every* bi or gay man felt that way, or perceived it the same as he did, but that's how he always found it to be. And right then, he was seeing the same thing in Alessio.

That fight.

This time, *he'd* give it.

Give *in*.

Next time was a whole other story, though.

So, Corrado gave him what he wanted. If he wanted *roughness* like he wanted the *fight*, then he could have that. He slammed a bruising kiss to Alessio's mouth as his hand wrapped around the front of his throat. Lips dragged over his savagely, determined to take the very breath out of him as he took Alessio down to the bed.

Hard bodies met, grinding as the two pulled harshly at what little clothes remained between them. Corrado didn't remember when that last piece of clothing hit the floor— when it was just warm skin and muscle meeting his, but there it was.

He felt Alessio's cock, already hard, slide against his own. Their hips moving in rhythm together to get that sensation, fast and desperate, he thought. That's what was thrumming through his bloodstream with his heart now.

Desperation.

"Fuck, *yeah*," Alessio groaned, mouth falling away from his.

Corrado's hand shoved between their bodies to get his hand where he needed it the most. He only leaned up just long enough to grab that bottle of lube before he popped the top open, and got the cool gel piled on his fingertips. He didn't keep the bottle, tossing it aside so he could get his hand back on Alessio's throat while his other started to *work*.

His fingertips pressed against the tight ring of Alessio's

ass. Just two, at first, working in with slow, twisting strokes. His fingers curved tighter around Alessio's throat as the man let out another one of those sounds.

Those *groans*.

And fuck, his moans.

His moans.

He was so fucking glad he wasn't new to this—himself, *and* Alessio. Learning sex was fucking *messy*, and this wasn't that at all. Not that he'd known that before this started, but he'd *assumed*. He knew he was right just by the way Alessio moved under him and *asked* for more. Any hesitations he had now were gone for sure.

"*Christ*," Alessio hissed when Corrado had two fingers stretching the man out.

Stormy blue met raging brown when Alessio's eyes lifted to meet his. And as much as he liked hearing those sounds, he wanted to *taste* them when they came out of the man. He got the heat of Alessio's mouth against his as he worked that third finger into his ass as his palm flexed against his throat.

Alessio's hands left the fisted sheets to grab onto Corrado's wrists. He could feel it, the push and pull of his hold on Corrado, the way he wanted to keep him right there, but push him back, too.

That fight ...

Against Corrado's roughness.

That's what he wanted.

He pulled his slick hand from Alessio and let go of his throat, too. Those fingers digging into the skin of his wrist hard enough to bruise loosened, and in a breath, Corrado had Alessio twisted around to his stomach on the bed. His teeth found the hard muscles of Alessio's back as he snatched up the packet on the bed. He made quick work of getting the condom open, and sliding it down. The lube on his fingers already soaking his length.

And *fuck*, he felt painful.

Throbbing and aching.

He stroked his dick, getting that lube all over as his mouth found Alessio's back again. The man pushed up against him, seeking *more*. His hands fisted into the sheets on the bed as Corrado fit the head of his cock against Alessio's ass.

He'd stretched him.

And he was still tight enough to hurt.

Alessio let out a shuddering breath, and Corrado slowed. He didn't need to hear his words to *know*—easy, easy. So, that's what he did, careful and fucking slow. Until his chest was so tight from holding back that it hurt, too. It was only when he was halfway to nine inches deep that he heard Alessio's voice, husky and *deep*.

"*Fuck*, yeah."

Corrado swore those two words rumbled along the bed, reaching his spot like a shot of heat right to his marrow. One hand splayed to Alessio's back, his other grabbing tight to the man's side.

It was only once he was seated entirely inside Alessio that *he* felt like he could take in a breath again. Still ragged and aching, though. His chest still felt too damn tight, and it wasn't going to get better until—

"Fucking make me *come*," Alessio murmured.

That.

Until that.

His hips pulled back from Alessio slightly faster than he'd worked his way in, and then flexed forward faster again. The rhythm became a little rougher with each push and pull. Alessio found Corrado's hand at his side, and yanked it under him.

He used Corrado's hand to tug at his cock, his own being

the one that worked him. He used him to get himself *off*, while Corrado used him to do the same.

"*Shit, shit,*" Corrado heard himself mumble.

He couldn't remember sex being so quiet. And he didn't want to remember it differently now.

So fucking intense.

Like it had turned into something else—something raw, a need that just had to be filled, and *now*. But *God*, where had this been?

His next thrust came *harder*, and Alessio let out a sound that felt primal. "Right there."

Alessio's back tensed. His fingers around Corrado's tightened, and pulled at his hand to work his length faster.

That sound came out of him again as warm cum hit Corrado's fingertips. "*Jesus*, Corrado."

He hadn't realized his own orgasm was so close until Alessio swore again, and his ass tightened around Corrado as he kept up his pace. But there it was, and he leaned down to splay his palm against Alessio's back, his teeth biting into warm skin as he came, too.

So fucking deep.

He couldn't speak.

Didn't want to.

Alessio let out a slow exhale. "What the fuck was that?"

Oh, fucking great.

So it hadn't just been him that *this* felt new for.

"Something good," Corrado mumbled against his skin.

"*Yeah.*"

As the shaking started to wane, his mouth trailed higher over Alessio's back. His teeth found the junction of Alessio's shoulder and neck, biting just hard enough for him to react. And he did—his semi-hard dick jerking in Corrado's hand. He tightened his grip just to let the man know he felt that, too.

"*Fuck*," Alessio mumbled. "Easy."

Corrado laughed. "*Now*, you want easy?"

"And?" Then, quieter, Alessio added, "I know I fucked up earlier … I didn't think because I didn't like *seeing* it—him taunting you when you were already down. So, I reacted."

Clearing his throat, Corrado pulled himself carefully from Alessio before rolling to his side on the double bed. Using his arms as a pillow, he stared hard at the ceiling for a while, saying nothing. He heard what Alessio told him; he understood it was *important*. Sometimes, things people said didn't seem all that deep on the surface, but it was the shit they *didn't* say that mattered the most.

He figured with this … the things Alessio said and didn't say were both equally important, and he needed to keep the fuck up.

Glancing over at his companion in the bed, Corrado replied, "I get it—you can't do it again, though."

Alessio, still on his stomach with his hands twisting into the edge of the comforter, curled his upper lip like the idea *offended* him. "What, protect you?"

Corrado frowned.

Was that what he'd thought he did?

"I don't think I can do that," Alessio said after a beat of silence passed between them. "But I'm not really sorry about it."

Yeah.

CHAPTER 11
ALESSIO

"What do you think he said?" Chris asked, his sarcasm heavy. "It's *Cree*, you figure it out."

"So, he basically told you no, but spouted some Yoda bullshit while he was at it."

"Yeah, and—"

"You didn't have to be here, though." Corrado made a noise under his breath, adding, "We told you that, but you decided to stay. I don't know what you want me to tell you."

"It's not about *being* here."

"I think it is."

"Corrado—"

"I don't know what else to tell you, Chris. You chose to stay. *This* is what it means."

Chris made a disgusted sound. "Fuck all of this."

Something crashed against the floor—a metal *ting* ringing out—before a few seconds later, Chris came flying out of the room where he and Corrado had been working for a good portion of the afternoon. Alessio, leaning against the wall because he'd figured it was better not to interrupt the brothers and their work, avoided Chris's gaze when he came storming out. Not that it made much of a difference, as he still saw the glare Chris threw his way before he passed him by without as much as a *hello*.

Alessio wasn't offended.

He didn't know much—if anything at all—about Corrado's twin, and not really for a lack of interest. There simply wasn't a lot of time here to bother with making *friends*. At least, not during that first year, unless someone was training you with a partner, or to be part of a team. Then, it was pertinent that you became friends with the person who you would be forced to trust with your life at one point or another.

It was strange, in a way, how he could easily pick out the differences between Chris and Corrado, and without much effort at all, too. But everyone else seemed more interested in finding all the things that made them exactly the same.

Alessio liked what made them unique.

He waited until Chris rounded the corner at the end of the corridor before he pushed away from the wall. Coming to stand in the doorway of the room where the two had been working, Alessio quickly found Corrado in the room.

Sitting at a large metal table, surrounded by dismantled pieces of *several* guns, Corrado stared hard at the wall, lost in his thoughts. His brow, dipped in concentration, knotted further before he shook his head. Still, he kept staring like he wasn't willing to get back to work.

This was meant to be a fun task, too, for the most part. Or rather, something that most prospects enjoyed. Getting set in front of a mess of dismantled weapons and being told to figure out what went with what was a hell of a lot easier than getting the shit beat out of you in the gym, after all.

"Problem?"

Corrado's head swung around at Alessio's question. He leaned against the doorjamb, arms crossed over his chest, and gave the man across the space a look. A silent, *well?*

"You spy a lot," Corrado muttered. "People don't like that, you know?"

Alessio shrugged. "Keeps me in the loop."

"Well, *stop*."

Probably not.

He didn't tell Corrado that.

"What's going on? That's the first time I've seen Chris get that pissed here."

And it wasn't like the other Guzzi twin didn't have a reason to get mad at The League. Everyone here had one reason or another to get pissed at someone or something. That was the whole point of this goddamn place—to push one's limits to the breaking point, and then beyond.

"It's nothing," Corrado muttered, and then, he held up a tiny spring, "is this for the AR or the AK?"

Alessio arched a brow. "Neither."

"*Fuck.*"

Corrado threw the spring back to the table, clearly disgusted that he'd been wrong. Folding his arms over the white T-shirt stretched across his chest, he glared at the many pieces he still had left on the table. No one ever told them *how many* guns were on the table, but it became obvious once someone started counting the clips and magazines.

Usually six to seven. All in as many little bits as they could be broken down into so that it could be more challenging. Little nuts and everything. Yeah, it was like a whole puzzle.

But with *guns.*

"Are you avoiding what that was all about with your brother because you're in a mood, or ...?"

Corrado glanced up, his brow furrowing as he took Alessio in again. "No."

"You sure?"

Because wouldn't that be typical Corrado?

Alessio figured so.

Corrado shook his head, dropping Alessio's stare as he reached for more parts to begin his task again. Negative reinforcement was a popular tactic at The League—this task wasn't any different than the others. So, if he didn't get those guns put together, now made *more* difficult by the fact he was doing it alone, then he was going to be here all night.

No dinner.

No bed.

No sleeping.

Nothing.

He would be here until he *finished*.

That's how it worked.

Alessio didn't miss that Corrado was quick to work, though. That he didn't care he'd been left alone to do the task, or that he would probably be here for a few more hours because of it, either. He didn't complain; he simply got to work.

That meant *good* things.

"Chris is in a different place than me," Corrado muttered as he eyed a small clip. "That's all. He came here with intentions that were way different from mine, and they're catching up to him. It's not about *me*, or even him … it just is what it is."

Alessio tipped his head to the side, considering that. "Because he stayed here for you, and you joined because—"

His words cut off, and he realized then that, in fact, he had no idea *why* Corrado chose to join The League as a new prospect. He'd never thought to ask. Then again, there was a lot he never asked a guy he now regularly woke up to sleeping next to him in bed, or even, found him waiting for Alessio when he went back to his rooms at night.

It seemed like that was just how the two of them transitioned. All it took was a moment in Alessio's rooms a month ago, and the next day, shit was different. Or, that's how it started, with different things between them, until the two of them found a routine that worked for them in their private, quiet moments. They didn't talk about shit—they just *did it*.

Alessio liked it that way, and he suspected Corrado did, too. Otherwise, they wouldn't keep doing it.

As for everyone else …

If someone noticed, they didn't say.

Dare never mentioned it to Alessio, and neither did Cree, but that wasn't unusual, either. As long as no one was being forced to do something, and it didn't affect what was happening at The League, they were willing to let whatever happen.

"Why'd you stop talking?" Corrado asked.

"I just realized, I never asked you *why* you joined."

Sure, he heard the things Corrado's father said in Dare's office that first night. Corrado *and* his twin had made passing comments. But he never outright asked, and got the information from Corrado.

"And you know, that there's a lot of other shit I don't ask you about you … or your life away from here," Alessio added.

Corrado looked up from the table again. "You want my life story, or …?"

He gave him a look.

Corrado replied in kind.

Rolling his eyes, Alessio muttered, "It was just a thought, that's all."

Corrado went back to work, seemingly pleased with himself when he found the *right* barrel for a specific body piece he'd been tinkering with for a couple of minutes. "Ha, fucking piece of shit, I got it."

Alessio smirked to himself. "Start with why you joined, then."

"Because I don't fit in anywhere else, and this seemed like the right place to figure out what I was made of without ruining my family's legacy, too."

"What?"

Corrado shook his head. "Cosa Nostra, what Guzzis *are*, is not a good fit for me and my ... lifestyle, as they would call it. Like it's a fucking choice that I like to fuck guys and girls. They act like you wake up this way, and decide *yes*, I am going to like both."

"Who said it would ruin a legacy to be bi? That sounds dramatic."

"The mafia is a lot of things—ragingly homophobic is sometimes one of them. Not so much my blood, but others ... people around them. It would be bad for the people I do care about, and I just never felt like I fit in."

Ah.

Alessio scoffed under his breath, thinking how ridiculous that sounded. "Being bi never ruined anything for *me*."

"You're not one of us, either."

Okay, *that* stung a little.

Not because Corrado was wrong, but because he also wasn't *right*. That pendulum swung both ways, and Alessio's mouth worked to tell the man exactly that before he would think better of it.

"Not that you know, but I'm the illegitimate son of Maximo Sorrento." Alessio saw the way Corrado's shoulders tensed at those words, and he almost wanted to laugh at the sight, but he held back. "*Yeah*, now you get it, huh? Maximo, who went mad before he died ... who almost ran his whole organization into the ground after having a stronghold on Vegas for decades. That's my father, and you can be sure there are enough people who didn't want to let me forget it, either."

He expected Corrado knew exactly who he was talking about, if only because Maximo, like Corrado's father, were *bosses*—or Alessio's father was before his death—of major Cosa Nostra crime families. That meant, business often exchanged hands between families when Italians were known for being distrustful to organizations beyond their own.

Corrado cleared his throat, still staring at the table. "Sorry."

"Doesn't matter. I barely knew him, I was two when he died. He was old enough to be my fucking great-grandfather, too, fucking someone who could have been the same age as his granddaughter. Everybody wears stains, you know?"

"Huh."

Shifting from foot to foot, Alessio added, "But it followed me *after* … probably didn't help that my mother made a mess of herself. Overdosed when I was ten."

Corrado never looked away from the table, but his jaw worked as he chewed over his words. Finally, he said, "It … wasn't like that for me and Chris. Never chaotic, and we weren't ever neglected. I sound like a selfish fuck to you, don't I?"

"Sometimes." Alessio laughed, adding, "But I don't fault you for it."

"Thanks, I guess."

"Are you going to tell me what your brother is pissed off about, or what?"

Corrado glanced up from the table, a storm brewing in his eyes. "He wants to speak to our father."

"Yeah, that's not going to happen for a while."

"But more our ma, I think, even if he won't admit it."

Alessio made a noise, dismissive and cold, although he didn't mean for it to sound that way. "Yeah, can't relate to that *at all*."

"Sorry about that."

"It's all right."

"It's not—I don't know what I would do without my ma."

Alessio eyed him, chewing on the inside of his cheek as a

million and one thoughts tumbled through his head. "What's that like, anyway?"

"Hmm, what?"

"Having a mother that loves you. I wouldn't know."

Corrado shifted on the chair, never looking away from Alessio. "It's …"

"Yeah?"

"Hard to describe. I love my ma."

Alessio nodded. "Wouldn't know what that's like, either."

"Recon and retrieval—Siberia, in a prison camp, we believe." Dare tossed the folder to the desk, but Alessio didn't bother to reach out and grab it. He was more focused on the image of the man in question that had apparently been missing for close to a decade. A prominent Russian mobster's son, who had disappeared during a war with a rival family. "We've had eyes on who we trust is him. The *team* will go in with you after you've done your recon and sent information back for the plan to be finalized."

Alessio's brow furrowed. "How long is the assignment?"

"Three weeks to a month, depending on how things go."

"And the client is—"

"The father, obviously. He knows it's a risk to go in and try to get the son out, but one he is willing to risk considering the man will die inside the camp otherwise. You are not to get close enough without the team that you might get caught. Do you understand me?"

Alessio gave Dare a look. "I'm not an idiot. I know how to do proper recon."

"I'm just—"

"If *you're* not ready for me to do an assignment, then just say that."

Dare swallowed hard, but straightened where he was standing beside his desk. "I do think you're ready."

"I didn't say me. I said *you*."

"That's not the same thing. The assignment is on the table, and it was given to you. That's what matters. There is no whether or not you want it, or if you would rather stand there and argue with me over *my* feelings ... you take that folder, and you do the job you were given. It's that simple, Les."

But was it?

He didn't think so, not after knowing he'd asked for a job since *before* he turned eighteen, and here he was almost two months later, still wondering why *now* was the time Dare finally gave him a job. It rubbed him the wrong way, and he wasn't entirely done with this conversation, but for now, he also didn't get a choice.

Dare was right.

The job was given to him.

The file was there.

He had to take it.

Alessio snatched the folder up from the desk, and turned to leave the office without another word. He didn't have anything else to say when it was already done, after all.

Dare made him hesitate with, "And the cameras to your rooms have been permanently turned off, by the way."

"Oh?"

"I didn't think to mention it, but ... you seem to be busy with something, you know."

Something.

Someone.

Same difference.

"I appreciate it," Alessio said, not turning around.

"You know the rules, Les."

Yeah, yeah.

Don't let it affect The League.

All that good shit.

"I got it," he muttered, leaving the office altogether.

How could he not?

What time did Corrado *finally* stumble into Alessio's room? Well, he wasn't sure, but it was far too early in the morning for him to be making *that* much noise.

The clock on the nightstand said four.

In the morning.

Alessio was still trying to grumble his way back to sleep when the bed dipped after the shuffling of Corrado shedding his clothes to the floor woke him up in the first damn place. "I *know* you have your own bed, asshole."

Corrado chuckled. "Yours is firmer."

Well …

"Is it?"

"Maybe. And warmer."

Alessio grinned, and turned to his stomach where he could bury most of his face into the pillow. Cracking just one eye open, though, he stared at Corrado who laid on his back, a hand splayed over his naked chest, while he stared at the ceiling. He said nothing, simply reached over to drag the tips of his fingers through the longer bit of Corrado's hair where his high fade started to darken.

Just as quickly, he pulled his hand back, the need to touch him satisfied. He was *there*. All was good to Alessio—he simply needed the reminder.

He never spoke it out loud, though.

It didn't make sense.

Why bother?

Corrado glanced over at Alessio, his dark eyes drifting

over him in the bed beside him before he stared back up at the ceiling. It was in their quiet moments where Alessio found *peace*. He had quiet before—time when he was completely alone, no distractions. And yet, it wasn't the same when it was just him and Corrado.

Here, they decompressed.

Here, nothing mattered.

Here, it was just *them*.

Silently, Corrado's hand slipped off his chest to find Alessio's against the sheets. His fingers curled tightly with Alessio's, and wove together, tucking their hands next to his hip where their bodies were close enough to hide the touch.

"If I *never* see another dismantled gun again, that would be great."

Alessio barked out a tired laugh. "Tomorrow, you'll have five new guns waiting."

"*Fucking bull*—"

"It's a good lesson to learn."

"*Right*," Corrado mumbled, scrubbing a hand down his unshaven jaw. "I'll remember that. What's that file for, anyway?"

Alessio stiffened.

Corrado didn't miss it.

"What?"

"The one on the stand?"

"That's the only one in this room, isn't it?"

Alessio's jaw clicked from how hard he clenched it to hold the words back. He wasn't sure why, all of the sudden, he didn't want to tell Corrado about his assignment, but the urge was *strong*. They were just starting to figure whatever this was out—if someone wanted to call it that, but he didn't know if he would.

Nonetheless, that didn't make it any less true. And here they were, at this unsteady point, and now he was about to head out to a whole different country for three or four weeks? That sounded like a problem waiting to happen.

"Les," Corrado murmured, waiting.

"It's … uh, a job."

That time, Corrado stiffened. "A job?"

"Mmm."

A beat of silence passed.

Then, another.

Alessio waited it out.

"Can you say what it's for, or no?"

"Recon and retrieval—Siberia."

"Interesting," Corrado replied.

"Could be a month, maybe a little less."

"Huh."

Alessio eyed him, trying to find *something*. Corrado's tone gave nothing away, and neither did his shadowed features in the darkness. Still, something just felt off.

"Hey," Alessio said.

"What?"

"What are we doing? *Us*, I mean. What is it?"

That seemed important to ask.

Wasn't it?

Shouldn't they get that part figured out here?

"Nothing, Les."

Alessio didn't move a muscle. "*Nothing*?"

Corrado looked over at him, still as blank as paper. "Yeah … I guess."

He wasn't sure if that was Corrado's pride coming out again to make another appearance at the worst fucking time, or if the man simply believed what he was saying. Either way, Alessio didn't like it, but he also wasn't in the mood to point out that for people who were doing *nothing* … they did it an awful lot, and Corrado *still* found his way to Alessio's rooms far more often than he did his own.

But all right.

They could be nothing.

For now.

Alessio rolled over in the bed then, and sunk back into the blankets, ready to go back to sleep. Corrado let him, at first, but then Alessio still felt him tuck into his back when he rolled over, too. The softest graze of his lover's mouth drifted between his shoulder blades, reminding him that even when he wanted to *hate* Corrado, he couldn't.

Not even a little bit.

The air caught hard in Alessio's chest as Corrado's arms snaked around him like bars. And then just as quickly, warm, rough hands slipped under his boxer-briefs to find his cock. It took Corrado no time at all to stroke Alessio alive under the blankets.

His mouth, still hot at Alessio's shoulders, skimmed higher. Corrado's teeth found the back of his neck while his fingers tightened and stroked him faster.

Dark words hit his skin.

"Like that, yeah?"

He couldn't speak.

Not when he was already *this* close to blowing his load. Not when those words caught in his chest because *damn*, maybe if he said nothing, then Corrado would say *more*. And there was something wicked and dark in his voice when he was like this.

Something Alessio *craved*.

There was one thing he found in men that he didn't find in women when he was in bed with them. Women gave *sweetness* in their sex, even when it was anything but. Men only gave darkness.

And when Alessio wanted *that*, he found it. When he needed sweetness, he could find that, too. Right now, he just needed the one.

Corrado had it all.

"Come on," Corrado mumbled against his skin, "fucking give it to me—I *want* it."

Alessio could feel him hard at his back, the length of Corrado's erection grinding into him in time with the strokes of his cock. In the next breath, he hit that *numb* place before he was thrown into the orgasm.

There was no holding that back.

He spilled on Corrado's fingers, and the sheets.

"*Shit.*"

Sinful, rough laughter filled his ears, and Alessio wanted to swallow it right up. He wanted all those dark, hard sounds against his mouth as he did the same to Corrado that had just been given to him.

Those feelings.

Those *sounds.*

Corrado needed to have them, too, he thought, and he twisted in the bed. Alessio found him already waiting as he reached back.

CHAPTER 12
CORRADO

"*Fuck*," Corrado hissed, lifting his gaze from the scope to glare down the barrel of the sniper rifle. He didn't need to check the sights again to know, in fact, he had *not* hit the goddamn target four miles away from the complex's roof where he was currently perched. Or rather, resting on his stomach with the gun in front of him. Behind him, Nathan, his current trainer, sighed loudly. "The wind is too—"

"The wind is fine."

"I adjusted the way you told me to."

"And inhaled when you *shot*."

Had he?

Fuck.

Again.

It felt like Corrado had been saying that *a lot* this last week. Propping himself up on his elbow, he used the tips of his fingers to massage at the spot on his temples that were throbbing. He'd woken up with a headache, the day was half over, and it still hadn't gone away.

"Fuck this," Corrado muttered.

Pushing up from the ground, he snatched up the gun to disassemble it the way he'd been taught. Nathan cocked his head, asking, "What in the fuck are you doing?"

"Not this. Not today."

"That's not your choice. Get back down there, and do it again."

Corrado laughed bitterly. "No."

"No?"

"That's what I said."

"Corrado, I don't know what stick got stuck up your ass this past week, but—"

Fuck that noise.

Corrado tossed the gun to the ground, uncaring that it was unsafe and *stupid*. He looked Nathan right in the face, so there was no mistaking what he said next before he got off that roof, and said, "Sometimes, people just need a goddamn *break*."

Right.

That's what he was going to tell himself.

It wasn't entirely a lie, either. From the point he came to this place, he had not gotten *one* chance to breathe. Not one day to do what he wanted. Hell, he still hadn't even spoken to his three brothers back home, or his parents. He'd been in Nevada for months, but had yet to see the lights of Vegas.

He didn't see anything but *this place*.

The League.

That was it.

And the fucking desert around it.

Screw that shit.

It was made slightly more bearable when Alessio was around because that took Corrado's mind off other things. Or rather, he looked forward to when the day and training was done, and he could head to the privacy of Alessio's rooms where *no one* bothered him. It was just him, and Les … nothing else mattered.

Except Alessio wasn't here.

He was fucking *tired*.

And today was *not* the day for this shit.

It just wasn't.

"Where are you going?" Nathan shouted at his back.

Corrado didn't even answer.

He just flipped his middle finger over his shoulder. *There.* Let the man make of that what he wanted because he was sure that he would. No doubt, he would quickly run it back to Cree or Dare, too, which meant Corrado would have to deal with that eventually.

He didn't care.

Not right now.

This bad mood wouldn't go away, accompanying him all week like a stink he couldn't get rid of no matter how hard he tried. *And he did try.* The problem was, he knew exactly why he felt this way, and the fact that it all led back to Alessio being gone.

He didn't like that.

None of it.

Corrado didn't do emotional shit—he found it much easier to deal with life and other people when he kept a healthy distance from it all. Then, stupid things didn't get brought in to play, too. You know, like someone's *feelings.*

Climbing down from the roof, he could still hear Nathan bitching up above. Then, it turned to Nathan getting on the phone to shout at someone—probably Dare, but he didn't care to listen and figure it out. It took him another twenty minutes before he was walking the corridor leading to his rooms.

Where he would be alone.

And *irritated.*

A great fucking combination.

The first thing he did once he was in his rooms was head straight for the connecting bathroom. It wasn't big—hell, Alessio's bathroom was bigger than his, *and* had a bathtub instead of a standing shower—but that's all he needed. Stripping down to nothing, he stepped in under scalding hot water, letting it pink his skin as he attempted to scrub away his frustrations, and clear his mind.

It didn't work.

Nothing worked anymore.

He needed quiet nights.

Conversations in darkness.

Fingertips keeping him awake when they glided over the ridges of his muscles because for some fucking reason, his body felt like a live wire whenever Alessio was near. A man who was *nothing* like him. And yet, he found familiarity in that same man, too.

He needed those things to get back to a *good* place, except he didn't want to need those things at all. That was where he found his biggest frustration, and he didn't know how to deal with it at all.

It was only once Corrado stepped out of the shower, dried off, redressed, and exited from the bathroom that he realized, no … he wasn't alone anymore.

Chris leaned in the doorway. He passed his twin a look, but when Chris didn't say anything, Corrado chose not to offer an explanation for his silence or tenseness, either. It was just easier that way. Life was always easier when he kept his problems to himself.

Besides, Chris had his own shit he was trying to deal with, but Corrado couldn't relate. He *wanted* to be here— even if he was struggling right now for reasons that he didn't want to face—but Chris didn't want to be there at all.

Not anymore.

You know, ignoring the fact Chris wasn't really saying that. Corrado didn't need his twin to say it for him to know it was true.

"You okay?" Chris finally asked.

Corrado let out an annoyed snarl under his breath. "What's it fucking look like to you?"

"Like you got a bad attitude."

"*Yeah*."

"And nobody fucking likes it."

Corrado turned around to offer his twin a sardonic smile. "Then, feel free to leave, Chris. The door is right there, and *look* … it's already opened for you."

Chris raised a brow.

He didn't change his stance, or attitude.

In fact, Corrado waved at the door and added, "Go on."

"Les has been gone about a week, huh?"

Corrado's jaw tensed. "What about it?"

"Don't you find it funny how a couple months ago, you could barely stand to look at him … and now lately, it seems like you become fucking impossible to deal with when he's not around?"

"No, I don't find that funny at all."

Truly.

He didn't.

Annoying.

Strange as fuck.

Not funny, though.

"Hmm."

"Get out," Corrado uttered.

Chris shrugged. "I'm just saying, you're in a mood lately. You should probably get that figured out, Corrado."

"Nobody asked you."

"And yet, I still told you."

Fuck that noise, too.

∾

His bad mood didn't go away.

In fact, it got worse.

Three weeks later, he felt like he could probably rip someone's face off if they looked at him the wrong way, but Corrado had somehow managed to convince his delusional ass that if he ignored his mood, then it wouldn't be a problem.

Wrong.

He wasn't willing to admit it, though.

His pride was a bitch.

How many times had he said that?

A lot.

Corrado heard the footsteps—several pairs, not just one—approaching his rooms long before the figures shadowed his doorway. He refused to glance up over the weapons magazine he'd snatched from the communal kitchen to greet the newcomers. This was supposed to be *his* day to relax, and he was trying his fucking hardest to do that.

Not that it was working.

Nothing did.

"What is it you want, Corrado?"

Cree.

He glanced up over the edge of the magazine, but instead of looking at Cree, his gaze drifted to the people standing just behind him. The *team*, it looked like. The same team that dragged him into those fucking rooms months ago.

He still didn't know who they were beneath their black masks. It could be Nathan, the sniper, under one. Or Oliver, the fighter, under another. Although, he doubted that simply because he figured now, he might *know* them just by being near them. He knew at least *one* was a woman considering her smaller build, and curves that were accentuated by the tight, black clothing. But that was as much as he knew—they didn't speak unless they absolutely had to, and he was sure their voices were not the same when they gave orders as it was when they were joking down in one of the communal areas of the complex.

Corrado tried *damn hard* not to show how seeing the team at his rooms made him feel—tight in his chest, and like a deadweight had come to rest in his stomach. He was not doing those fucking rooms again. He had news for them, if that's what they thought.

"Are you listening?" Cree asked.

Corrado's gaze cut back to the man in question. "No."

Cree's expression didn't change.

Nothing new there.

"The last month—three weeks, give or take, but who wants to be specific?—you've been struggling," Cree noted.

"And?"

"What is it you need, hmm?" Cree tipped his head to the side, considering Corrado as he said, "Your brother wanted contact with his parents ... he needed motivation, we'll say. He earned it, and got what he wanted. Did you know that?"

"*And?*" Corrado asked again.

Because yes, he did know. And no, he didn't see what it mattered.

Chris was Chris.

Corrado, despite looking the same, was not actually *the same*. Why was that so hard for people to figure the fuck out?

"I have an offer for you," Cree said, tipping his hand over like there might be something waiting in his empty palm for Corrado to see; there was nothing, obviously. "I don't think it'll be exactly what you want, but some things can't be helped ... and, if anything, it might help with the fact you're a little stir-crazy."

He looked to the people behind Cree again.

"What kind of offer?"

"The team—they'll drop you off about twenty-five miles from here, even further out than we already are. You'll have to the end of the day."

Corrado blinked. "*To do what?*"

"Get back alive."

What?

Cree smiled slightly, as though he could see the questions forming in Corrado's mind. "For one, it's a good way to put some of the skills you've been learning to a *real* test. Out in the real world, so to speak. The team will be near, or close enough to cause you trouble here and there. Think of it like a—"

"Hunt," Corrado interjected.

"Well, yes."

"And what do I get … if I make it back, I mean?"

Cree shrugged. "You'll make it back, that's a certainty. It'll be whether or not they need to carry you back, or if you'll walk in with your own legs that'll make the difference."

"That's not that I asked."

"A night away," Cree said. "Whatever you want to do, wherever you want to go … *within reason*, keep it to the state, you will be able to go. You'll be provided with every-thing you need—vehicle, fake identification, just in case, and whatever else. No babysitters watching you. Prove you've learned something these last two months, because the past three weeks have put you back several steps, and we'll see what we can do for you."

Corrado chewed on his inner cheek. "Hmm."

"There is an expiry on this offer. Ten seconds is what you have to decide."

"Where will they drop me?"

"I told you, twenty-five miles—"

"No, *where* exactly?"

Cree smiled. "Nowhere. It'll seem like nowhere because that's exactly what it is."

Huh.

Corrado looked at the team again.

"Three seconds," Cree said.

"All right," Corrado muttered, pushing off the bed and tossing the magazine aside, "what's it going to hurt?"

Cree laughed.

An unusual sound, considering the man *rarely* did it.

"That's what I want to hear," Cree said, slapping him on the back as he passed. "Try not to fight the team too much when they put the hood over your head, yeah?"

"*Great.*"

Corrado was shoved to his knees roughly, and he *felt* the fucking rocks on the ground dig into his skin and bones through his pants. Something dropped to the ground beside him with a heavy thud, and then that hood was ripped from his head. It took him far too long to realize he was surrounded by *cliffs*. Red dirt, dry plants, and a few towering trees keeping the sun shaded.

Where the fuck was he?

He focused in on the man kneeling in front of him. Ten feet away from him was a helicopter that had landed in the only spot that seemed safe and wide enough for it to do so, considering the rocky ledges that led hundreds of feet down into *more* rocks.

Fun.

"Hey," the guy said.

Corrado swallowed his nerves, saying, "Yeah?"

"Here's where I let you go, huh?" Without warning, the guy pushed the mask up over his face, giving Corrado the first peek at *one* of the people on his team—the team that trained him. Dane, one of the few members of The League that Corrado liked … strange how that worked … gave him a grin. "Everybody else got dropped off in vehicles at different points. Nobody is going to kill you, but it might seem like it when they get a little close. Don't stop moving, because that's when predators find you, find your way back—keep going east. Do you remember how to tell if you're moving east?"

Corrado glanced at the rocky ledge.

Yeah, he knew.

East meant going right over that ledge.

"I know how to keep going east," he muttered.

Dane chuckled. "*Now* you get it. This isn't going to be easy, but if you keep going east, you'll be fine. At some point, if you're going the right way … you're going to start recognizing shit from things you've done in training, or whatever else."

He wasn't wrong.

Some training *had* taken place in areas around the complex. Miles into the desolate land that surrounded the area.

Dane pointed at the bag next to Corrado. "There's a satellite phone *if* you need it, and it's preprogrammed with the only number you can call from it. You want water? *Find some.* You've got one small blade in there—get it out, and have fun getting your ties cut. Then, start moving. Sound good?"

Corrado smirked. "Sounds like hell, really."

"Depends on who you ask. This was one of my favorites. How else are you going to learn to *survive*, Corrado?"

Something beeped.

Dane checked his watch. "And that's my signal. Stop wasting time, Corrado."

That said, Dane straightened to his full height, and turned to head for the chopper. Corrado had about a million and one questions he still wanted to ask, but he figured Dane was right. Those things didn't matter, and he was losing seconds right now.

He bet even those were going to count here.

Seconds would make the difference to him succeeding with this or failing. With hands still tied, he used his booted feet to drag the small bag back closer. Then, he used his teeth to rip the zipper down as far as he could get it.

Corrado had the knife balanced between a rock and his boots as he ran the edge of the blade against the zip ties at his wrists before the helicopter had even lifted from the ground again.

And then he heard it.

A *whistling*.

The dirt next to his knee exploded, peppering his body, and making him jerk sideways to protect himself. The knife slipped from his grip and hit the dirt. Not that it mattered, despite slicing his skin a bit, he also cut the ties enough to break them when he yanked his wrists apart.

He was more concerned with the fact a bullet just hit the ground next to him, though. Looking up, he found Dane resting along the side door of the helicopter, sniper rifle aimed right at him. The man looked up over his scope, winked, and waved two fingers.

Yeah.

It kind of was a hunt.

Except … he didn't like to be prey.

Damn.

"Let's fucking go, then."

No one else could hear his mutter, sure, but that was fine. He grabbed that bag and the knife tight in one hand, and headed for the rocky ledge leading to the cliffs. But first, he had to fucking climb.

All the way down.

CHAPTER 13
ALESSIO

"Now *why* would you put metal in your face?"

Stepping off the escalator leading in from arrivals, Alessio grinned, knowing *exactly* what Cree was griping about. Raising his hand while giving Cree a look from the side, his fingertips drifted over the two small, golden hoops he had put side by side—with about five millimeters of space between each—in his right nostril.

A bit of spare time on his hands, a tattoo shop across the road from where he was hiding out when he wasn't working in Siberia, and *yeah*. Shit happened. Things like that always happened when Alessio became bored.

That's how all his tattoos got on his body, too.

Besides, now he had something to remember this hellish month by—and since he liked his new body modification, he'd think about that instead of the rest.

Certain places were wastelands, okay?

That's what he felt like he just came back from.

Dropping his carry-on bag, which was nothing more than a black backpack that made travel easy but also had the essentials he needed should his luggage disappear, to the airport's tiled floor, he gave Cree a smile.

"Nice to see you, too," he said.

Cree chuckled, and folded his arms over his chest. "I already know how it went, but go ahead and tell me."

Alessio shrugged. "It was fine."

"That's all you want to say? Your first assignment, *alone,* too, and it was fine?"

"Yeah."

Boring.

A little too easy, all things considered. His main part of the job had been the recon mission, which was basically doing nothing except watching, looking for shit, and staying out of sight. Then, when he had confirmation the Russian mobster's son *was* in fact in the isolated prison camp, he could prove it, and also had a good idea of the man's schedule inside the place, he called it into the team.

It was up to The League's team leader on whether or not he would be allowed to take part in the retrieval, and he had. Not that it had been anything exciting, either. They went in at night, armed and ready, took out the main security that would be a problem, grabbed the guy from his building where he was housed, and then blew out the side of the cement fence that was also wired to electrocute people who touched it.

Simple.

"Well, come on, then," Cree said, tipping his head sideways a bit, silently saying the two of them should get going. No one from The League liked to linger too long in a public space like an airport after a job in another country. "Let's get out of here."

"All right."

Alessio picked up the bag he'd dropped before and followed behind Cree until they were at the luggage carousel waiting for his to come around. Cree stayed quiet as brightly colored bags passed them by on the conveyer belt. He didn't mind the silence, as it gave him a chance to relax a bit, more so than he had over the past several weeks.

Nevada felt like home.

In a way nowhere else did.

He watched the people gathered around the conveyer, some leaning close to talk, others laughing, and a few looking as though they were simply ready for the day to be over. It was funny because he related to every single one of them.

For different reasons, obviously.

Did it feel good to be out and finally doing a job?

Yeah.

It also felt good to be back here. For the past three weeks, he felt like that last conversation with Corrado had left a lot of shit unsaid between the two of them. They had unfinished business, and that's where Alessio's mind continued to go back to every time he had a moment alone to think while on assignment.

He didn't need that distraction.

Didn't want it.

But here he was, so …

Alessio wasn't going to dwell on the *whys* of it all, because a part of him knew that was obvious, but he figured now that he was back, the two of them could settle out some shit. Then, he could put that behind him and get back to work. He wouldn't be kept awake at night by thoughts of a guy who clearly didn't know what in the hell he wanted where Alessio was concerned.

Or, whatever.

Who knew?

"You're quieter than I expected you to be after coming back from your first assignment," Cree murmured as Alessio's bag finally came around, and he could pick it up from the belt. "I thought you'd want to tell me *all the things.*"

Alessio passed him a look as the two turned to navigate the busy arrivals area so they could leave the airport entirely. "Is that what you want me to do?"

"I want you to do what you *need* to do, Les. That's what I spent years teaching you, even if you didn't realize it."

He did realize, though.

He'd simply never said it out loud.

"I left some business unfinished back here with someone else," he said, refusing to explicitly state Corrado's name, not that it would have made a difference to Cree either way. Still, if there was anything Alessio learned from watching the men he was closest to, it was that things like relationships—and the fickler, *love*, if that's even what this was because he didn't know—was not something you offered out for public consumption. Not in this life. "And it's followed me for weeks."

Cree nodded. "That happens."

"I'm not a dweller. I don't *dwell*."

"Except when it's important. Then, you dwell entirely too much, overthink, and usually … overreact about it all. That is what you do."

Well …

"You're not wrong," Alessio muttered.

Not *happily*, though.

He caught sight of Cree's amused smile, but the man was quick to hide it by looking away. He wasn't sure whether to be annoyed that his affections for someone else was so clearly on display for those he was closest to, or that he should be grateful someone knew him well enough to see it at all.

This shit was confusing.

A mess.

And he still didn't know if he liked it.

Once the two were outside of the airport and had found Alessio's smoky gray Mustang parked in the underground garage where he'd left it three weeks earlier, Cree turned to him with a sleek burner phone in his hand.

"Here, one more quick job for you … although this one can end when you're ready for it to, I suppose," Cree said.

"My car is on the other side of the garage, and I can find my own way back to the complex, I'm sure."

Alessio took the phone, his gaze drawn to the red, blinking dot on the middle of the screen. "What's this?"

"Something I suspect you need."

"I don't—"

"Find the dot, Les, whatever happens after that is up to you. You know how to get yourself back, and besides, I'm not worried about you leaving. Where would you go?"

He gave Cree a look. "I wanted to go home."

"I know."

~

Alessio found the red dot.

Corrado.

He found him sitting at the bar of an upscale hotel in the very heart of Las Vegas. The drive following the little red dot move around the city wasn't exactly hard, except for the fact Alessio hadn't known *what* he was looking for.

That was annoying.

Until he found it.

Alessio suspected whatever phone Corrado had on hand was being tracked, which was where the red dot came into play. He almost wondered what Corrado had been doing all evening, and why he'd been allowed to leave The League's complex before his first year of training was up, but those thoughts quickly drifted away as he watched him from afar. Nursing what looked like a glass of whiskey on ice, Corrado didn't even notice Alessio just twenty feet away standing in the entrance of the hotel's bar.

Despite being *only* eighteen, and not at all legal to drink, Alessio didn't think Corrado looked out of place at the bar in his dark wash jeans, and leather jacket. He tipped that glass up for another drink and shook his head when the bartender came around like he was going to offer another round, if he wanted it.

Alessio bet—because of rare occasions, he knew Dare let people have a free day away from the complex—that Corrado had been given whatever he needed for the night. A vehicle, likely, and IDs to get him by; probably cash, too, if not black cards without a spending limit.

He was content to watch Corrado for a while, and not interrupt his time alone, but that idea quickly went away when he realized the man sitting next to him at the bar was leaning closer. To his benefit, Corrado wasn't paying the guy *any* attention.

Not a lick of it.

That didn't stop the man from trying, though. In a silk dress shirt, top two buttons undone around his throat, and a grin that said he was *interested* ... the man leaned closer still, his hand coming to smack Corrado's arm.

All things Alessio instantly *hated*.

The guy could simply be attempting a friendly conversation. He might have noticed another quiet man at the bar and decided to make a friend.

Or maybe it was something else.

An attempt at *more*.

It didn't matter.

Alessio didn't *like* it.

He'd felt a lot of things in his life; far too much anger and bitterness from his childhood, and the loss of a father and mother that had never really been his to begin with. Abandonment and loneliness sometimes felt like his best friends when he was alone with his own thoughts at night, in a cold bed. Pride was something he'd learned to let go of years ago because someone always wanted to take it from you. He knew affection and loyalty because those were some of the first things Dare and Cree taught him when they took him in at only ten, and those emotions *sharpened* for him over time, but especially to those he cared for.

Right then, though?

All he felt was a hot, burning jealousy searing through his chest. It cut right through his fucking ribs, and stabbed him in an organ he liked to pretend didn't exist a lot of the time —*his heart.*

And he'd never felt that.

Not like this.

Not *that* strongly.

It was so strong and piercing inside his body and mind, in fact, that it propelled him forward across the floor of the hotel's bar before he had even thought about it. His legs taking long, sure strides until he came up behind Corrado, and the man that felt way to close to someone that Alessio felt like was only *his.*

Corrado was *his.*

He wasn't sure when he decided that fact—possibly that day he saw Corrado in the knife room, and the man didn't care to take his shit like everyone else did. Or maybe it was that first taste of him, mouth bloody, but *damn*, he still found something perfect there. It could have been late nights in his rooms where conversation wasn't always present, but Corrado's *presence* brought him the closest to the feeling of security that he'd felt in years.

He didn't care when it happened.

It just *was.*

And that man was too close to something that wasn't his. It couldn't be his when Corrado was Alessio's … even if he didn't think so.

Yet.

He would know soon.

The man beside Corrado saw Alessio approaching first,

his eyes widening a bit. Maybe it was just the fucking aura Alessio gave off—a *back off* kind of vibe—or it could have been the severe expression he couldn't shake, not that he bothered to try.

At the man's obvious distraction, Corrado turned to look over his shoulder. His gaze slammed into Alessio's, and for a second, it felt like the world slowed down around them. Gone were the sounds of a busy bar, and chattering people. The music in the background was dulled, and he barely felt the floor under his feet.

None of it mattered.

Not when Corrado's gaze skipped over his face and the rest of him like he was trying to correlate what he was seeing to *real life*. Like he didn't believe he was standing there for a moment, and he needed to make sure it was really happening.

"That's new," Corrado said, pointing over his shoulder at Alessio's face.

At the nose rings, likely.

He arched a brow. "I guess so."

"What if they get ripped out?"

"That'd be shit, I bet," Alessio replied dryly. "Say goodbye to your friend here, we've got other things to do."

"Excuse me?"

Alessio didn't look away from Corrado, not even bothering to spare the man beside him any attention. He wasn't fucking around here, and if he didn't put some distance between Corrado and the stranger, someone was going to get hurt.

Because apparently, Alessio wasn't good at this. He didn't do well with jealousy. And since he was more than capable of causing some serious bodily harm to another human being, it was better if he just corrected the problem causing him the issue in the first place.

Like *now*.

By getting Corrado away from the man.

If it seemed like Alessio was being an asshole, then so be it. They could deal with that later. At least, people would remain *alive*.

Right?

Yeah, jealousy was not his friend.

At all.

Learn something new every day.

"Say goodbye," he murmured.

Corrado's brow lifted, clearly hearing the heat in Alessio's tone. Yeah, he couldn't even hide what he was feeling, for fuck's sake.

This was ridiculous.

Downing the rest of his drink, Corrado set the glass to the bar, and pushed off the stool to stand toe to toe with Alessio. Alessio had all of a half of an inch on Corrado's six-foot-two height. It wasn't a lot—barely there at all, really. For the most part, it still put them damn near eye level.

He didn't say goodbye to the guy, who was now slipping off the stool that had been beside Corrado's, and moved further down the bar away from them entirely.

Corrado only looked at Alessio.

"Better?" he asked.

Alessio wasn't going to lie.

"Not yet."

"Yeah, I can tell."

"Don't sound so fucking smug about it," Alessio returned.

Corrado smirked. "Kind of hard."

Jesus.

Alessio needed to get off this conversation. He didn't need his weaknesses available to the rest of the world for public consumption. "Do you have a room here?"

"And a fake ID, some cash … twenty-four hours to do whatever I want." Corrado shifted from foot to foot, glancing away. "I didn't know you were back."

"Clearly."

Okay, that came out cold as hell.

Even he heard it.

Corrado looked back at him, a fire blazing in his gaze. "Do you have something you want to say to me, or what?"

Why lie?

"Yeah, but I don't think you want to hear it."

CHAPTER 14
CORRADO

"Which room?"

Alessio didn't even look over his shoulder when he asked that question. Corrado watched his hand flex tightly around the black bag that dangled from his fist, and the way his shoulders tensed with every step he took.

Pissed all over.

Or ... Alessio was something else altogether.

Jealous.

"Room *208.*"

Alessio made a noise under his breath, still walking straight down the hallway without bothering to look at Corrado behind him. "All right."

He wanted to deal with the fact that Alessio randomly showed up when *no one* was supposed to know where he was —that was Cree's deal, right? If he made it back to the complex before the sun went down, then he would get one free night to do what he wanted *without* babysitters watching him the whole time. So, how the fuck did Alessio know where to find him?

At the same time, he didn't mind. Or rather, he didn't care that it was Alessio that showed up. Except going into that meant handling the fact Alessio was jealous. Because he didn't like what he found when he showed up.

Not that it had been anything.

Or meant anything.

Corrado didn't even know that guy's name, or what the fuck he wanted. He'd been trying to have a drink before he went upstairs, and passed out on the king-size bed. He'd wandered around the city for a while earlier, trying to decide *what* he wanted to do. And maybe, had Alessio been there with him, he might have picked a half of a dozen things just because.

Instead, he wanted to be alone.

Drink.

Sleep.

Feel fucking normal.

He'd been content to ignore the guy at the bar, whether his friendly attempt at conversation was just that—friendly —or whether it was a hint for something else. Which was exactly what he had been doing when Alessio showed up.

Not that Alessio realized that.

Or saw it.

Corrado could tell.

The bigger problem?

He liked it.

Corrado wasn't a liar, or he tried hard not to be. So, it'd be a damn lie if he tried to say the warning—one for him, and for the other man at the bar—that flashed across Alessio's face because he *thought* he knew what was going on there didn't make Corrado feel some kind of fucking way.

Not that he wanted to feel that way.

Or any way.

He didn't know what the hell he wanted.

Alessio stopped in front of the room that belonged to Corrado for the night. Stepping aside so he could lean against the wall while Corrado pulled the keycard from his pocket to unlock the door, Alessio asked, "Would you have done that, then?"

Corrado's hand froze at the card reader, hovering overtop

but not pulled down to drag the keycard through the lock. "Done what?"

"That guy—*him*. Would you have brought him back here had I not shown up? Spent the night with him? *Any* of it?"

"Why don't you just *say it*, huh?" Corrado returned.

"Excuse me?"

"You're jealous, Les. *Say it.*"

"That's half the fucking problem, isn't it?" Alessio let out a dark laugh, making Corrado's chest clench from the sound. *God*, he loved that sound. "The fact you don't *want* all that shit to be out there, right? Because once it's out there, Corrado, we don't get to take it back. You get stuck in your fucking pride, because you don't know how to deal, and there we'll be. That is the *problem.*"

Corrado's jaw flexed, holding back words and anger. Because frankly, Alessio wasn't wrong, and he didn't know how to admit that without sounding like a fool. Nobody wanted to be the idiot with a foot stuck in his mouth.

"Yeah, I know," Alessio added when Corrado continued to stay quiet.

Raging blue met dark brown when the two stared at one another in the hallway. The silence stretched on, heavy and loaded with *a lot* of shit Corrado had been leaving to the wayside where he and Alessio were concerned. Things like *feelings* and what the fuck was even going on between them. The labels he hated because once *you* labeled yourself, the rest of the goddamn world thought they got the right to do the same. Or even the fact that he'd never connected with someone on a level like he did with Les—like the man just *knew* the craziness in Corrado's mind without him ever needing to open his mouth to say it.

And he recognized those same things in Alessio, too.

These things?

It was too much.

Too deep.

Things that he figured, once they were said, there was no going back. And maybe that bothered Corrado because it scared him. He didn't like to be scared of shit—didn't *want* to be, either—but he didn't know how to tell Alessio that without the rest of the shit in his mind spilling out, too.

Like the fact he didn't know how to do this.

How to be *someone* to someone else.

How to be a *them.*

A thing.

And despite a part of him not wanting to admit he wanted to be exactly that, even if that meant he would need to deal with things he'd shoved down where *nobody* could find them, the other part was louder.

"You didn't answer my question," Alessio said.

Corrado arched a brow. "You didn't answer *mine.*"

"I already said you don't want me to."

Right.

"And that's *your* problem," Corrado replied, shoving the keycard through the reader to unlock the room door, "because you don't listen nearly as well as you fucking talk, Les."

"What does that even mean?"

Corrado shook his head, opening the door and entering the hotel room. He dropped his jacket to a chair, kicked off his shoes, dropped his bag, and headed for the bathroom. All the while, he ignored Alessio behind him as he called after him.

"Hey, I'm fucking speaking to you. What does that mean?"

No.

He was done talking.

For one, this wasn't a conversation he wanted to have. And for two, because even if he did want to have it, he didn't know where to begin. Not without admitting he didn't know if he could ever *be* something with Alessio.

Maybe a part of Corrado was just broken.

Or *wrong.*

Who knew?

"Corrado!"

He let the slam of the bathroom door answer Alessio's shout of his name. Maybe he'd get the hint, then, and back the hell off. Corrado hoped for too much, because as he was tugging off his shirt while turning on the shower taps in the large bathroom, Alessio came right in.

Like he'd been invited.

"We're not done here," Alessio said.

Corrado made a harsh noise under his breath, shrugging off his pants, and yanking off his socks. *Fine.* If that's what Alessio wanted—an answer to his damn question—then he would get one. "*No*, okay? No, I didn't even know that guy existed until you made it into a thing. I was too busy thinking it would have been a *far* better day had you been here to show me around the city." He stood straight, fingers hooking around the waistband of his boxer-briefs to shove them down before he could step into the shower. "There, is that what you wanted to hear?"

"You think *that's* what this is about?"

"No, I think you want something from me that I'm not even sure I can give, Les. *Why* can't I give it to you? I don't know, so don't ask. But if you're looking for that, you're not going to get it."

"I—"

"Get out so I can shower."

Alessio stood firm. "No."

"Fine."

Fuck him.

Corrado shoved his boxer-briefs down, and stepped into

the shower, closing the frosted glass door behind him to keep Alessio out. Not that it really would if the man wanted to come in, anyway. He didn't need *Alessio* to be done with the conversation to keep doing what he wanted to do. He was sure that frustrated the hell out of his companion, but whatever.

Even beneath the spray of heavy, hot water from a shower head that was the size of a dinner plate, Corrado could still hear Alessio when he spoke. "I keep thinking it's your pride that does shit like this, but I don't know anymore."

Staring at the brown and beige tiles, Corrado willed his ears to stop working. If for just a second because he didn't *want* to know he was fucking this up. He didn't want to know he was hurting someone he cared about.

Someone he *loved*.

Because he wasn't ready to say that.

It couldn't be *real*.

Once it became real, then he had a whole bag of other shit to unpack, too. Like the people in his life who would say he was wrong and *weak* for loving who he did. Like the people who would shame his father, his family … their entire legacy because he loved another *man*. That culture—the mafia—was caustic when it came to people like him, and it wouldn't matter that he wasn't *in* it. It wouldn't make a difference because there were still expectations for him, and his family, regardless if he was made or not.

He knew it.

He heard them his whole life.

People like him?

They were shamed.

Shunned.

Forgotten.

God knew he never wanted to put his family in that position—he never wanted to make his parents or his brothers feel like they had to choose between him, and the life they'd always known. It didn't matter that they would accept him because there would be plenty of others around them that wouldn't. And when they chose to fight *for* him, it would only leave them with a target on their backs because of it.

That's how the mafia worked. When one didn't fall in line, even if that *one* was the boss, then the rest seemed to take that as a sign of weakness. A problem that had to be culled before it could get worse.

He loved his family.

He loved where he came from.

Those were things Corrado was *not* willing to give up, not for anything. And if he was going to keep them, and maintain the delicate line he'd been walking his whole life, then nothing could change. He couldn't give more to Alessio than he already had without sacrificing something else. It would always be that way.

It was Corrado's burden to carry.

He didn't expect Alessio to understand these things. He didn't think the man would care, either. Because in reality, they weren't at all alike, and they didn't come from the same *world*.

That pride of his ...

It was still a bitch, but that was only because pride was the only thing that kept Corrado sane a lot of the times.

"I should have listened, right?" Alessio asked outside of the shower, his voice muffled by the water pouring down on Corrado's tense form. He heard the shuffle of fabric before Alessio added, "I asked what this was, and you said *nothing*. Man, yeah, I should have fucking listened when you said that."

His teeth clenched, holding back words and *pride* and the truth. "Les—"

Corrado's back hit the tiled wall when, without warning,

the shower doors were thrown wide open. Cold air rushed in with the man that stepped inside, too, both wrapping around Corrado, but in entirely different ways.

The cold *chilled* him, slinking around his skin and muscles with a featherlight touch that had him shivering just beyond the spray of water.

Alessio, though?

He made Corrado *hot*, taking away that icy air as Alessio's hands landed to either side of his head, smacking against tile and effectively pinning him in place. He wasn't even *touching* him, but Corrado knew there was no way he was moving, now.

Not with Les so close.

Not with that *heat*.

"Except you're a fucking *liar*." Alessio murmured, his lips coming dangerously close to Corrado's as he spoke low, "because we can't be nothing when from the start, we were *something*."

Shit.

He hadn't even taken his clothes off. Corrado was all too aware of that right *now*. The way the water soaked through Alessio's clothes, making the fabric mold to his body. And as much as he liked the way it looked, he couldn't focus on that when all he could see was an ocean of blue bearing down on him.

Ready to *drown* him.

"You're right," Corrado said thickly. "You are."

Alessio's stance didn't soften a bit. "*But*? Because I can hear that—even when you don't say shit, I hear it, Corrado."

"But this is what I can give you. I can't give more. Either this is good enough for you, or you get nothing at all. That's how it has to be for me, and for *this*."

Silence echoed.

Alessio's gaze blazed brighter.

Then, his palm slapped the tiled wall next to Corrado's head hard enough that he felt it vibrate through the back of his skull. Yet, he didn't flinch; he wasn't *ever* concerned that this man would strike out against him in a physical way —not now.

People didn't hurt things they loved.

Life taught Corrado that.

"*Fuck you,*" Alessio muttered, his jaw tight, and his mouth twisting with his anger. "Fuck you for that, too, because you know, right? You know it's better to have a *piece* of what you love than to have none of it at all."

"I'm sor—"

"Fuck you for doing that to me."

As fast as Alessio had come into the shower, he turned and left.

"Les, wait," Corrado called after him.

He got nothing.

Not even a *noise*.

"*Fuck.*"

He hit the switch on the shower turning the water off, so he could go after Alessio. The cold air slammed into him again when he stepped beyond the glass doors, but he barely felt it. He was more concerned with the fact that the bathroom was now empty, the only sign of Alessio's presence being the droplets of water on the floor leading out. Grabbing the towel on the rack, Corrado tightened it around his waist as he headed out of the bathroom.

Alessio hadn't gone far.

Across the hotel room, the other man stripped out of the sopping wet clothes, leaving only his underwear, with his back turned to Corrado. There was no way he didn't hear his approach because Corrado didn't bother to be quiet as he came up behind him.

Still, Alessio said nothing as he pulled dry clothes from

the bag. He stood straight, shoving the boxer-briefs down around muscular thighs as he *finally* turned around to face Corrado. Like now he had enough give-a-damn to allow the man his attention.

"Aren't I always the one running away from you?" Corrado asked, bitterness coating every word. "Not the other way around."

Alessio chuckled, nodding as he fisted the dry clothes in his hand. Standing there naked, he didn't seem the least bit bothered by it. Not that Corrado expected anything different from him. Shame was not something Les was well acquainted with, to be honest.

"What, you don't like a taste of your own medicine?"

"Don't be a fucking *child*, Les."

"I'm not." Lifting his shoulders, Alessio added, "See, it changes *nothing* here, Corrado. You said what you needed to say to keep your pride right where you like it—but it isn't what you want to say. And it changes fuck all."

"What does that even—"

"We're still something, and you're still mine."

Corrado blinked.

Stunned.

Alessio smirked a bit, clearly liking the reaction he got for that. "Yeah, because if *you* get to decide shit just because without considering me, then I get to do the same. And I decided *that*. You're mine, and while we're doing this together, keep that in mind."

He stepped closer.

Corrado didn't move an inch.

Just like in the shower, Alessio crowded him until all he could see was an ocean of stormy blue coming for him. Those eyes of Alessio's always told the truth of things far better than his mouth did.

He was *hurt*—he wouldn't say it, though.

He was *pissed*—it was just an afterthought right now. Corrado did that.

He hated it.

"How's that for you?" Alessio asked.

"Depends on what it means," Corrado returned.

"It means while I'm fucking you, or you're fucking me ... or we're playing this stupid game with each other, then it's *just* us. It's you," Alessio said, pointing a finger at Corrado, and then turning it around on himself as he added, "and *me*. That's it. No other man gets to have you while I do, you got me?"

That's what he wanted?

Corrado cleared his throat. "That's what you want? Exclusivity?"

"No, *loyalty*. Because if you can't give me anything else, then you at least owe me that. And if you can't give me that, either, then this isn't happening at all."

All right.

Corrado let out a slow exhale, both annoyed and amused. But wasn't that what Alessio had always done to him? Frustrated and fascinated him to no end? Challenged and tested him every step of the goddamn way?

Why would this be different?

"Well?" Alessio demanded.

He was so close now, his mouth nearly grazed Corrado's as he spoke. And yet, it was still the intensity in his eyes leveling on Corrado that kept him ensnared, unable to move.

"Just you and me," Corrado replied. "Any other rules you want to slap on this while we're here?"

"Is that what we're going to call it—*rules*?"

"Why not?"

Alessio sighed harshly. "Don't joke. This isn't a *joke*."

"I'm not. I'm *trying* to give you as much as I can. You

want control here? Fine, you have it. What are the rules, Les? Tell me. I'm listening."

"Just that one, then."

Alessio inched closer. Not that there was much space between them left to close now. In fact, this put the two of them practically skin to skin, but he was fine with that. Closer was always better with this man. Like this, he saw more; *found* more that Les liked to hide. Maybe they weren't all that different, after all.

Corrado felt Alessio's knuckles as they grazed the line of his stomach just above where the towel rested on his hips. It was a soft touch—barely there at all, if he were being honest. Except it was there, and that was important.

That was *Alessio*.

It was him being okay.

Connection in his silence, and that's what he offered. Corrado would take it. Even if it was just knuckles stroking his skin. He'd always take what Alessio gave him. No questions asked.

"No other men, got it." Corrado grinned a bit, murmuring, "Women are okay, then?"

That touch stilled on his stomach.

Alessio's head snapped up, and his gaze leveled on Corrado at the same time his tongue peeked out to swipe along the seam of his lower lip. Maybe it was the way the blues of his eyes darkened a bit, or it could have been how that soft touch against his skin turned into rough fingers grasping tightly to his side.

Whatever it was, Corrado saw it.

Felt it.

He just wasn't sure what *it* was.

"What was that?" he asked quietly.

Alessio's throat jumped when he swallowed thickly. "I

was just thinking about that." He made a rough noise, adding, "It was a nice picture, and … yeah."

Huh.

He wasn't going to pretend like he didn't like the sound of that because he did. Probably a little too much for it to be healthy, but now wasn't the time. Even if his cock, perking to life under the towel around his waist, had an entirely different idea.

"More rules, then?" Corrado asked.

"We'll work on that," Alessio replied huskily.

"All right. Where do we go from here?"

"*Forward.*"

Alessio's fingertips dragged along the line of Corrado's stomach, then curled into the line of the towel to pull it away at the same time his other hand came up to circle around his throat. The kiss that came after, as the towel was dropped to the floor, reminded him exactly why he was here doing this in the first place.

The *war* of it.

The fight in it.

There was passion there, stoked by pride and words unsaid, emboldened by a touch that made him feel like a live wire, and strengthened by a man who was willing to cut his own heart out and hand it over if it meant keeping what he wanted.

Corrado knew that too well.

Here he was, doing the same.

Even if it was for different reasons.

He'd keep Les.

He needed to.

It just had to be *this* way.

Alessio's hand grabbed the back of Corrado's neck, and he dragged him down closer to the floor even as he continued kissing him. He was lost in the roughness, too lost to understand that Alessio had grabbed a small bag from within his backpack on the floor until he threw it across the room.

The small bag hit the top of the bed.

That didn't matter, either.

Not really.

What mattered was the palm hitting flat to his chest, pushing him back while the hand at the back of his neck kept him right there, connected to that kiss until he felt like all he could taste and breathe was Alessio. It was only after his back had hit the bed, when Alessio had crawled on top of him, that Corrado realized this was *different*.

Up until this point in their fucking and moments, it had always been him that felt in control—the one making the demands. And this was not the same. Not when it was Alessio's rough movements and kiss that had Corrado arching up to get more when the man dared to pull away.

Because now he was fucking desperate.

Now he wanted this.

Soft sheets slid against his back, Corrado found Alessio watching him as he reached for that bag. It seemed that's what *he* wanted, to watch Corrado as he took him—as he was given what he wanted.

And he did.

Watched him as he sheathed the thick length of his dick in latex. Watched him as cold lube and deft fingers stretched him open while Alessio's mouth worked his cock until he felt like he was going to come from that alone. Watched him when he was ready to *beg* to come when Alessio started working the head of his cock against Corrado's ass.

Never had he let a man take him.

Until *now*.

That ache was deep—the pain sharp even as something dark and *fucking amazing* started licking at his nerve endings.

Still, it was slow. Too fucking slow, maybe. It felt like that heightened the pain, but also sharpened the pleasure trailing right behind. Enough to make him want to *stop*, though that teasing promise of more kept him right there, lost in that place.

And still, Alessio watched him.

A hand splayed to his chest, and another sliding under the roof of his jaw. He pushed Corrado's head back to the pillow as he continued staring at him. It was only when that pain started to ebb, when it became *better*, and Alessio was fucking him until he felt like he couldn't breathe that the man finally looked away from him.

Alessio's forehead hit his chest, and Corrado tipped his head back to stare at the ceiling, his lips falling open with a hard moan.

Because there it was.

Fuck.

How many times had he come before?

Felt *that* pleasure?

More times than he cared to count.

It never felt like this.

Never took away his sight, his vision, and everything else, too. Like he was drowning in Alessio, and *sensation*.

"Jesus Christ," he heard Alessio grunt, lips grazing his chest as he stilled, coming almost in perfect tune with Corrado.

Jesus Christ was right.

Corrado still couldn't breathe.

He felt the soft glide of Alessio's fingertips drifting over his chest, leaving a trail of raw nerve endings as his hand left where it had been resting. It was only then that Corrado realized he'd been fisting the sheets at his sides.

"You should have told me," Alessio murmured. "Told me you'd never—"

Corrado looked down as that hand fell from his jaw, finding Alessio's chin resting against his chest as he stared at him. "Why ... I wanted what I got, Les. It didn't matter."

Alessio blew out a breath, the warm air skipping across Corrado's skin. "Yeah, don't I know that."

PART TWO

ALMOST FIVE YEARS LATER

CHAPTER 15
GINEVRA

"His name is Andino Marcello, and he is who I picked for you to marry."

She used to be a normal girl.

And then life happened.

Or rather, someone's life collided with Ginevra's, and she realized that, no, her small world wasn't at all normal. She had simply been living in a delusion that someone else created for her. A pretty bubble that was opaque, so she was unable to see the truth happening all around her.

Last month, she had been normal.

A twenty-one-year-old woman with two younger sisters, a mom she loved, a dad who was distant but kind when he came around, hopes and dreams, and a *life*.

This month, she was something else.

The daughter of a dead mobster, a half-sister to three new siblings, and a woman with a life that was no longer her own to do with what she wished.

"This is the way of *Cosa Nostra*," Kev told her.

Ginevra sat on her mother's couch, hands twisted into tight balls where she could hide them at her sides, *willing* herself to stay quiet, and say nothing. She saw what happened when her new half-sister, Siena, tried to speak against Kev, or even their other brother, Darren. They weren't kind about telling them to shut up, or simply striking out to *make* them shut up with a slap.

Beside Ginevra, her mother, Marie, stayed silent, too, staring at the wall behind the brothers standing at the other side of the living room. She was immovable, a statue, even.

Matteo died, and everything changed.

Everything.

"This is the Calabrese way," Darren added when Ginevra and her mother stayed quiet on the couch. "And whether you like it or not, our father gave you the Calabrese name when you were born, and so you're now expected to *own* it."

"The way we want you to." Kev raised his thick brows when Ginevra *almost* opened her mouth to tell them right where they could shove their demands. His look shut her up instantly. "This will be good for you, and for us. Surely, you've heard of the Marcellos? You must know the family, Ginny. It's a good match."

"She knows *nothing* about that life," her mother said softly. "Matteo didn't want me to explain, and we were removed from it all, Kev."

His gaze drifted to her mother, his lips forming a thin, grim line.

Disappointment.

There was no denying the fact that Kev was his father's son, Ginevra thought. God knew he looked just like their father, even if a different woman had brought him into the world than the one that gave her life.

Still, they shared similarities.

Like Ginevra to Darren, or even Siena.

The dark hair, the shape of their oval faces, and even the way they all *smiled* the same. She'd taken her brown eyes from her mother, though, and she was grateful for that in moments like these. Because when she looked into Kev's eyes, all she saw was *coldness*. She knew her stare was not the same as his.

"I just ..." Ginevra struggled to find her words, to say

something that would make these men understand this was not what she wanted to do. It didn't matter to her that the blood inside her veins said she was the same as them. It didn't matter that her father—now dead—had once controlled a major mafia family. She wasn't *like them*. She never lived like they did. Their way was not her way. "This isn't my life; I don't want to do this just because you say it's what I should do. I'm allowed to make my own choices. I'm twenty-one, and—"

"It's been decided," Kev replied dryly.

"And you will see it through," Darren added for his brother, "whether we have to force you down the aisle, or you walk down willingly. If you think we don't have the means and the motive to see it through for you, test us, Ginevra. It is going to happen."

"It *will* happen."

She sucked in a sharp breath, using her fingernails to dig into the palms of her hands to keep her emotions under control. These men were *horrible*. They would enjoy seeing her tears all too much, even if they were simply a byproduct of her anger.

To them, it would be a battle won.

To them, she was just a *girl*.

A stupid girl for them to use.

"I know you think because you weren't brought up in the same life as us that you can somehow ... escape the same expectations that we were given," Ken said, making Ginevra wish he would just shut the fuck up, and get out of her mother's apartment, "but that isn't actually the case at all. With our father dead, *we* are expected to carry on his legacy, and make the choices that will further our family in the criminal world. That's how it works. And you are the thing we plan to use to do that."

"Do you understand?" Darren asked.

Ginevra bit the inside of her cheek hard enough to draw blood. "I won't do this."

"You will. Or we will make sure you do. You continue to think you have a choice here, Ginny—"

"*Don't* call me that."

Kev let out a sigh. "Now, be nice. It's just a nickname."

No, it wasn't.

It was the name her mother had called her since she was a girl. It was the name her sisters shouted from the other end of the apartment when they wanted her to come help them pick out an outfit so maybe they could finally get their crush at school to notice them. It was the name her professors— which she would no longer be allowed to attend classes, according to Kev—used when they directed questions at her in classes.

It was not, however, a nickname her father gave her. It did not come from the fucking Calabrese. And she didn't want the rest of them using it.

"Don't call me that," Ginevra muttered, keeping her gaze down.

Kev, seemingly reaching his level of patience with her for the day, smacked the wall with his hand loud enough to make Ginevra and her mother jump on the couch. "I won't say it again after this, but it *has been decided.* You will marry the Marcello man within a couple of months. We'll nail down an appropriate date, and let you know. If you run, Ginevra, we will find you. If someone here thinks that helping you get away will help your case, then they will be *removed.* I won't tolerate someone going against me—I don't give a fuck if you are my blood. Do you understand me?"

God.

She hated him.

All of them right now.

"*Do. You. Understand. Me.*"

Ginevra lifted her head, and met Kev's stare from across the room. She felt her mother's hand find hers on the couch, and grab tightly to keep her grounded. Right now, she just had to get through this day. They could figure out the rest later.

Surely.

"I understand," Ginevra lied.

Lied, because no.

She would not marry someone chosen for her.

She wouldn't do anything they wanted.

Kev's gaze narrowed. "You know, I can see that fight in your eyes, Ginny. All of us Calabrese … it all looks the same, and I see it."

Good.

She said nothing.

"But don't worry," Kev added, smiling in that cold way of his, "you will learn, and I will break you like I did the rest of them. Remember, you were warned."

A cold chill slipped down Ginevra's spine, but she refused to show her fear. Like her anger or heartbreak, her fear would make them think they had won, too. They didn't deserve anything from her, not even the emotions in her heart.

It was only once her half-brothers had left Ginevra and her mother alone in the apartment—although, not before explaining they would have guards posted at the door to watch them—that her mother finally turned to her.

Teary eyed, Marie grabbed both of Ginevra's hands as the wetness slipped down her cheeks. Usually, her mother was a ray of happiness. Always smiling, so strong, and never sad. Lately, it seemed like sad was all she knew how to be.

That broke her heart, too.

Ginevra dragged in a ragged breath, and for the first time, a tear streaked down her own cheek. She didn't try to wipe it away, her mother's hands keeping her from moving.

Not that she cared, now. Her mother could see the emotion. It was *them* that couldn't.

"It's okay," her mother whispered, nodding fast, "I promise it'll be okay, Ginny."

"It won't."

Marie shook her head. "It *will*. I will figure out a way to get you away from them, and this *marriage*. I will, I promise."

"Ma, don't—"

"They don't scare me. It'll be okay, Ginny."

Except it wouldn't.

It *really* wouldn't.

It was the quiet whispers from the hallway that made Ginevra and her mother pull away from each other. A quick check over her shoulder confirmed what she figured, her seventeen and fifteen-year-old sisters waiting at the end of the hallway, standing close together like they were the only things keeping each other up at the moment.

They probably were.

"It's okay," Ginevra whispered to her sisters, seeing the tears in their eyes. This was not *their* life, either. This wasn't what they knew, or how they expected to be treated. They shouldn't have to watch their *new* half-brothers force their sister into a marriage she didn't want with a stranger, but this was their new reality. And it was terrifying. "Greta, Giulia, it's okay, I promise."

It would have to be.

For them, for her mama … she was going to have to be strong. Because if not *her*, then would Kev or Darren go for them next?

Ginevra couldn't safely say no.

That left her to keep them safe.

"Come here," she told her sisters.

The oldest, Greta, came first. Giulia was quick to follow.

Just a month ago, they had been normal girls, too. Experiencing high school, and their worries filled up by things like what jeans looked best with what shoes, and if they were going to pass their upcoming tests. Now, they had far greater worries.

That shouldn't be how it was.

Once her younger sisters were sitting with her and Marie on the couch, Ginevra felt a little better. It felt good to hug them, to promise that things were going to be okay.

"Why are they making you marry—"

"It doesn't matter," Ginevra said quickly, hushing Greta as she shot a look to her mom. "You don't need to worry about me. I am going to be *fine*."

And so would her little sisters.

Somehow, she was going to make sure of it.

~

"Ginny?"

"Yeah?"

Giulia looked away from the casket a few feet in front of them to stare at her oldest sister. "I don't know how to say goodbye to Mama."

Greta made a soft noise under her breath—it sounded like an agreement—but she didn't look up from her hands. She'd been doing that for a week, now. Staring silently, but saying very little, and not engaging.

Ginevra worried more and more for her sisters with every passing day. For now, though, she had to worry about getting them all through this horrible day. "You don't have to go up and say goodbye that way, if you don't want to, Giulia. Mama knows that you love her, okay?"

Her youngest sister nodded.

"But I'm going to say goodbye, now. Are you both okay here?"

The girls nodded.

She didn't believe them.

None of them were okay, now.

Ginevra left her sisters behind in the pew, and headed for the altar. She glided her fingertips over the chrome decals of the shiny, black casket sitting atop the altar. For now, the church was quiet ... but not for long. Soon, it would fill with grieving people who had known and loved her mother, ready to send Marie off to a better place.

They would *never* know the truth. Not her sisters, or the people coming to the church today.

They would never know that her mother was killed trying to save her from a fate nearly as bad as death itself. That those scars on Marie's wrists weren't self-inflicted, no matter how much money the coroner had been paid to say so. That Ginevra blamed herself *every single day* for this.

I'm sorry, Mama, she thought. *I'm so sorry.*

She stroked the closed casket again, wishing she was *better*. Because then, she might have been able to stand having the top opened, so she could look at her mother's face and say those same words out loud. Instead, she was stuck like this.

Wishing she could be better.

I love you, Mama.

Peering over her shoulder, Ginevra found her young sisters —still teenagers, and now left with her to take care of them— sitting in the first pew. The priest had suggested the girls be allowed to have a few minutes with their mother's casket alone before the funeral started. He thought it might help them to say goodbye, but Ginevra didn't know if it mattered.

They were still heartbroken.

Still crying.

Still *alone*.

And now, terrified, too.

Because their *brothers* had done this. People who were supposed to be family had taken away the one person they loved more than the world and life itself.

Ginevra needed to be better for them, too. For Greta, and Giulia. No one else would be here to take care of them, and make sure they weren't pawns for Kev and Darren's fucking games. For now, they were too young … they couldn't be used in a way to further the brothers' agenda, but eventually they would be older.

Eventually, they too would be on Kev or Darren's radar. Ginevra needed to make sure that never happened. And she didn't want them to be used against her, either. Not like her mother had.

Marie thought to help her.

Kev made sure she couldn't.

That couldn't be her sisters, too.

"Ginny," came a soft voice to her left.

There, she found Siena standing a few feet away. For the most part, her half-sister, yet another sibling she didn't know existed until Matteo died, was *nothing* like her brothers. Siena was sweet, kind, gentle, and all the things Kev and Darren didn't know how to be. She showed true empathy and sympathy for the situation Ginevra had been put in, and she constantly stepped in between her brothers and sister when she thought she might be able to help Ginevra in some way. Even if it meant Siena got in trouble for it, too.

At the very least, Ginevra thought she could trust Siena. That was saying a hell of a lot more than she felt regarding most *other* people in her life. She didn't feel anything at all for them, now, except her sisters.

Everyone else just fell in line.

Except Siena.

"Yeah?" she asked.

Siena offered her a small smile. "You okay?"

She shrugged. "Not really."

"Yeah, I … get that."

Ginevra put her attention back on the casket, knowing she only had a few more minutes to spend alone with her mother before the funeral would start. Once the church filled with guests, she would be expected to put on her mask, and keep up the charade. Kev and Darren would expect nothing less from her, now.

She would do it.

She *had* to do it.

For her sisters.

But it killed her inside. It was taking a piece of her every single day. The closer she came to the date her brothers chose for the wedding, the worse she felt. In her heart, and in her *soul*. This was wrong, and all kinds of bad.

This was not how it was supposed to be.

"Hey, hey," she heard Siena whisper. "It's all right."

Ginevra didn't realize it until she had been thrust right into the middle of a panic attack, but she bent over at the knees beside her mother's casket. One hand stayed on the smooth, shined wood, while her other pressed overtop her racing heart to slow it down. She swore that if it didn't calm, it was going to race right out of her chest. Or *explode* altogether.

God.

"It's all right, Ginny, it *is*," Siena said softly.

She felt her half-sister's hands on her shoulders, and then one rubbing across her back like she thought that might help, too. She bet her younger sisters were watching from the pew, seeing yet another horrifying thing to remind them that nothing about their life was normal anymore.

Everything had changed.

Again.

Now, with their mother's death.

It was all wrong.

"Come on," Siena murmured, forcing Ginevra to stare up at her through watery eyes, "look at me, huh? Don't let them come in here and see this, all right? Don't let them see what they're doing to you—they don't deserve that. I promise they don't."

Ginevra dragged in lungful after lungful of air. She willed her anxiety and raging emotions to calm, but while it helped, it still felt like a whole war continued to battle on inside her heart and mind.

"What am I going to do?"

Siena blinked. "What?"

Ginevra swallowed the lump in her throat.

It *ached.*

Like the rest of her, too.

"What am I going to do, Siena?" she whispered, lips trembling. "If I run, they have my sisters. *If* I can even run, because I never get the chance. And if I stay, then I have to marry a man I haven't even met yet. What am I going to do?"

Siena's fingers tightened around Ginevra's shoulders. "For right now, you're going to get up, let me fix your face, and then we're going to sit down in the pew like nothing is wrong. You're going to get through this day, thank people who offer their condolences, and make sure Kev and Darren think you're doing everything they want. Okay?"

"I *can't.*"

"You can. You've been doing it. This doesn't change that."

Ginevra let out a slow stream of air. "And then what?"

Siena's eyes burned brightly. "Never worry about those girls, Ginny. *I* will look out for them, if you can't. I promise you that. Don't ever think you have to stay for them when there are people here who will take care of them, too."

"I can't just leave them to Kev and Darren."

"*Stop.*" Siena gave her a look. "They'll be *fine*. They are too young to be married off, and right now, they wouldn't even consider those girls for anything else. What we have to figure out is how we're going to get *you* out of this."

"You shouldn't help me," Ginevra mumbled. "Look what happened to my mama."

Siena nodded. "I know, but I can't stand back and do nothing, either. That's not who I am."

Which was why she was different, Ginevra knew.

It was why she could trust her.

"What am I going to do?" she repeated.

"Give it time. We'll figure something out."

But would they?

The first time Ginevra met her *husband-to-be*, Andino Marcello said very little to her. He was kind, of course, and polite, but that was as far as it went. He didn't seem interested in discussing the wedding with her brothers, and he certainly didn't care to talk about it with her.

Not that she minded.

Even she was doing the very bare minimum that she could regarding the planning. If someone asked her for an opinion, she gave one, but that was it.

It wasn't like she wanted it.

Why should she care?

The couple of meetings that happened after that first one with Andino were basically the same. Safe, kind conversation that didn't make Ginevra think he was anything different than the other men in the mafia life. The only obvious difference about Andino was the fact he was actually an heir to a criminal empire.

The next boss, she was told.

You should be grateful, Kev had taunted her. *We picked you a husband that women in this life would kill for, in a position they would give anything for. And you cry about it?*

Like she should be happy.

She wasn't.

It wasn't Andino as much as it was everything else. She didn't blame him, either, and she tried to be polite to him— not only because her brothers threatened her, but it was who she was, anyway—but that didn't mean she wanted any of this.

"Do you talk at all?" Andino asked.

Ginevra looked up from the gross salad in front of her, and frowned. "I do, I'm sorry."

Andino tipped his head sideways at that reply. "Why?"

It took Ginevra entirely too long to respond to that. Mostly because she didn't know *how* to respond. No other man around her, but especially not her brothers, seemed to give even one damn about *why* for anything in her life. They didn't ask her questions, they simply told her what to do, and expected her to follow through.

It was that simple.

Andino's question surprised her.

"Why, what?" she asked.

"Why are you apologizing to me?"

She focused her attention on her plate, using the fork to play with the salad as she spoke. "For not being ... whatever you would like, I guess. That's what I was told to be today— whatever you would like. And with everyone else, that usually means staying quiet and out of sight, if possible. I can't exactly be out of your sight when I have to sit right in front of you at the table, so being quiet seemed like the way to go. Sorry if that's not what you want."

Ginevra didn't miss the way Andino glanced a few tables over at her brothers where they sat enjoying their steaks and potatoes, while she had been forced—by them—to order a salad. The other thing she didn't miss?

The *anger* in Andino's face.

What was that?

What did it mean?

"I neither want, nor need, for you to be a piece of art beside me," Andino eventually replied.

Her brow knotted as she met his gaze, confused.

"Pretty, but inanimate," he added after a moment, shrugging. "If that's what they expect, then that's another story. When they are around, you can behave however they deem appropriate as to not cause yourself trouble. With me, you can be whatever you feel like in the moment."

"Right now, I would prefer to be anywhere else."

Andino smirked.

That surprised her, too.

Mostly, this man seemed like a statue. Cold, and immovable. Like he didn't have emotions at all, or rather, none he outwardly showed to those around him. It was why she found it so hard to read him. It was why she didn't understand his motives here.

"I do appreciate a woman who isn't a liar," he said, "but for the sake of appearances, let's at least play nice."

Okay.

He didn't want a liar?

She could do that.

"I don't want to marry you, Andino. I don't want to be here, and I certainly don't want to pretend to give a damn about anything you want to talk about right now. So, if it's okay with you, I would much prefer to sit here and occasionally nod when you talk so that you might think I give a shit. But really, we'll both know I don't."

It took a second for him to reply, but when he did, it stunned her.

Silent.

"Oh, good. Then, we're on the same page."

He didn't want to marry her, either.

Then why were they here?

Ginevra didn't get the chance to ask.

Just as quickly, he asked, "Did they choose the salad for you, too? Because I wouldn't willingly eat that without some kind of steak to weigh it down."

She almost smiled.

Almost.

"They did—heaven forbid you thought I ate too much."

Andino made a noise, shaking his head. "I prefer women who enjoy themselves, actually. Not that it'll matter what I prefer from you. Some other man, perhaps, but not me. You would do well to remember that."

She met his gaze again.

Andino smiled back.

"What does that mean?"

Because she was *desperately* hoping it meant one thing.

That this wedding wouldn't happen.

But *how?*

Andino pushed his plate of chicken parmesan across the table for her to take, winking as he did so. "You'll find out when the time comes. And here, take my food. At least, you won't leave here hungry, and my mother taught me to always make sure a woman was happy when she left a table with me. Eat up."

She did.

Still wondering if she could trust him.

Or what might happen now.

CHAPTER 16
ALESSIO

"Holy Christ, *Les*."

Alessio licked the salty, heady flavor of Corrado's cum from his lips as he slinked over his lover's body, using his hands to fist into the sheets covering their mattress as he hovered above him. Corrado lifted to kiss Alessio, his tongue slashing against his like he was ready to take the taste of him back.

"Fuck," Corrado said, falling back to the bed.

Grinning like the asshole he was, Alessio flashed his teeth, letting that cockiness of his come out to play. Because that's what he did, and Corrado liked it. If only because he could challenge it.

Corrado was probably the only person in Alessio's life—and that had never changed in the nearly five years that they'd been doing this shit together, whatever *it* was—who could deal with his nonsense. Not to mention, give it back just as hard.

He needed that.

Craved it, really.

Alessio dealt with all sorts of people on a daily basis. People he couldn't stand, and people that drove him up the wall. He came across too many personalities to name, and very rarely did he find one that actually *interested* him, or kept his attention.

His job, still being an assassin for The League, meant he

went from one person to the next, taking on assignments and seeing the world over and over again.

Yet, he still wanted to be *here*.

In this bed, or this penthouse.

With Corrado.

It was where he found peace.

And happiness.

"Why …" Corrado let out a hard breath, his tongue snaking out to lick the corner of his lips as his hands drove through the longer bits of hair at the top of his head. Out of breath, his chest still heaved from that orgasm. Alessio like that sight more than anything else. He liked knowing he affected him. Why lie? "Why were we doing that again?"

Alessio dropped to the bed beside Corrado, propping himself up with his elbow, and resting his head on his hand. "That chick—the Poland job."

Corrado nodded. "*Yeah* … shit, yeah, okay. She was a screamer. How did the talk of the Poland job turn into you sucking my dick, though?"

He chuckled.

"Good memories."

Mostly, Alessio wanted to make Corrado shout, too.

He'd done that.

It worked.

Why did he have to explain it?

"And I just got back," Alessio added, rolling to his back to stare up at the glass shard chandelier that hung above their four-poster bed. Tucked against floor-to-ceiling windows in the penthouse's master bedroom, they had ample view of the busy Vegas city, although they were just high enough that unless someone was watching their windows with fucking binoculars, no one was seeing what they were doing. And if they were watching …

Well, shit.

Alessio hoped they enjoyed the show.

Nightly.

Corrado shifted to his side, and Alessio caught his gaze with his own. Not saying a single word, he reached over and pressed his thumb to the corner of Alessio's mouth. The pad of Corrado's digit dragged across his lower lip with the softest touch.

The silence stretched on, but that was okay. He'd learned after all these years with Corrado that, sometimes, quiet was better. It was in their stillness where they found the *best* connection.

They didn't always need words.

They just needed *moments.*

Quiet, soft moments.

Sometimes, they came when neither of them expected it, too. Between bursts of busy schedules, and chaotic careers that sent them both running all over the world doing jobs for The League, and different clients. After the danger waned, and the violence was gone, it was just the two of them again.

They ended up back here.

In their life.

Together.

Quiet.

Alessio knew that from the outside looking in, he and Corrado didn't make sense to other people. They didn't have a *label.* Far too many overlooked them, and assumed they weren't a thing together. Not that they ever gave people a reason to know the truth, either.

You know, beyond living together.

For nearly five years …

Still, people didn't know.

They could only assume.

He partly blamed himself, and Corrado, too. Not that he ever said that to anyone, or his lover. A long time ago, they'd decided *this* was what they were going to be. Together, but only to each other. A thing, but it wasn't open to public consumption.

Alessio was willing to do that.

It gave him what he wanted.

Corrado.

Somehow, they found a familiar rhythm like this. He didn't push for something else, or for more, because what else was there to have when … in a lot of ways, he had it all.

Or did he?

People wouldn't understand.

They shared *everything.*

A life.

Work.

A home.

Women.

Sex.

There was nothing in their lives that wasn't somehow touched by both of them. So much so, that those closest to Corrado and Alessio thought the two of them were often extensions of the other. Without one, the other wasn't *right.*

Nothing was right.

"What are you thinking about, huh?" Corrado asked, his voice thick with sleep and *bliss.* Probably still humming from that orgasm, and if all went well, Alessio would be the next one. "You're quiet over there."

"You like that, anyway."

"Sometimes."

Alessio grinned.

Corrado smirked right back.

Reaching over, he drifted his fingertips down the line of Corrado's jaw still shadowed with a few days' worth of scruff. "You do like it when I'm quiet. Admit it."

It was true.

Corrado thrived on attention.

Alessio just liked to *watch*.

"And when you're a shit," Corrado added.

He laughed. "Yeah, that, too."

"And don't deflect. What were you thinking?"

Alessio sighed, his gaze going back to the large, glimmering light fixture above the bed. Only Corrado would know something was going on in Alessio's mind when he was quiet. No one else saw him in his silent moments and thought, *something's happening there*. They were all too willing to let him stew, even if they didn't know that's what he was doing.

Not Corrado, though.

He often wondered, how, at eighteen—although now, just a month or so shy of his twenty-third birthday—had he found his *person*. He knew some people went their whole lives without ever finding that person that was meant to be only theirs.

He found his early.

Corrado was still there, too.

God.

And he loved him.

Loved him fucking *stupid*.

Loved him enough to still be here even when shit held Corrado back, and forced them into his strange place where they were something, but they weren't at the same time. Where they shared women in bed, and had a whole life together behind closed doors, but out in the world … they weren't anything. Where they dictated this thing between them with rules that had followed them from damn near the beginning, but neither of them said three little words to cement it.

I love you.

But that was too deep.

Corrado didn't do deep.

So, Alessio lied.

"I was thinking one of us needs to take the black Porsche out, and open it up," he murmured, swallowing the emotions in his throat, "it's been a while since it's been taken out."

Corrado glanced over at him, and if he knew he was lying, he didn't say. Not that he ever brought up that kind of shit; it might open a can of worms that he wasn't willing to face yet, and Alessio had a bad habit of letting Corrado have what he wanted.

Even if it hurt him.

"Yeah, all right," Corrado replied.

Crisis averted.

As per usual.

The ringing phone on Corrado's nightstand saved the two of them from saying anything more. Corrado rolled over, and snatched the phone while Les pushed out of the bed, and started grabbing the few clothes he'd discarded earlier. A shirt, his pants …

Corrado had *nothing* on.

He tossed his clothes over, too.

"Thanks," he mouthed, answering the phone at the same time. "Marcus."

Alessio stilled, shooting a look over his shoulder. Not that it was unusual for Corrado to get calls from his family because that was all *too* normal. Usually a couple a day, really. If not his mother, then it might be the man's twin, his father, or any one of his other three brothers.

All of which Alessio knew.

And well.

It was one of the reasons why this thing between them didn't make any fucking sense, not that Corrado liked it when he pointed it out. Alessio wasn't *hidden* from Corrado's family like he was a dirty secret to be kept. He sat at their dinner table—he attended their parties, and celebrations. They knew him.

And he suspected, they knew why he was there.

But no one asked.

So, no one told.

He just didn't understand.

Why?

What did it matter after all this time?

"But can't they just—" Corrado sighed harshly, telling his brother, "Fine, Marcus. *Yes*, they can throw a double birthday party for us, and you."

Then, Corrado added, "I assume Les will come, why wouldn't he? Tell Ma yeah for that."

Alessio went back to pulling on his clothes, slightly annoyed. Not so much at the conversation happening behind him, but the *topic*. His family just expected Alessio would be around for something like Corrado's birthday party his mother and father wanted to throw in a few weeks—although his birthday was sooner than that—because they had to *know*.

They had to know what he was to Corrado.

Why he was important.

That this *thing* was a fucking thing.

Why were they still playing this stupid game together?

He also knew that at least a handful—or a couple, anyway—of people, like Corrado's twin, knew a lot more about Alessio and Corrado than anyone else did. Like the fact their poly lifestyle in the bedroom often had them sharing women, and otherwise.

But never men.

Those rules, again.

Although, Les was to blame for *that*.

It made him see fucking red to think of Corrado sleeping with another man, but it didn't bother him at all to know during his last job, his lover hooked up with a woman at a club he frequented. And it wasn't different for Alessio, either. He had the same benefits in this mess that Corrado did.

The only thing was no other men.

And they *always* told each other the truth.

Simple as that.

Alessio just didn't understand why they were still here, deeper into this mess together than ever before, when it seemed like the only people who mattered around them already knew the truth. Even if no one was saying it out loud.

"I'll see what I can do," Corrado said, "and yeah, I'll talk to you soon, Marcus."

The call ended.

Alessio kept his back facing Corrado as he headed for the walk-in closet where their collection of *everything* stayed safe behind glass counters and shelves. There, he found a particular watch he wanted—encrusted with diamonds around the face, with a black background, and gold hands to tell time. He affixed it to his wrist, adding a couple of beaded bracelets around it that cost a fraction of what the watch did. A black cross made up of miniature, worn metal skulls attached to a leather cord dangled from his hand before he quickly slipped it over his head, letting it hang from his neck.

On jobs, he didn't wear jewelry.

Nothing but *black*.

Nothing to distinguish him, or give him away. He'd just come back from a quick trip with the team over in Romania, but he doubted he would have another job for a while. Dare tried to space them out a bit, unless something came up that couldn't be helped.

When not on assignment, Alessio wore whatever the fuck he wanted, his style a mixture of dark grunge, and *excess*. Like the watch. Corrado, on the other hand, looked like every other fucking Guzzi that Alessio had ever met. Dripping in wealth, and carefully put together. Not a hair out of place, and suits were preferred to jeans.

Although, Corrado did like his leather jacket.

It worked, though.

"You good?" Corrado asked, coming into the closet to stand just beyond the doorway.

Alessio shrugged. "Why wouldn't I be?"

"I don't know, I just got that feeling, Les."

Right.

That feeling.

"This whole thing with us is all about that *feeling*, yeah," Alessio murmured.

"What does that mean?"

Corrado had his *thing*.

Nobody asked about what the fuck was going on with him and Alessio, so he didn't offer the information willingly.

Alessio had his thing, too.

He dwelled on everything, overthought it all, and when all else failed ... he managed to overreact, too.

Corrado wasn't working on his thing.

Alessio was *trying* with his.

Like now.

"Nothing," he said, willing to drop it, "I'm just running off at the mouth, and—"

The phone in Corrado's hand rang again.

Alessio wasn't even offended.

He just got back home from a job that had him away from this place, and his person, for three long goddamn weeks; he didn't want to fight. Especially not about something that had never changed in nearly five years.

What did it even matter?

"Les," Corrado said, ignoring the call, "are we good?"

He looked back at his lover.

His.

That was the thing.

Corrado was still his.

Nothing else counted but that.

"Yeah, man, we're good," Alessio said "Answer your phone."

CHAPTER 17
CORRADO

Keeping his gaze locked on Alessio, because Corrado figured this conversation wasn't over, he answered the call ringing through to his phone without checking the ID. Alessio ignored him all the while, confirming to Corrado that despite what his lover might be saying, there *was* something wrong.

He planned on figuring out *what*.

Right after this call.

"Corrado here," he said into the phone.

"What's it been, Corrado, two or so years?"

He stiffened at the unmistakable voice on the other end of the call. "About that, Andino. Can't say that time bothers me, though."

Alessio tipped his head up, and eyed Corrado curiously at the mention of a man's name who lived in New York. Way the hell across the country from them.

Andino Marcello chuckled. "That's fair. I could say the same for you."

Something like that.

"What do you want?"

"My uncle. Lucian, remember him?"

Shit.

Yeah, he remembered.

The way this conversation was going, Corrado decided here wasn't the best place to have it, all things considered.

Turning his back to Alessio, he headed out of the large walk-in closet, and back into the comfort of their spacious bedroom.

"What about him?" Corrado asked, coming up next to the chair Alessio liked to use when he tied his combat boots back around the ankles. "And spare me any bullshit. I don't have the time."

"Still as moody as ever, huh?"

"*And?*"

Andino sighed. "A couple years back, you were in New York on a job, and one of his people ended up caught in the mess. Lucian stepped in to help sweep that under the rug, and you promised him a—"

"Favor," Corrado muttered, his hand curling around the edge of the chair. *No one* was supposed to know about that favor—Lucian gave his word. Corrado hadn't been *new* to The League when that fuck up happened, but it had been one of his first few solo jobs. He didn't want to go back, and say he'd caused problems with a crime family as big as the Marcellos, so he worked something else out. "Well, what does he want, then?"

"Oh, he's allowing *me* to cash in the favor instead of him."

Great.

"And what is it?"

"Seems I'm supposed to be getting married on the twenty-fifth of July to Ginevra Calabrese. She's twenty-one, new to this whole ... mafia bit, and whatnot. Ever heard of that family?"

"A bit," Corrado admitted. "I don't see what you getting married has anything to do with me or this favor I owe, though."

"Oh, I don't plan on actually getting married. See, that's where you're going to come in. I need that girl to disappear."

Corrado blinked. "*What?*"

"I didn't stutter."

"You want me to take out a woman you're supposed to *marry?*"

Because *fuck*, that was kinda cold.

A little bit.

Then again, Andino was known for being a manipulative asshole when he wanted to be. He didn't give a shit who it was, either. Blood or not.

"No," Andino said, laughing darkly. "She needs to go away for a while. This *marriage* … it's a sham. A way for her family to try to get a place within the Marcello ranks, and I won't allow it to happen. And so, she needs to *go*. And by that, I mean somewhere else, out of this country, for a spell of time. A few months, maybe. I figure, you have dual citizenship to Canada, I'm sure you have homes to use there, and I *know* you have the means and motives to keep her safe and out of sight for a while. It's perfect for me."

"But not for *me*," Corrado returned. "I have a fucking job, man. People I answer to, and things I have to take care of myself."

For the most part.

But a few months away?

Could he even swing that?

It was hard to say. Dare would likely allow him time off from The League, if he asked. He hadn't taken any time since becoming a full-time member, whereas others usually took a bit of time off every year, and some, after every finished job.

Everyone needed something different.

But it was more than The League, too.

It was also—

Alessio came out of the walk-in closet with his combat boots hanging from his fingertips. Corrado moved aside as the man came to sit in the chair he was standing next to, and watched as he slipped his feet into the shoes before lacing them around the back.

He had someone else to think about, too.

A few months was a long time.

"And I need this kept *quiet*," Andino added after a moment. "No one can know the details—the less people that know, the more unlikely it is that she'll be found. I don't want to have to worry about killing the woman's brothers, while at the same time, have to think about whether or not someone has figured out where *she* is. Do you get me?"

Fuck.

"Yeah, I get you, but—"

"A favor is a favor in this life. You say you owe it to someone, then they can cash it in *whenever* they fucking want. Am I right, or no?"

"You're not wrong."

"Hmm."

Asshole.

Corrado scrubbed a hand down his jaw, and eyed Alessio from the side. He was done with his boots now, and leaning back in the chair with his hand resting at the line of his jaw while he stared out the large windows surrounding their bedroom.

"I was thinking," Andino continued, "that since they have her so protected, the *only* time they might give us the chance to get her away from them is on the wedding day. If you could drive in, because I don't want *any* paper trail attached to someone the Calabrese might recognize or know coming into the city, then—"

"I'm in Vegas. That's across the country."

"You have three and a half days. Drive *fast*."

Perfect.

This was just … great.

"She's dark-haired, brown-eyed. About five-ten, or so.

She'll be wearing a large church hat that'll cover her face. She *will not* be in a wedding gown. Make sure your vehicle is in front of the church to grab her as soon as she comes down those steps."

Andino gave the name of a well-known cathedral in New York City, adding, "I need to know what vehicle you'll be driving to let her know which one to get inside."

No questions.

Just a demand.

So, they were really doing this, huh?

Seemed so.

Corrado thought about the Porsche, if only because Alessio had mentioned it earlier, it did need to be opened up —what better way than fifty over the speed limit on the highway—and it was probably the fastest car they owned between them. "A black Porsche."

"Good."

Alessio glanced away from the window at that, his brow furrowing. Corrado shook his head, not wanting him to worry. This didn't involve his lover, and he didn't want Alessio getting messed up in this, either.

It wasn't that the Marcellos were bad people—in the underworld of criminals, they were more like *royalty*. He simply figured it would be better if he handled this mess alone, and let Alessio continue on doing what he always did without worrying about Corrado at the same time. He'd been the one to fuck up, so he would be the one who fixed it.

Easy.

Clean.

Just how he liked it.

"Better get on the road," Andino told Corrado. "I'll be in touch."

The man didn't even wait for him to agree, or say good-bye, before he hung up the phone. That might have pissed

Corrado off any other time, but he was now focused on the fact that Alessio was looking his way with a question in his eyes.

Because, of course.

"What's going on?" Alessio asked.

Corrado stuffed his hands in his pockets, keeping a tight hold on the phone at the same time to hide it away, too. "Something I have to do—last minute, it just came up."

"A job?"

It wasn't unusual for Dare to send Corrado or Alessio on a job without telling the other one. He left that to them to figure out between them, and whether or not the details were something they could or should share.

"Something like that," Corrado replied, "but more like a favor. Outside of The League's business. Nothing serious, but I need to head out."

"For how long?"

Yeah, *damn*.

He didn't want to lie.

He also didn't want Alessio asking too many questions.

"Could be a while," he replied, but then quickly added, "I can't really talk about it a lot."

It was the shadows that darkened Alessio's expression that told Corrado he didn't like that answer, and was more than willing to ask more.

"I have to look after someone for a while, keep them out of sight, and whatever else," Corrado explained, hoping it would be enough for Alessio, "but they don't want too many people in the loop about it. It's just a favor ... it won't cause trouble."

"Yeah, all right." Alessio cleared his throat, and looked up at Corrado, his blue eyes stormy again. That's where his emotions always showed, even when the rest of him was blank. "Where are you going, then?"

"Back to Toronto, I think."

"And it's going to take a while?"

"Seems so."

"Didn't Marcus say, when he called, that they wanted to have a birthday party for you, Chris, and him?"

Yeah.

"It'd be better if you stayed here, especially if I'm still taking care of … this issue," Corrado murmured.

"Is that it, or is it something else?"

"What?"

Alessio shook his head, his jaw tightening as he turned to look out the window again. "Nothing, man."

"You're not good at deflecting, Les."

"Maybe not, but I also don't hide things people already know, Corrado."

Ah.

Okay.

Now he knew what was wrong.

Except he really didn't have time to do this with Alessio right now, not considering he had a very short window of time to get on the road, and start the drive to New York. It certainly wasn't enough time to sit here and argue about *this*.

Again.

"I have to head out," Corrado said, "so can we come back to that?"

"*Right.*"

"Les."

Alessio looked back at him, and shrugged. "Yeah, we can come back to it. Where the hell else am I going to be, Corrado? I'm always here, right?"

He was.

Sometimes, Corrado wondered if he wanted to be, though.

Well, he knew what he wanted.

He always had.

Leaning down, Corrado kept his hands on the arm of the chair as he dropped a quick kiss to the side of Alessio's jaw, feeling the man's cheek twitch under his lips. "*Cette partie de mon coeur est à toi, hmm*? I'll call you, yeah?"

There were things he should say ...

Things he needed to say ...

Corrado never knew how to say them without needing to deal with the aftermath of it when for too long, he'd been used to *this*. Them being like they were, it was comfortable.

Cette partie de mon coeur est à toi.

This part of my heart is yours.

Alessio swallowed audibly. "You know, Kass has been teaching me French whenever I go into the complex, huh? Thought it was hilarious that it bugged me you two could speak, and I didn't understand, so he started teaching me some things. I didn't think to mention it, or whatever."

Corrado stiffened.

Well, then ...

Alessio let out a breath, and tipped his head to the door of the bedroom. "Better get on the road if you really need to go now."

"Yeah, I guess."

"So, go."

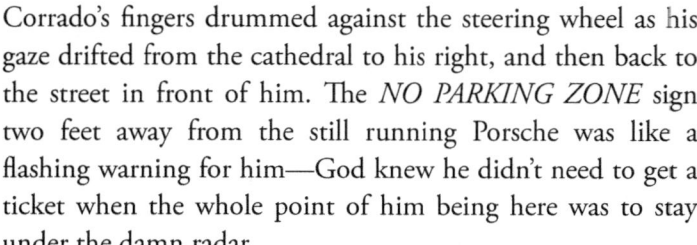

Corrado's fingers drummed against the steering wheel as his gaze drifted from the cathedral to his right, and then back to the street in front of him. The *NO PARKING ZONE* sign two feet away from the still running Porsche was like a flashing warning for him—God knew he didn't need to get a ticket when the whole point of him being here was to stay under the damn radar.

Not that it mattered.

He had to stay here.

Until someone else got here, too.

Sighing, Corrado dragged his hand down his jaw while keeping a tight grip on the steering wheel, and a foot on the brake pedal. Because yeah, if Ancino wanted him to get out of here quickly after he picked up this Calabrese chick, then he planned on doing exactly that.

He hadn't given her—Ginevra, was it?—much thought during the long drive across country. She was a job, and something he had to do. He didn't plan on making friends with her, so he didn't see why it would matter if he considered her or her situation when he was just there to hide the woman, and keep her out of trouble for the time being.

Instead, his mind focused elsewhere.

On a man he'd left back in Vegas.

Alessio.

He'd left things unsaid, and business unfinished there. He knew, without a doubt, the next time the two of them were standing face to face, Corrado was going to be pushed into a conversation that had been a long time in the making.

Shit that hurt Les.

Him, too.

Both of them, really.

Corrado wasn't sure when his family and people started putting things together about him and Alessio, but a lot of them knew the truth. It was kind of hard not to when they had lived together for the last few years and were practically inseparable except for when they were on a damn job.

It didn't matter.

Nobody *asked.*

Maybe they didn't want to.

Corrado didn't know.

He still didn't *tell.*

A part of him found comfort in that—in not feeling like he ever needed to justify why he loved Alessio, or in not needing to explain the complexities of their relationship. After all, it was *theirs*, not everyone else's.

Why did they need to know?

Corrado kept circling back to the customs and culture of his family's connections to the mafia, too. The fact that his sexual orientation could be used against them as a way to shame or harm them … well, that about killed him.

It wasn't his fault.

It wasn't *theirs*.

He just …

Didn't want to put them in that position.

At all.

Was that so fucking bad?

Les wouldn't understand.

Corrado was so lost to his thoughts that, for a moment, he'd forgotten where he was and why he was there. So stuck in his mind, in fact, that he didn't see the young woman approaching the Porsche until she had practically ripped open the door, and threw herself into the passenger seat. He didn't see her face at first, although he heard the sob that ripped out of her chest. He didn't know what she looked like, but he saw her hands balled into fists against the leather of the seat, and *shaking*. The dress she wore—it looked like something someone might wear to a wedding, but not on the bride—had ridden up around her thighs in her haste.

And then she looked up.

The wide-rimmed church hat likely hid her face when she was looking straight on, or even down, for that matter. Her dark brown hair had been pulled back into a sleek chignon, and while the makeup on her face had taken hell from streaks of tears …

He still had to look twice.

Take a breath.

Blink.

Soft, dainty features set off her whole face. Small lips, and a thin nose that curved up at the end just a bit. Oval face, with wide, doe-like eyes that made her look entirely too *innocent*. Tanned skin, and curves that filled out that dress *perfectly*.

Shit.

Corrado didn't know what in the hell he expected from Ginevra Calabrese. He hadn't given her a lot of thought—why should he?

He was looking at her now, though.

She was filling his thoughts *now*.

This felt like trouble.

A lot of it.

He just didn't know why.

"Drive," she snapped.

Angry.

Terrified.

So why did she sound musical?

"*Drive!*"

Corrado said nothing, simply checked his mirrors, and then let off the brake as he hit the gas hard. *Time for the second part of this damn road trip.*

CHAPTER 18
GINEVRA

How long had they been driving now?

An hour?

She checked the clock on the dashboard of the Porsche, still kind of stunned she was in a Porsche at all. About an hour and a half of driving, it seemed.

The man in the driver's seat continued his stretch of silence—he'd not said one word to her from the moment she got in his car. Or ... she suspected this was his car. Who else would it belong to?

Glancing over at him, *again*, Ginevra took in his profile. With the sun still high in the sky, she didn't have to imagine anything about the way he looked when it was all there for her to see. From his strong jaw dusted with a bit of dark facial hair, to the dusky olive skin tone with just a touch of tan. His fingers—long, and *deft*, she thought—flexed around the steering wheel in a rhythmic fashion, as though he was thinking about something, and his hands told the story of his thoughts.

She wondered if he had been stressed about something before she got in the car—maybe about picking her up—if only because where his high-fade hairstyle melted into the longer bits of hair at the top of his head was messy. Like he'd been running those fingers through it, and the strands fell out of place.

Not that it looked bad.

Nothing about the man looked bad.

What was his name again?

Andino said it when he brought her a *gift* for their wedding day to her private suite. Her *get out of jail free* card, she thought, sadly. A way out, he'd told her.

But what was his name again?

"Corrado," she said softly, remembering it all at once.

Just as fast, the man in the driver's seat reacted, his head swinging in her direction for the first time since she had entered his vehicle. His profile did *no* justice to his rugged features when he looked at her head-on.

Strong lines.

Brown eyes, flecked with gold.

Intense all over.

"*What?*"

His tone, as sharp as the edge of a blade, shocked her. He seemed angry, his jaw tensing as his gaze flicked over her, but she didn't know why. Maybe he didn't want to be here, or to help her. She understood that—who would want to help someone they didn't know?

A part of her didn't want to be here, either.

She left her sisters back there.

With *them*.

It made her heart ache.

She had to make a choice—her own freedom, or to sacrifice it. Except, when that freedom had been dangled in front of her fingertips, with the promise that it *might* be okay in the end, the first thing she had done was snatched it right up.

Greedy hands shaking, and all.

Was that selfish?

She didn't know.

"What?" Corrado asked again, his tone softening slightly the second time.

Ginevra swallowed hard. "Sorry, I just remembered your

name, that's all."

"And who told you my name?"

"Andino."

Corrado nodded. "Don't trust very much *he* says, let me tell you."

"He's the one who gave me this chance," she replied quietly, "so all I have to go on about him is that he made the right choice for me."

The man glanced her way again. "Arranged marriage, was it?"

"Not one I wanted."

"One rarely does."

He'd said that so dryly, and yet, managed to sound amused at the same time. Ginevra found, the longer she stared at him, the more confused she was about him, and *who* he was. How did Andino know the man, and was he someone she could trust? Where was she even going with him; where was he taking her, and what in the hell were they going to do once they got there?

She had too many questions.

And no fucking answers.

Ginevra's heart grew heavier the longer she thought about it. Her sisters, without her *and* their mother … the fact she was now a girl on the run with a man she didn't even know, that the engagement ring she had been made to wear was *still* on her fucking finger.

"*God,*" she mumbled.

Corrado glanced her way again.

She was quick to wipe away the tears that slipped down her cheeks, but that didn't really help. The stupid things kept coming, like a floodgate had been opened, and now she couldn't control it. She went from silent tears to hiccupping *sobs* in a blink, and she felt foolish for it, too. Not that she could stop it, now.

"Stop that," Corrado muttered.

Ginevra dragged in a ragged breath. "I'm *trying*."

"Try *harder*."

His sharp tone was back.

It made her cry more.

What was wrong with her?

"I don't *do* tears, fix your face."

"Excuse you?"

"I can't handle a woman that cries all the time, so quit it."

Fuck him.

"Would you *shut up*?" Ginevra barked back. "You have no idea what my life has been like lately, or what happened to me today! Just … shut up!"

Corrado blinked, murmuring, "You're kind of a mess, *donna*."

"And you're kind of an asshole. What about it?"

Those tears still hadn't stopped flowing. Corrado let out a harsh noise, but that time when he looked her way, a sympathy stared back from him. She didn't know what happened until the tires of the car crunched on gravel, and they slowed to a stop. He came across the seats after throwing off his buckle. He snatched a couple of napkins from the cup holder between them, and with a soft, but quick, hand, wiped the wetness from her face.

And likely what was left of her ruined makeup, too.

He kept stroking away those tears, never saying anything the entire time. Part of Ginevra liked that *far* too much—the way he looked as he focused on his task of wiping away her tears, and how he did it with such silent intensity that it struck her quiet.

And made her stop crying at the same time.

Finally, she whispered, "Thank you."

Corrado shrugged one shoulder. "Don't mention it."

"Where are we going?"

"Home. Or, a place I used to call home ... I'm sure they'll be surprised to see you with me when I arrive."

She frowned.

What did that mean?

Who else would he show up with?

"For how long?" she asked.

"Apparently," Corrado drawled out, sitting back in his seat and buckling up again, "until I am told otherwise. Settle in, I'm sure it'll be fun."

Yeah.

But would it *really*?

"Home sweet home," Corrado muttered, dropping Ginevra's box—the one Andino had given her with the forged passport, and other things she might need—to the floor. "Feel free to find a room you like, except the master bedroom, it's ... mine," he said, after hesitating. "And yeah, that's about it for now."

He didn't say anything else, simply headed down the hall without taking off his blazer, or removing his shoes. Ginevra didn't feel comfortable enough to walk through this Toronto penthouse without taking her manners into consideration. If he owned the place, then he could do what he wanted—she hadn't been raised that way.

Hanging up the hat that she had used to hide her face as she escaped from the church, Ginevra noticed the coats hanging along the rack on the wall. It wasn't that there were coats there that made her hesitate, but more the fact that they were two entirely different styles.

Leather.

Blazers.

She kicked off her shoes, and moved them into one of

the cubbies underneath the row of jackets, noticing there, too, were different styles of shoes. And not *just* a selection of loafers, but rather, combat boots, a pair of Doc Martens, and then next to those, runners, Armani loafers, and a pair of shined, black leather dress shoes that would work with any suit.

And just with a quick glance, she could tell the shoes were two different sizes. Like they belonged to two people.

Two men.

Did someone else live here?

"Is this yours?" Ginevra called after Corrado. "This penthouse, I mean?"

He didn't answer her back.

She tried not to be annoyed.

Not knowing where he went after he disappeared past the large entrance, decorated in black and white marble, Ginevra headed down the hall. That same sleek and stylish décor followed her deeper into the penthouse. She passed by a sitting room with an entire wall covered by windows overlooking a busy part of Toronto's center, and another that held a television large enough to be a projection screen. The black leather sectional sitting atop a similarly colored rug looked inviting, and God knew she needed to relax, but she had questions.

Only one man could currently answer them.

Overtop the couch hung a chandelier made up of metal fragments that mirrored the light from the inverted lights in the ceiling. Hardwood floors gleamed under her feet. Artwork covered the walls, and fresh flowers rested in a vase that she passed as she moved toward the noise coming from a room over.

Did someone change them regularly?

A maid?

The place screamed *excess*.

Money.

From the sturdy, huge bookcases she found in what looked to be a library-slash-office, to the black marble standing shower and matching clawfoot tub in a bathroom directly across from a state-of-the-art kitchen.

The kitchen was where Ginevra found Corrado nursing a glass of amber liquid. Whiskey, given the bottle sat in front of him on the gray, granite countertops. Stainless steel appliances and white cupboards surrounded him in the large space, and yet, somehow, he still dominated it. Her attention was only on him, and that *haunted* look in his eyes.

What was that from?

"There were keys in the bowl near the door," she said.

Corrado looked her way. "And?"

"I just … thought it looked like someone had recently left and planned to be back or something."

"Or something," he replied.

"Do you have a roommate here?"

Corrado laughed. "I own this penthouse, and we use it when we're in the city to visit my family."

"We?"

He cleared his throat, setting the glass to the counter a little harder than was necessary. She could tell just by the look in his eyes that *moody* Corrado was back—oh, he still looked the same, sure, still devastatingly handsome, but that attitude screamed back off without him even needing to say a word.

Was it because of this place?

Or her asking questions?

"Don't you have something else to do?" Corrado asked. "It was a sixteen-hour drive, find a place to sleep."

"So, no one else lives here, then? I don't want to wake up to someone—"

"I have to make some calls."

With that said, Corrado moved around the kitchen island, and crossed the space. He passed her by in the doorway without as much as a look in her direction, and that only left Ginevra more confused than ever.

He'd said *we*.

She heard it.

What did that mean?

"Fuck, thanks, I'm sure she'll be grateful to have something to wear," Ginevra heard Corrado say, his voice muted from how far it was traveling through the penthouse. "I'll take her out in a couple of days, or something, and let her grab the rest, but at least she'll have something to wear until then."

"No worries."

At the new male voice, Ginevra left the safety of the library where she had been mulling over the events of her life that led her to this place, and trying to find a book to take to bed at the same time. She couldn't do anything to change her circumstances at the moment, so she was content to distract her mind until something happened.

She lingered in the hallway as the conversation near the entry of the penthouse continued on between Corrado, and the newcomer. He hadn't said anyone would be coming over, so she wondered if it was maybe the *other* person who lived here.

"You want me to let Ma and Papa know you're here, or what?"

"I'll call," Corrado said. "They were expecting me, anyway. I just showed up a little earlier, that's all."

"Right, and they won't ask questions at all."

"I can't answer all of them even if they do."

"Yeah, I get you. The League, or …?"

"No," Corrado murmured. "Do you want a drink, or do you have somewhere to be?"

"I could have one drink, but I need to head out soon. A meeting tonight with some of the Capos, you know. It never ends."

"You always were a better made man than you were an assassin, Chris. I'm glad you figured that out before it was too late."

Chuckles echoed down the hallway. Ginevra came to the end, and peered around carefully so she wouldn't be seen. For a second, she thought she was seeing doubles as she found the two men standing at the end of the entrance hallway.

Like mirrors of one another.

It took her a second.

Then, *two*.

Twins, she realized.

Corrado had an *identical* twin.

If she hadn't known the clothes Corrado was wearing earlier, she might have needed to look twice to try and tell the difference between the two. They stood the same facing one another, arms crossed over their chests, and features looking as though they'd been cut from stone. Corrado's brother—Chris, wasn't it?—wore his hair a bit longer, and his three-piece suit was a contrast against the simple black slacks and silk shirt his twin wore.

There were differences.

But not many.

And they were *surface*, things. Clothes, hairstyle, and so forth. Nothing really physical about them was different, or at least, not that Ginevra could tell from this far away.

"Does he know," Chris started to ask, "that there's a chick here, I mean?"

Corrado shook his head. "Didn't mention that … yet."

"Probably should, man."

"Yeah, I will."

Ginevra was too caught up in the fact that the two looked so similar that she missed part of their conversation. She didn't really understand what they were talking about, now.

"We have a guest," Chris said, his gaze drifting to Ginevra.

She was quick to dart back around the corner, but not before Corrado turned, and laid eyes on her, too.

Shit.

She caught that look he had.

Intense, again.

Contemplative.

Like he didn't know what to make of her. It was the same stare he'd had in the car, and she didn't know what to make of it. Or how it made her feel, or *why* she felt anything about it at all, really.

Why did it feel like everything was changing? That this was going to end up being *more* than just her hiding away from her half-brothers while New York waged a mafia war?

"Yeah," she heard Corrado say, "I think I found trouble with that one."

"Seems like you find trouble a lot, man."

"That's unfair, and—"

"And you're not a liar, so."

"You know what," Corrado said, "fuck the drink, get out."

Chris laughed loudly. "I missed you, Corrado."

"Can't say the same."

"*Lies.*"

Ginevra slipped back down the hallway, and into the library.

No one came to find her.

She didn't mind.

CHAPTER 19
CORRADO

"How long do you think you'll need?" Dare asked.

"A couple months, maybe. I'll let you know if I need more time off."

Dare made a noise on the other end of the call, but didn't question Corrado on *why* he needed time off. That was thing about The League—being an independent contractor, essentially, allowed him more freedom than other members who went up on the auctions, and signed years of their lives away to buyers.

Corrado would never do that.

No one owned him.

"I thought you wanted to do that upcoming job with Alessio. The political hit in Albania, I mean," Dare said, "because this will fall in that time frame, according to the details I have for that assignment."

"It didn't need two people on it."

He just wanted to go with Les.

Things changed sometimes.

It couldn't be helped.

Dare cleared his throat, asking, "Things are fine, aren't they? You're not … having trouble with anything, are you?"

Corrado almost laughed.

That was about as *deep* as Dare cared to get with one of his people. He didn't care if they had personal shit going on in their lives as long as it didn't mess with The League, and what the organization was doing. On the opposite end of the coin, Dare and Cree were some of the *few* people who knew the complexities of Alessio and Corrado's relationship.

So, when Dare asked something like *that*, he was really asking about Alessio and Corrado without outright saying it. Corrado wasn't stupid.

"Why, so you could send Cree to set me straight?" Corrado asked.

The man had the decency—or gall—to laugh.

"I only send Cree when you give me no other choice."

"Right," Corrado murmured. "And no, nothing is wrong. I just need a break. Other things to handle for a bit, and then I'll be back to work."

"Noted." Keys clicked on the other end before Dare said, "That's it, then. Call me if you need to change something, yeah?"

"Will do."

Corrado lingered in the library, that also doubled as his office, for a while longer after he ended the call. Staring out at the busy city below, one of the only rooms in the penthouse that didn't have full floor to ceiling windows, he found a strange comfort in this space.

Designed to be useful to him—he liked the office area—and to Alessio, who needed a million and one books because he could never find enough shit to read, the two of them often found themselves in here more often than anywhere else in the penthouse when they were in the city. It wasn't lost on Corrado how Ginevra also seemed to favor this room since her arrival here. More often than not, she gravitated to the books, and settled into one of the sitting areas to crack it open for hours on end.

Alessio would enjoy that. Someone to entertain his need for words and knowledge until long after the fucking sun set, and the rest of the world was sleeping …

Not that Corrado needed to be thinking about that *at all*. Yep.

Quite enough of that.

Spinning on his heel, he left the office library before he could think better of it. He didn't need to be thinking about shit that didn't matter, anyway. Strolling through the penthouse, he rounded the corner at the end of the hallway, and came to an abrupt stop in the entryway that led to the sitting room.

The *hint* of a smile curved his lips as he found Ginevra standing in front of a television screen that was as tall as her, and as wide as the entire wall. With a game controller in her hands, she pressed a button and laughed when her tank on the screen blew up her opponent behind enemy lines.

For the most part, he tried to give her space. He liked his own, after all, and figured most people were the same. Since she didn't try to seek him out, he offered her the same respect.

Like now, he would usually walk away.

He *should* walk away.

Instead, he stood there in the entryway, watching her from the side as she fiddled with the game, and her features lit up each time she succeeded in doing something right. He was reminded again, then, as her bow-shaped lips curved with her happiness, and her brown eyes widened with joy, that she was an *exceptionally* beautiful woman.

If not innocent …

It was a silly thing, really. *Simple*, and not at all something that he would find amusement in any other time. That was a game he liked to play to chill a few years back, but he hadn't touched it in a long while. It had been too long since he and Alessio came back to Toronto for a visit, anyway.

He shouldn't be watching her at all, or *caring*. Not that

she found happiness in his games, or that she enjoyed spending her time with Alessio's books.

That didn't mean *anything*.

Right?

Except, Corrado wasn't that simple, and neither was his mind. He was detail-oriented. He liked to know *all the things* about people, and what made them tick. Ginevra wasn't an exception to that rule, and if anything, he found himself *more* curious about her than he had anyone. How did she feel to be twenty-one, and in the position she now was? Who had she left back in New York? What had she wanted to be or do *before* this?

All those questions, and no answers.

Unless he talked to her.

That could be a problem.

"Do you want to play, or are you going to keep standing there watching me?"

Corrado found Ginevra staring at him from the side, unbothered by his presence. "It's my home, Ginevra."

"I prefer Ginny." She smiled brightly—*sweetly*. "That's what my mom used to call me, and my sisters."

Corrado dragged in a heavy breath, feeling the sense of time he had never been able to forget because it was seared into his brain coming back in a flash. That time, and that man, it melted together in his brain with this woman.

He saw her face.

He heard her words.

And he also saw Alessio—heard him, too.

I prefer Les.

That memory hit him hard.

All at once.

Like a punch to the gut.

He'd been this curious once a long time ago. He remembered that day vividly—that knife room, and those few words he shared with a man that would change his whole life. This felt different in ways, and in others, the same.

Because the curiosity was *there*. God knew it was going to be his curiosity that got him in trouble. It always did.

Like fucking *déjà vu*.

Yeah, a problem.

That's what this woman was for him.

Corrado knew it right then.

Because he had *interest*.

Nothing was ever simple when he found interest in something, but especially because *nothing* interested him anymore. Nothing but the man back in Vegas, and apparently, this woman standing in front of him.

"Well?" she asked. "Do you want to play?"

"I don't think I should," he replied, honestly.

Her smile fell. "Oh. Okay."

"Don't let me stop you from enjoying it, though."

She didn't reply.

He didn't mind.

Corrado left Ginevra to her game, and he went back to Alessio's library. Shit felt easier there. He could breathe better in that space, further away from her, and the confusion he now felt.

Except that was a lie, too.

Nothing was easier.

"*Fuck*."

Corrado glared at the digital clock on the nightstand that displayed a time *way* too early for his fucking phone to be ringing. Even if the sun was up, it didn't matter. *Nobody* needed to wake his ass up before seven-thirty.

Unless someone was dead.

And even then, it depended on who died.

"*What?*" he snarled into the phone.

"Woke you up, did I?"

Corrado's brow knotted as he took in the familiar voice, and then eyed the clock again. Seven o'clock in Toronto meant it was four in the morning in Las Vegas. "Why aren't *you* sleeping, Les?"

The man on the other end of the phone made a grunt. A good sign he didn't want to answer the question, but he was probably going to do it anyway simply because Corrado asked. So was their way.

"Well?" Corrado pressed.

Pushing over in the bed, Corrado rolled to his back while keeping the phone at his ear. He waited for whatever it was Alessio had to tell him as he sat up, and used the black velvet of the headboard as a place to rest his back.

He needed to wake up.

Alessio was still quiet on the phone.

Across the hall from his master bedroom—without Alessio, Corrado *rarely* closed his bedroom door—he found a familiar form sleeping. Apparently, Ginevra also didn't know how to close her door when she went to bed, although this was the first time Corrado had woken up before her in the week that they had been staying together in this penthouse. Usually, he had found other ways to distract himself when the woman was around, so then they both had their space.

He didn't know *why* he did that.

She didn't upset him …

He just felt odd around her. Like when she'd started crying in the car when he drove them to Toronto, and his first reaction was to be *rude*. And then just as quickly, he found he needed to fix that and her because he didn't want to see her cry.

He shouldn't care at all.

She was a fucking job.

"Corrado, are you listening?"

"Yeah," he muttered, coming back to the conversation at hand. Although, he was still staring across the hall even as he said it, half amused by the fact Ginevra slept *on top* of the blankets, and also slightly bothered by it at the same time. Not because he thought she might be cold—the penthouse was warm—but more because he noticed at all. Like he noticed the shape of her thighs, and the way her legs looked under the pair of cotton shorts she'd pulled on. *Fuck.* He needed to get back to Les. Now. "What's going on?"

"You asked for time off from The League?"

Corrado stiffened in the bed, scrubbing a hand over his face at the same time. "Who told you that?"

"Who do you think?"

"Dare, likely. Cree doesn't pay attention to that shit."

"You're not wrong," Alessio grumbled.

Across the hall, Ginevra rolled over in the bed, a soft sound escaping her at the same time. It *almost* sounded like a moan. Add that onto the fact that Corrado was still admiring the swells and curves of her body, not to mention, the fact he was *quite* aware that she was a beautiful woman, and he suddenly needed to ignore a raging erection under his own sheets.

Great.

That's just fucking perfect.

Another woman, under entirely different circumstances, and Corrado might have acted on his attraction. He would have let Alessio know the shit he was feeling, that he was attracted to the chick, and it would have been done.

That was their rule.

It was *fine.*

Except this was different. He wasn't *just* attracted to Ginevra—he was also interested in her, and what brought her here to him. Things he had no business feeling, and he didn't know how that factored into the way he and Alessio had always done things when it came to women. Not to mention, he gave his word about the job with Ginevra; he wasn't to tell people where she came from, or who she was. Including Alessio.

It was a fucking mess.

This was trouble.

That woman was *trouble*.

Why, or for what reason, or even *how* … Corrado didn't know those things, but he knew this. He could tell already, one week into watching Ginevra, that she was going to be an issue for him. For more reasons than he cared to admit, if he were being honest. Sometimes, Corrado just got a feeling about something or someone, and he was *rarely* wrong.

He'd had that same feeling about The League.

Or Alessio.

Different jobs.

He didn't ignore it now.

"It's for that favor, right?" Alessio asked. "Andino Marcello?"

Corrado cleared his throat and forced himself to avert his eyes from the figure across the hall. As it was, the guilt had already started to compound in his chest. "Yeah, that's what it is."

"And you still can't tell me what it is?"

"Not really. I gave my word, that's all."

Although, Corrado was starting to think that was probably a lame fucking excuse. There was no one he trusted *more* than Alessio. Life had taught him that, and Alessio only proved it time and time again.

He could, at the very least, explain the *gist* of the job, and the fact that he had a woman here with him. Except, then he was wading into dangerous fucking territory with that—he would still be omitting important details to Alessio.

Like his interest in her.

The attraction.

So, no.

Corrado refused to say *anything*.

Because he didn't plan to act on it.

None of it.

Simple.

Or that was the lie he was going to tell himself. He'd fucked up here. From the moment Ginevra got inside his car at that church, the first thing Corrado should have done the *second* he could was call Alessio.

Been honest.

Gave every detail.

But he didn't.

And now here he was, a week into this *thing* ... and he was just digging the hole deeper. It wouldn't be as simple, now. He couldn't just tell Alessio the truth, and the man shrug it off. That wasn't how *they* worked.

That's not how their thing worked.

The fact that he didn't tell Alessio *from the start* would be a nail in the coffin. Corrado didn't need confirmation from Alessio to know it was true—it was their goddamn rule. Except he hadn't done anything, and as long as he continued on that path, then there was nothing to tell.

Right?

Yeah.

The guilt compounded deeper.

Fuck.

So, yeah. He was going to say nothing. *Do nothing.* He wouldn't act on a damn thing—not his attraction, or his interest. He was going to get this fucking job done, and go back home to Alessio like he'd planned to from the start before he looked at Ginevra after she got in his car, and got *that* feeling.

That same feeling he had when he met Alessio for the first time. A feeling that said *this is going to change everything for you.* Because what else could he do? He'd already dug this fucking hole, he might as well keep digging until he was out of it, too.

"I'm just saying that I don't like finding out shit from Dare instead of *you*," Alessio said on the phone, bringing Corrado back to the conversation again. "And you know how Andino Marcello is—he doesn't care what shit you step in for him, so are you sure this *job* is even on the up and up with him?"

"Les—"

"Since when do you hide shit from me, Corrado?"

Yeah.

Shit.

"I'm not hiding anything," he said.

There was just nothing to tell.

Not yet.

Across the hall, Ginevra made another noise before she rolled to her back. He saw her eyes flutter open, and she stared up at the canopy above the four-poster bed.

"Corrado—"

"I have to let you go," he said quickly. "I'll call you back."

He hung up the phone, and tossed it to the bedsheets without waiting for a goodbye from Alessio. His chest became tighter—that pain, growing *sharper.*

But he probably wouldn't call back. Not when it meant needing to hide things from Alessio because now, Corrado just didn't want to *lie.* That guilt was a *killer.*

Corrado still wasn't sure how he got to this point simply by taking a goddamn job to pay back a favor. All he had to do was open up his fucking mouth. Tell Alessio the job was a *woman*. And because it wasn't as simple as it seemed, his dick decided to get involved, and maybe his curiosity, too.

That was it.

That's all he needed to do.

He was making it more complicated than it actually was, but he didn't know how to fix it. Nothing was ever simple with him and Les, even if on the surface, it might seem like it. Those were lies, too. They'd made this complicated.

Corrado blamed himself for that, too.

CHAPTER 20
GINEVRA

Ginevra eyed the landline cordless phone charging on the counter as she stirred the sugar into her steaming coffee. It'd been a week, and not once had she considered using any one of the many phones throughout the penthouse to call out.

Except she was doing that now.

Maybe it was because she woke up, and realized this was the longest she had ever gone without speaking to her siblings. Even after she turned eighteen, and moved out of the house to begin classes at a community college, she still called them every single day. And her mama, too.

She'd made an effort *not* to think about it since coming here. She knew it was dangerous, and calls could *easily* be tracked. This morning, it was all she could think about.

Funny how that worked.

What was happening in New York, now?

Were her sisters safe?

Had Siena kept her promise?

What was happening?

Nothing could drive a person to do crazy things more than the unknown. She'd spent the last week acquainting herself with the penthouse, and the different things to do inside it. She bet Corrado paid a good amount for this place.

Ten rooms.

Three bathrooms.

A few thousand square feet.

There were lots to do, too. Like the gaming systems in the sitting room, or the library. There was also a small gym with the same floor to ceiling windows that overlooked the heart of Toronto. A hot tub on a balcony that was enclosed with more glass walls.

Despite the fact a maid came three times during the week to clean, and bring in groceries, she also had a whole stack of takeout menus for restaurants she could order from. Corrado had also taken her into the city to shop, and grab whatever she needed by way of clothing or personal items.

Mostly, she tried to stay busy because then, she didn't focus on those unknowns back in New York nearly as much.

And still …

Here she was, eyeing that damn phone.

Ginevra sighed, and *forced* her damn gaze away from the phone so that she could focus on something else. It didn't matter how much she wanted to call, the rules were clear—she *couldn't*. Not until she knew it was safe.

Because that was the thing, right?

It was more than just her.

It was her sisters, too.

She had to be smart—and strong—for them. She was sure they were terrified and wondering what in the hell happened to her. She highly doubted their half-brothers were treating the young girls well, but at the same time … they couldn't *hurt* them, either. Greta and Giulia were literally Kev and Darren's last thing to use to reach for the top, right?

That's what Siena said.

Trust them, her mind whispered.

Except, who exactly was she trusting?

A man who led her to believe he was going to marry her right up until the point she was almost ready to walk down the aisle? A half-sister she barely knew, but always seemed kind enough for her to let down her defenses?

Corrado?

A man who *barely* spoke to her.

Who was Ginevra supposed to fucking trust?

Maybe that was the thing that bothered her the very most. Beyond the fact she was in a whole new country, or couldn't speak to her sisters. Separate from the fact she felt stir-crazy here, and didn't know anything that was going on back in New York.

It was that she didn't know *their* motives.

Andino.

Siena.

Corrado.

None of them.

She didn't know their motives, alone or with *her*, and that bothered her. The very last thing she ever intended to be was someone else's pawn, but right now … that's exactly what she felt like at the end of the day.

A pawn.

Being moved.

No control.

It was only once she had poured a bit of cream into the mug that she turned back around to sip on her coffee, and stare at the phone again. She didn't know what made her reach out to pick it up, but she did. Staring at it, but not deciding to make that call, she simply *held* it.

She didn't hear Corrado until he was right there, *grabbing* the damn phone from her hand. He moved like lightening, silent and dangerous. She jumped when he came up behind her, and nearly rammed right into his naked chest when she spun around fast to face him.

With the phone in one hand, he cocked his head to the side, and smirked a bit. "What were you doing?"

"Uh …"

It was hard to focus—hard to *talk*—when he was

standing this close to her. She could blame it on the fact he wore nothing but a pair of boxer-briefs, and she had a glorious view of the hard lines, and ridges of muscle that made up his lean, yet muscular, form. He reminded her of a runner in the way he was built, and the way the waistband on those boxer-briefs rested against the hard V of his groin had her gaze lingering before he cleared his throat.

Ginevra's gaze traveled back up his body.

Jesus.

Skin uninked.

Though he had scars.

A few.

Yeah, she could have blamed her inability to speak on the way he looked—because he was shamelessly gorgeous, and he probably knew it—but that wasn't what did it. No, it was the way Corrado *stared* at her that always seemed to silence her.

He did it when she was looking.

And when she wasn't.

Did he even know how intense his stare was? Like he'd found prey, and was ready to go in for the kill?

A part of her wouldn't mind that.

Being his prey.

Not at all.

Corrado's right eyebrow arched when Ginevra's gaze drifted over his strong features, and she couldn't stop that heat from rising up her cheeks. *This close*, there was no hiding the fact she just stared at him like a foolish girl for at least two minutes.

Just *stared*.

He was kind enough not to say anything.

His smirk deepened, though.

"Well?" he asked.

"I was just … looking at it," she said lamely.

Corrado cocked his head to the side. "You know the rules."

"Yeah, but—"

"No calls out. Yes, I can take you out of the penthouse, we can go do things, and whatever else, but if there is *any* chance someone could track you back here, then that's a no-go. From what I understand, you were mostly unknown back in New York, being that you were only recently brought into the folds of the Calabrese family, right?"

Ginevra swallowed hard. "Yeah, my mom … was Matteo's mistress for a time. We were kept a secret until—"

"They needed someone to marry off."

"Basically."

"So like I said," Corrado replied, shrugging one shoulder, "you're mostly unknown, and that means you'll be able to do other things here besides stay hidden away in this penthouse. But if you go off doing stupid things like calling people, which will make it *far* easier to track us, then we're going to have to move again. I doubt you'll like where we'll go, or the fact you won't be able to leave the place. Got it?"

Well, when he put it that way …

She nodded.

What else could she do?

"I understand."

"*Perfetto.*"

Corrado leaned around Ginevra, making her entire body seize when heat shot through her gut at the feeling of his body grazing hers—*how?*—and he froze, too. She felt the way he stiffened, and a jolt of *something* passed through her before he sucked in a quick breath, too.

Like he felt that, too.

Electricity, maybe?

A *shock*.

Ginevra lifted her stare to find he was staring at her

again, his hand holding the phone hovering over the charger like he forgot what he was supposed to be doing again. She didn't know how long the two of them stared at one another like that—a few seconds, or more, but it could have been longer, too.

It felt like forever.

She found heat in his gaze.

Interest.

Something unknown.

And she liked it far too much.

Not that she understood that, either. She didn't know anything about this man.

"Are you like them?" she dared to ask.

Corrado's tongue snaked out to wet the edge of his bottom lip. "Like *them,* how?"

"Mafia. *Made.*"

"No."

"I don't know if I believe that."

He felt like them, in a way. Dangerous, and dark. Like he held secrets in his eyes, and in his heart. He didn't feel *average,* and God knew she had met enough average men over her lifetime to know it.

No, he felt like something else.

"I'm not like them," he said, "but I am a little worse."

She hesitated to ask more.

What did that mean?

Corrado seemed to take her hesitation as a chance to break their moment. Whatever in the hell that had been … that touch, the heat, that fucking *feeling.* She didn't know what that was, and while she might like it, it also terrified her.

Because she didn't know him.

And she still didn't know if she could trust him.

He placed the phone back on the charger. As fast as he was touching her, he was gone.

It didn't matter.

He still lingered.

She felt it.

Everywhere.

What in the hell was *that*?

Corrado cleared his throat, and wouldn't meet her gaze. She wondered if he felt that, too? God knew he didn't say much to her. For the most part, he'd spent the last week avoiding her as much as was possible when they were alone together in the penthouse.

"Would you like me to cook you breakfast?" he asked, a thickness roughening up his tone as he reached for the cupboard beside her.

Ginevra was back to feeling like she couldn't speak, so instead, she whispered, "Sure."

"And you can tell me about your sisters," he was quick to add, shooting her a smile, "maybe then you won't feel like you need to talk *to* them, if you're talking about them."

"You want to know about my little sisters?"

Corrado shrugged. "Why not?"

Well, okay.

Like he said, why not?

"So, there's Greta," Ginevra said, "and she's seventeen. And then there's Giulia, and she's fifteen. They're typical teenage girls. We're all close … I guess because us girls are all we really had growing up since our dad just came and went. Usually when he came around, it was to give our mom money. So, we all leaned on each other."

"What about your mom?"

Ginevra stiffened, and Corrado didn't miss it. He turned to look at her, raising his brow in question at her sudden silence. Something painful came to wrap around her heart, and she swore those tears wouldn't be very far behind.

Did he see that?

She didn't know.

Not when she was too busy trying to hide it.

"Don't do that again—those tears," he said quickly when she peeked up at him. "I can't do the tears, girl. You might as well stick a fucking knife in my chest, and finish the goddamn job while you're at it. It kills me."

Ginevra did her best to hold back the emotion.

Barely.

"They killed my mom," she whispered, "Kev and Darren, I mean. My half-brothers. They made it look like a suicide, but I knew. They told me what they would do if she tried to help me, and that's what they did. Because she tried to help me get away."

Corrado let out a fast breath. "Hey, that's not your fault."

"Isn't it?"

"No. And I'm sorry. About your ma."

Yeah.

She still hadn't gotten the time to deal with that. It was like one minute, her mama was there, and then the next, she was gone. Except she had to move on to taking care of her sisters, and dealing with the upcoming wedding. Her *brothers*, the bastards. And everything else, too. The wedding day, Andino letting her escape, Corrado, and coming here.

One thing after another.

It didn't stop.

Not for one second had she really been able to handle her grief for her mother. Until now, really.

"It's worse at night," she admitted. "Maybe because that was the time I used to spend the most with her ... we would read, or talk."

Corrado made a noise under his breath. "I know, I hear you crying."

She kind of wished he didn't say that. It just made her feel worse to know that someone was a witness to her pain, and couldn't help.

Nothing helped.

"You're allowed to grieve," he said quietly, leaning against the island and giving her a bit of breathing room. "And you're allowed to do it however you need to. If that means crying at night when you're alone, then that's what it is."

"It doesn't make it better, though."

"I don't doubt it."

Ginevra glanced away. "Then, I ran away, and left my sisters there."

"Hey," he murmured, his hand coming up fast so that his fingertips could graze down her arm with a soft touch. That light stroke was enough to send heat licking up her arm, but somehow, she ignored it. "I think someone else made that choice for you, and you're doing the best you can with it. Because what were the options, huh?"

"Well—"

"What were your options back there?"

"To marry a stranger."

Corrado nodded. "And your sisters ... you were told they'd be taken care of, I'm sure."

"But what if they *aren't*?"

"And you think, what, calling them, getting tracked down, dragged back there, forced into a marriage, possibly being hurt for running away ... do you think that will help *their* situation at all?"

"When you put it *that* way."

"Perspective helps everything," he murmured.

Sure.

Still ... "That doesn't make the guilt easier to swallow."

"Yeah, you're not wrong." Corrado smiled crookedly. "I know that. All too well."

Did he?

"What makes you feel guilty, then, Corrado?"

He straightened in place, the widening of his brown eyes telling her that he hadn't expected that question. Still, he continued pulling items from the cupboards, before moving to the drawers where he found utensils. "I don't know what to make of you, Ginevra."

"I'm sorry?"

"You continue to surprise me."

"Is that a bad thing?"

"I haven't decided yet. People rarely surprise me anymore. I'm not sure what to do with the ones that manage it."

"You know, you didn't answer my question. About what makes you feel guilty, too, I mean. Instead, you deflected it back to me."

He pointed a butter knife at her, and winked. "You're absolutely right. And look at that, you're surprising me again."

That said, he moved around her with the grace of a predator, opened the fridge, and pulled a carton of eggs out along with butter. That gave her an answer, too, even if it wasn't the answer she wanted: he wasn't going to tell her what made him feel guilty.

She didn't mind.

Now, she could watch him cook.

CHAPTER 21
ALESSIO

"Why are you in New York?"

"Pretty sure," he replied to Dare, "that I didn't have the chip put in for you to track me *just because*."

"No, it was for emergencies only, but—"

"This is not an emergency."

"You didn't pick up my last three calls, or reply to Cree's texts," Dare said quietly, "and *yes*, to me, that is warrant enough to check up on your tracker."

All League members had them—or most. It was an option they were given simply because it was one thing to be forced into having a tracker put into your body, and it was another to willingly accept it. That was just about one of the only choices The League allowed the assassins to make for themselves.

Alessio understood the need for it. In their business, they made a lot of fucking enemies. A client one week could be a problem the next when a new client came in to take out the previous, or attempt it. Their business was dirty, no doubt about it.

Sometimes, in an attempt to get back at The League, the first thing someone tried to do was go after the members. The trackers at least gave Dare and Cree a chance to retrieve their man or woman, and hopefully, still alive, if they moved fast enough or got the team out. It didn't happen often, but even once was too much.

Corrado opted for a tracker, too.

"I'm not on a job, right?" Alessio asked into the phone.

Dare sighed. "No."

"Then, I can be wherever I need to be."

"Answer my calls, and I won't check in."

Something *akin* to guilt stabbed Alessio in his chest. He should have picked up those calls, or at the very least, answer one of Cree's many texts over the last week or so. It was entirely unusual for him to ignore both of them, never mind the fact he hadn't been into The League's complex since Corrado headed out two weeks ago for that … fucking *favor*.

"What's going on?" Dare asked.

"Nothing."

Lies.

Alessio wasn't a liar.

He *wasn't*.

He would be right now, though, for Corrado. Because if this favor for Andino Marcello was something that might get him in trouble with The League—not that Alessio knew that was the case for sure—then he wasn't going to be the one who delivered the news.

"Then why are you in New York?"

Alessio gave the café he passed a quick glance, trying to figure out a way to end this conversation so he could get on with his plans, and the day. "I have something to handle."

"Corrado?"

"Corrado is in Toronto, which you know."

"That doesn't change the fact—"

"Everything is *fine*."

"Alessio," Dare murmured, "I am not asking about things for The League right now. I know you think that's all I care about most of the time, but you have been my priority from the time you were ten."

His walk slowed until he came to a stop altogether.

People blew by him on the sidewalk, but Alessio simply stared up at the cloudy July sky. In Nevada, the heat would be *dry*, which he liked. Here, it was fucking humid.

Which he hated.

And still, here he was looking for answers because he couldn't *not* seek them out. When it came to Corrado, Alessio didn't know how to leave things alone, but especially not when something just felt *off*.

This favor?

Andino Marcello?

Yeah.

It all felt off to Alessio. Like something was going on, or whatever was happening might bring Corrado a world of trouble, and Alessio wouldn't even be able to help him because he *didn't know what it was*. For two weeks, he'd practically crawled out of his skin with the feeling that something was up here, and it was going to end badly.

So, here he was.

In New York.

Alessio was going to get those fucking answers one way or the other. He knew where to go, and how to go about doing it, too. If Corrado couldn't—or wouldn't—tell him, then he would go to another source to get the details.

Simple as that.

Because *God*.

What in the fuck would Alessio do without Corrado? That, more than anything else, was what had been keeping him awake these past two weeks. He didn't like not knowing things, but especially when it meant something could be wrong.

Add Corrado into that mix?

People were *begging* to feel pain.

Alessio didn't fuck around.

"Les—"

"I just have business to handle," he said, stopping Dare before the man could ask more. "That's it, and that's all."

"Business dealing with *him*, no?"

"Even if it is, that's for me to take care of."

Dare sighed. "I wish you would learn the difference between something *healthy* and something that … turns you into someone you don't recognize when you look into the mirror at the reflection staring back, Alessio."

Funny.

"I don't even remember who I was before him."

"I can tell."

Alessio smirked, though Dare couldn't see it. "And I'm fine with that."

If it were possible for the ground to combust simply from Alessio glaring at it, then the pavement would be ashes under his feet currently. No doubt, it was his mood and current surly expression that allowed him a wide berth of space on the New York sidewalk as he headed down the busy block. People avoided him, parting the crowd for him to walk straight through.

He wasn't going to complain.

This city *was not* Vegas. Of that, he was most sure. Even in the bright light of day, New York still had a dreary, dark quality to it. Now, that would typically be Alessio's style. He liked all things moody and *black*—it reflected himself, after all.

Not when he was in this mood, though.

Alessio came to a stop in front of a Brooklyn restaurant. The gold lettering on the windows spelling out the name, and the satin curtains pulled back to expose the lavish décor let him know he was not dressed appropriately for the place in his black jeans, combat boots, and leather jacket.

He tipped his head to the side, considering.

Fuck it.

When had he *ever* cared about that?

Never.

That's when.

Taking one last drag from his cigarette, he tossed it to the sidewalk, and headed for the entrance of the fancy restaurant. Taking the steps three at a time, Alessio yanked open the door, and stepped into the smells of rich sauces, and lingering spices. Something that, on another day, he might have stopped to appreciate.

Not today.

Today, he had other things to do.

The girl dressed in a tight, black dress behind the podium looked up and met his gaze when the bell above the door chimed at his entrance. With a tablet at the ready in her hands, she opened her mouth to greet him.

As she should.

It was her job.

Alessio simply passed her by before she could even ask her question. Her shout of *hey* at his back fell on deaf ears because he didn't give a shit. His task was simply to find the man who owned this place, and have a chat. All it took were a couple of carefully placed calls to the right people— everyone in this *life* had contacts to use, him included—and Alessio knew exactly where he had to go to find Andino Marcello.

He heard the woman's heels clicking against the floor as she followed him through the bustling restaurant, still hollering at his back like he gave a single fuck about her. He didn't. Not at all.

His contact said if Andino wasn't having business in the

private dining section of the place, then he would be in the back office at the far end of the kitchen. Passing the private area with a quick glance said Andino was in the office, so that's exactly where Alessio went.

Cooks in the kitchen yelled at him, too.

Fun.

He ignored them as well.

"Sir, you can't be back—"

"Who the fuck are you?"

Alessio came face to face with likely one of the biggest men he had ever seen in his life when he turned the corner around a rack in the kitchen. At least four inches taller than Alessio's nearly six-foot-three height, and probably a good sixty pounds of extra muscle than him, too. He had more of a boxer's quality. This man looked like he needed to be on the defense line of a fucking football team.

The guy stood in front of the open doorway that led into the office, and directly behind his very wide shoulders, he found the man he wanted to see sitting at his desk.

Beside that desk sat a ruddy-colored pit bull.

More fun.

"Me?" Alessio asked.

The muscle—no doubt, an enforcer for Andino's crime family who kept him protected while he worked—cocked an eyebrow like he wasn't here for this shit. Well, *surprise*, asshole … neither was Alessio.

"Who else am I looking at?" the enforcer snapped.

"Well, I'm not important," Alessio said, smiling just enough to piss the man off. If the guy wanted to try to make a move on Les, then he was more than welcome to come right on ahead and *do it*. All he had to say about that was the bigger one was, the harder they fucking fell when Alessio punched them in the throat. He pointed around the man's large shoulder, saying, "That man right there is who matters at the moment, and I have a meeting to speak with him."

"No, you don't."

"I do, actually."

The enforcer's lips flattened into a grim line. "Listen, I don't know who the fuck you—"

"Pink, let him in."

Alessio had all he could do not to laugh. He grinned instead, staring up at the bigger man with all the cockiness he could muster as he said, "*Pink*, huh, that's cute."

"I will fucking kill you."

"Yeah, you could certainly try."

"Well, as amusing as *this* is," Andino muttered inside the office, "let him in, Pink. Stay nearby, of course."

"If you're sure, boss ..."

"I am sure."

Pink stepped aside, and Alessio winked at the man which only made his brow furrow, before he took a second look at him. Like he wasn't quite sure what to make of Alessio, and it put him on edge.

Good.

It should.

"Don't stand out there and continue to taunt him," Andino said, sounding entirely bored behind his desk, "because then I won't be responsible for what he does once you're out of my sight. Like Snaps here," he added, gesturing down at the mean looking dog next to him, "Pink only minds when he is in my view. I'm sure you understand."

Noted.

Alessio gave the enforcer a look from the side before he entered the office and closed the door behind him at Andino's gesture to do so. The man didn't offer him a chair to sit in, however, but that was fine with him. He would much rather stand for this.

Eyeing the dog next to the desk who looked like he was considering whether or not he wanted to find out what Alessio *and* his leather jacket might taste like, he asked Andino, "What is your business with Corrado Guzzi?"

"What is *your* business with him?"

Ah.

That question.

Well, that was not simple.

Part of Alessio and Corrado's thing of not being public with their relationship dealt with the fact one of them hadn't truly dealt with his bisexuality. Not that Alessio was naming names, but it wasn't him. The other part of it came down to *this*—when they were open and people knew, it gave others the power to hurt Corrado and Alessio by using one against the other.

It was one of the only reasons, next to the fact as long as he had Corrado, then he was happy, that he kept this fucking game up between them for all these years. *No one* would ever have the control to separate or hurt them. If that happened, it was because they chose to do it, not because someone with a touch too much power decided to put their hands in the pot, too, so to speak.

Alessio took his gaze off the dog and leveled it on the man behind the desk instead. "The League—business, that's all."

Andino sucked air through his teeth and rested back in the chair. "What, did The League send out one of their dogs to check up on another one of their dogs, or …?"

"Step *very* carefully from here on out with your words," Alessio warned the man, "because I take insults as a challenge, Marcello, and you don't want to know how I answer those."

"He owed us a favor."

"Us as in—"

"My family—the Marcellos. What else do you need to take back so they'll let me cash that in, and fuck off while I do it, huh?"

Right to the point.

Alessio would have appreciated that on another day, or about any other topic *except* his lover. When it came to Corrado, he couldn't appreciate anything that might put him in danger that would take him from Alessio.

Not that Andino knew that.

"Details," Alessio said, "that's what we want, just to make sure it's not something that will overlap with the rest of our business. I'm sure you understand that could be dangerous for him, and for the rest of us at The League."

"*Right*," Andino drawled, "well, there isn't much to tell, and if he keeps anyone in New York that would know who Ginevra Calabrese is away from her, then none of us will have to worry about any trouble coming his way. Certainly not The League, regardless of what happens. They arranged my marriage to Ginevra but as I didn't plan on following through, she needed to go away for a while—hence, Corrado watching her. I doubt *anyone* in Canada knows that woman I sent him off with. Most people here didn't know who she was, and her face is a dime a dozen in New York. Canada doesn't mix very much business with the Marcellos, so I assume she is essentially a ghost there with him. Something pretty on his arm, I would say."

Alessio blinked.

What?

"Excuse me?" he asked, his voice a murmur.

Andino arched a brow. "Did I not speak slow enough for you?"

"He's looking after … a woman."

It wasn't even a question.

Just … a statement.

Why wouldn't Corrado tell him that?

They had rules for a reason—those rules between them kept the men honest, and their relationship open and *safe*. Telling each other everything was more than just showing their trust but offering their loyalty.

It didn't make sense that Corrado wouldn't explain *that* detail. He could have simply said there was a woman with him, and at the same time, keep the rest from Alessio if it might mess with this favor he owed to Andino.

Except he didn't.

He kept *her* a secret.

Why?

How long would Corrado keep that information from Alessio?

How long would he lie?

Alessio wet the corner of his lip with his tongue. "Ginevra, you said?"

"That's her. If you wouldn't mind, I need that info kept quiet because she needs to stay out of sight for the time being. We have a situation here in New York, a little war, nothing big … and I would prefer if she wasn't brought back before I kill her useless brothers, and all."

"That seems like a strong reaction to an *almost* marriage."

"No, strong would have been blowing up the church with everyone inside when they thought they could marry me to her without giving me a choice. *That's* a strong reaction. Instead, I figured out another way. And all I have gotten for it is grief, and since I don't know who the fuck you are, or why you give a shit, I won't be taking any of that grief from you for it, too."

"Huh."

Andino nodded at the door and lifted his hand to gesture along with it. "And if that's all, you can get the fuck out. Do be sure to leave Pink alone on your way out—I can't stand his attitude when someone pisses him off."

Right.

Sure.

The last thing Alessio gave a fuck about right now was Andino's enforcer. He had other things to consider, now.

CHAPTER 22
GINEVRA

Thwack.

Ginevra's eyes flew *wide* open at the loud sound. It came again less than three seconds later, letting her know that no, she was not dreaming, and someone was making way too much noise at … she rolled over in the bed, and blinked at the digital alarm clock on the nightstand.

Five-thirty?

In the morning?

What the fuck was wrong with people?

Thwack.

Ginevra jumped in the bed at the noise again. What even was that, and *why*? Why at five-thirty in the morning was someone—probably Corrado—doing it?

She wasn't lazy. In fact, she was usually the first one awake and around doing anything in this penthouse in the mornings. A month into living here, and she had quickly learned that, if he could help it, Corrado didn't roll his ass out of bed before *nine*. She was usually up around seven, and ready entirely for the day, including breakfast, before he even stepped out of his room.

So, what changed?

Ginevra didn't know, but she sure as hell planned to find out. If that meant going down the hall where that noise was coming from to tell him to knock it the hell off, then that's exactly what it meant.

Who said she was pleasant in the mornings?

She wasn't.

That's why she woke up earlier than everyone else, so she could get over her shitty morning mood, and be her usual sweet self by the time she had to even think about looking at another person. Seemed simple, right?

So, why was Corrado making it *hard* right now?

Huffing, Ginevra climbed out of the bed, ignoring the cold hardwood floors pressing against her naked feet as she padded out of the bedroom. She didn't bother to close her door at night because from the time she was a little girl, she'd been terrified that something in her room would magically appear, and it would be the closed door that stopped her from getting out.

Stupid and silly, sure.

But it carried into her adulthood, too. Not so much the fear, but rather, the habit of sleeping with the door wide open just in case she needed to get out quickly.

Bleary-eyed, she rubbed the back of her hand against her face to wipe away any remnants of sleep as she followed that damn noise. Every couple of seconds, another *thwack* would make her startle again, pissing her off even more.

Too early. This is way too early.

Finally, she found the noise.

Ginevra had to blink to take in the sight in front of her, and make sure it actually *was* what she was seeing. Other than running on the treadmill in the gym once a day or so, she really didn't put the space to use. She was lucky that it took very little effort to keep her body healthy and fit, but she found that running was a huge stress relief.

And she ran at night.

Before bed.

It also acted like a sleeping pill.

Never in the morning, though.

Across the gym, Ginevra found the source of the noise. Corrado, turned to the side so she had a good view of his profile and the hard lines of his body in nothing but gym shorts, flicked his wrist back before he let *something* fly out of his hand. She only realized it was a knife when he flicked another from his opposite hand into his palm, and let it fly with nothing more than a jerk of his wrist over his shoulder.

Her gaze followed the path of the twisting, spinning knife until it embedded itself right into a wooden block at the other end of the gym about twenty feet away. Along with the other five knives that he had apparently already thrown into the middle of the target.

Nearly perfect shots every time, it seemed.

This one, though, landed a few inches to the right. Corrado tipped his head to the side, his eyes narrowing on the slightly fucked shot as he made a grunt. That disappointment flitting over his features only served to roughen his face up more.

She liked that.

A lot.

Kind of like the way she enjoyed watching the carved-from-stone lines of his body move as he prepped another knife, the last one he held, before he threw it, too. There was something about his focus, that intensity setting his lips into a hard line, as he worked that made her mouth a little dry.

And her body *hot*.

She'd seen him look like that before—when he thought she wasn't looking, and he stared at her. He held that same intensity, that same *fire*.

Huh.

Corrado let his last knife fly, and the weapon quickly embedded itself right into the middle of the target, between two other knives. A perfect shot this time. It was the tilt of his mouth at the corners that gave away his pleasure at having gotten it right that made her realize it wasn't just her dry mouth or hot body that loved the sight of this man.

She ignored the ache between her thighs, though. It was easier. God knew she wasn't innocent when it came to men— she'd had fun and experimented. A part of her didn't think Corrado would be the same *at all*.

One could simply tell.

All men were different.

He was certainly *that*.

"Say something, but don't just stand there and *stare*."

Ginevra startled at Corrado's sudden statement, his tone surly, realizing his blazing dark gaze had turned to the side, and leveled on her. She drew in a quick breath, unsure of how to handle this man when he was in one of *those* moods.

They came and went, she noticed.

More so in the evenings, though.

Despite being told to *stop* staring, Ginevra couldn't help but to continue. All over again, she found her gaze traveling down the length of his body, from the gym shorts hanging loosely around the hard muscles of his hips, to the way his stance didn't move an inch from his feet being firmly planted at shoulder width apart.

Like he'd been taught that.

Corrado made a sexy noise, although whether or not that was his intention, Ginevra didn't know. Part of her felt like she was constantly walking on egg shells around this man. Electricity followed them day in and fucking day out. The closer they became, the more it *snapped* all around them.

His gaze followed her.

Her attention focused in on him.

It never ended.

She simply didn't know what—or how—to do anything with it. If he was interested in her, and she was *clearly* interested in him, then why hadn't he done something about it? That's what *she* wanted to do.

Instead, she was waiting on him.

Ginevra was just about done waiting. If she was going to be stuck here in Toronto with this man until God knew when, then why couldn't she have a little bit of fun while she was at it? Besides, it wasn't *just* the attraction. No, it was more than that.

Something about Corrado danced like a flame.

She was the stupid moth coming a little too close.

What would happen when they met?

Something amazing, she bet.

"I think you like my staring," she replied.

Corrado's tongue peeked out to wet the corner of his mouth, showing off rows of white teeth that made her wonder what it would feel like if he used those teeth on *her*. Okay, wow. She went there quick.

Yeah.

"You don't know that I like anything you do, actually," he returned.

No, because he was very careful about that. Quick to put distance between them. Fast to give her space when he thought the two of them were getting too close. He always made sure that they never got *too deep* when they talked. Not since that morning in the kitchen.

She didn't like it.

"Right now, I know," she said.

Corrado arched an eyebrow in challenge. "Oh, tell me how, then."

"I don't think you want me to."

A laugh answered that back. And *God*, he sounded and looked so fucking good doing it, too. Except in her distraction at enjoying the sight of him carefree and sexy, she didn't realize he'd crossed the gym floor and came to stand in front of her until he was right there.

Right fucking there.

Brown eyes bore into hers.

He was close enough for her to touch.

Ginevra stared up at him, words catching in her throat as that heat shot through her nerves all over again. *Electric.* It really was the only appropriate way to describe what she felt whenever this man was near. Like something was buzzing around them— something different and important and *amazing*.

He seemed willing to ignore it.

She wasn't.

Not anymore.

"Tell me how you know, then," he said, his head dipping lower so that she could feel the warmth of his breath whispering along her lips. "I'm waiting, Ginny."

Her gaze dropped between them.

And then, it came back up.

She couldn't manage to feel embarrassed about the heat staining her cheeks as she whispered, "You're hard."

And he was.

Under the thin, satiny fabric of the gym shorts, the ridge of his erection was plain to see pushing against the material. She didn't think he was wearing anything else under the shorts, not that she minded. It gave her a good view.

It proved something, too.

She *affected* him.

Corrado blinked once, slow and considering, his stare drifting over her face, down her throat, and then back up again where his eyes lingered on her lips. The action alone was enough to make her wet her lips, and swallow hard.

"You shouldn't poke a monster," he murmured.

"I only see a man, Corrado."

"It's what's hiding in the man that might scare you, *amour*."

"Just how many languages can you speak?"

Corrado's mouth edged higher at the corners. "*That's* the question you want to ask right now."

"Why not?"

"Surprising me again, Ginny."

She finally figured out what he meant when he told her that, too. Everyone else would ask the obvious question, and she didn't. She asked the things he wasn't expecting, and it constantly kept him on his toes.

"How many?" she asked.

"I grew up speaking three," he replied. "French and Italian from my father's side of the family—French from the *Quebecois* side, and Italian from … well, we're a touch more Italian than French. And also English, of course."

"Is that all?"

"I know a bit of Russian, enough to get me through a conversation. Some German, but not nearly enough. And I might take on something else, if it interests me."

Ginevra nodded, and her gaze dropped between them again … *just to check*. "And you're still hard. Is that all it takes, just a conversation with me to get your cock up, Corrado?"

"I shouldn't be feeling anything about you at all, but certainly not *that*."

"But why?"

He inched closer, his body molding against hers all at once, taking away her breath, and making her incredibly aware of every nerve ending inside her. He smelled like leather and musk—maybe a touch of whiskey, too.

It stunned her.

"You are far too innocent to be playing that kind of game with a man like me," he said, his tone dipping dangerously again. "I promise you that, Ginny. The things I've done in bed would make you *run*. You're looking for something that's going to be fun for you, and I only like to ruin things, woman. I take beautiful things, and I wreck them."

She didn't think so.

That only made her hotter.

And *curious*.

"Would you tell me those things?"

Corrado let out a dark sound, a noise that seemed like it tore right out of his fucking chest. Except, she didn't get the chance to admire the sound, or the way his features shadowed because in the next breath, he was kissing her.

There was nothing soft about the kiss—nothing *sweet*. The roughness of his lips slamming against hers was enough to have her stomach clenching, and her heart racing. His tongue swept the seam of her lips, *demanding*. Like the rest of his kiss, and touches, too. One of his hands tangled into the waves of her hair, and the other landed hard to her hip, fisting into the thin cotton shorts she'll pulled on for bed.

He took and took and *took*.

Lips that worked harshly against hers, their tongues warring, though he controlled that, too. And then his teeth slid against her lower lip before tugging. His mouth moved lower, a sharp heat following the same path when his teeth grazed her skin. Just as quickly, he came back up to claim her mouth again with another bruising kiss that felt like he wanted to suck the fucking soul right out of her.

She'd give it to him.

If he asked, he could have that.

He dragged her closer, grinding her body against his, and making that heat travel lower. Until her thighs ached from it, and she was sure her shorts were wet, too.

Then, all at once, Corrado stepped back from her. It happened so fast, that she didn't know what to make of it, or the sudden stiffness in his body as he refused to meet her gaze. She could see the need vibrating through him, the way his jaw flexed as his tongue swept his lower lip, tasting *her* there.

Still, he kept that distance.

He stayed stiff.

"Corrado—"

"Don't," he said thickly, a shake of his head punctuating the words.

Something painful hit her in the chest.

It felt like rejection.

Why wouldn't he look at her?

"There'll be a box on your bed later," he said, turning away from her. "I trust that the girl at the shop picked out something appropriate, and that you'll like it. I know that you picked up your makeup and whatever else women like when we went shopping, so put it to use. Be ready for six—we have somewhere to be."

Ginevra, refusing to show the hurt she felt, asked, "For what?"

"A mutual birthday party. For me, my twin, and my oldest brother, Marcus. Our birthday already happened, but Marcus's is coming up. Our parents like to … do a big thing for it."

Oh.

"When was your birthday?"

Corrado looked at her, then, something unknown flashing across his face. "Huh."

She blinked. "What?"

"I just … wish you would quit doing that. Surprising me, I mean. You should tell me to fuck off right now, not ask when my birthday was. Don't *care* about me, Ginny."

"Why not? Is that such a bad thing?"

"Because I'm only going to hurt you."

She shrugged.

"But will you really, though?"

Corrado's jaw tensed, and he let out a hard breath that almost sounded like defeat. "Girl, you have no idea the mess you just walked into here. *No fucking idea at all.*"

Probably not.

A part of her still didn't care, either.

"Now, go," he uttered.

Ginevra did, but not because *he* told her to. No, she spun around and left the gym because the ache between her thighs was so deep now that if she didn't do *something*, then there was no telling what might happen. She was positive Corrado had been able to see the heat climbing in her cheeks, and the way she clenched her legs together in an effort to soothe that ache.

She didn't need to be *more* humiliated.

This was enough.

And yet, even as she put distance between her and Corrado—one step after another until she was inside her bedroom, and slamming the door behind her—it did *nothing*. Nothing to help the heat curling around her throat like it was his hand there, squeezing tight. Nothing to make the *need* coursing through her bloodstream go away. Nothing to help the clenching of her muscles, or the fact she couldn't catch her breath. Nothing to make that fucking stupid ache better.

How did a kiss make her that crazy?

That stupid?

That high?

God.

It was unfair.

And she just needed to feel better.

Ginevra's back hit the door, and she acted on her need, and nothing else. Slipping a hand under the waistband of her cotton sleep shorts, she found her pussy wet already. Not that she was surprised, she'd felt the fucking wetness back there with him. It'd been far too long since she'd had release, or even thought about it, really.

Life was more important.

Everything else came first.

She came last.

But not right now.

Ginevra's fingers worked that wetness she found at her slit higher, rubbing it into her throbbing clit with small, tight circles that had her whining, and grinding into her own hand. *More*, that's what she needed.

So much fucking more.

She thought about *him*, then, and the way he watched her when he thought she didn't see. The way his mouth felt as it worked against hers. How his hands felt splayed along her skin, or grabbing tight like he didn't want to let her go.

Those circles at her clit came faster.

Her noises became louder.

She could have tried to hide it …

She *should* have tried to be quiet.

Ginevra couldn't.

And when that orgasm finally came, it felt as punishing as it did *good*. Like ice water down her spine, numbing her entirely as a broken cry fell from her lips, and a heat shooting straight down to her pussy to remind her she was still empty.

It had been entirely hollow.

Fuck.

Ginevra stared at the bed, and the mussed sheets where she had been sleeping not too long ago. Or rather, the comforter that had been pulled back a bit because she tended to sleep on top of the blankets instead of underneath.

Beds were always cold with only one person.

Too cold, maybe.

This whole place felt cold right now.

She didn't want to think about that, *or* what she had just done. Feeling sticky, and sweaty, she just wanted a shower, and to go back to bed.

Pushing away from the door, she turned to grab the handle, pulled it open, and froze right where she stood. Across the hall, leaning in the doorway of his master bedroom, was Corrado. He didn't look up at her; he didn't move at all.

But she could see it.

That tightness in his jaw, and the way his tongue peeked out to snake across his lips like he might still be tasting her there. The shadows on his face, and how his next exhale came out harder than the last. His eyes, lowered but *dark*, when he dared to look up just a bit, although still not enough to look her in the face.

And his erection, still straining against the line of his shorts.

He'd heard her.

He'd listened.

And she didn't know how to feel about that at all.

What did this man want with her?

Ginevra slipped down the hall toward the main bathroom. Corrado turned, and went into his bedroom, slamming the door loudly behind him.

Apparently, *this* was what they were going to do.

Say nothing, acknowledge nothing.

Perfect.

CHAPTER 23
CORRADO

The sky, streaked with colors as it began to darken from the evening, was the backdrop to Corrado's thoughts as he waited for Ginevra to meet him at the front of the penthouse. He didn't quite know what to expect for her outfit, but for the fact he told the lady who sent it over from the private boutique what kind of party it would be.

A *Guzzi* event.

That meant something spectacular.

If he had needed Ginevra in a ballgown or something like that, then he would have let the woman know that, as well. Really, she just needed to look *good*, and as though she belonged on his arm for the evening. The rest, he was sure she could handle without help.

Still, as his thoughts drifted to Ginevra and the upcoming evening, he also thought about someone else. Or rather, the fact that his cell phone was quiet, and had been for several days. Other than calls from his family, and one to confirm yes, he wanted the white Maserati removed from storage for the night, his phone was silent.

Completely abnormal.

Alessio called *often*.

It could be possible that Alessio took on a last-minute assignment from The League that took him out of the country, or required him to drop off the radar for a while. Even then, though, he would always let Corrado know.

The silence bothered him.

Something felt wrong.

Corrado couldn't think on it for long. The click of heels coming down the hallway toward the penthouse's entrance had him turning his head away from the view at the window in just enough time to see Ginevra come around the corner.

And *damn*.

What a sight.

It would have been a shame to miss that.

The gray, silk dress with thin straps over her shoulders was tight around the bodice, and cut *low*. Showing off just a peek of the beige lace bra cups underneath that made her chest look fucking fantastic. His gaze traveled lower, taking in the tightly cinched waist of the dress, and the way it fell over her hips and came to a stop quite a few inches above the knees.

It was *short as hell*.

She showed off all kinds of leg, and he loved it. He *really* did. She held tight to a matching clutch in her hand. The strappy, five-inch heels put her at damn near eye-level with him, and every step she took showed off a little more of the olive-toned skin of her thighs. And apparently, a diamond garter around her right thigh that only peeked out when the slit in the skirt of the dress opened with her steps.

It matched the choker at her throat.

And the studs in her ears.

Christ.

Which took his gaze right back up to her face. There, he found her lips were a stark red, and she had somehow managed to paint her innocence away with dark strokes of kohl that smoked her eyes, and mascara that fanned her lashes.

"Beautiful," Corrado murmured.

Entirely unable to stop himself, too.

He just said it.

It *needed* to be said.

Like he needed more reminders of just how fucking attractive this woman was because apparently, his body didn't let him know enough on a daily basis. Like their little moment that morning in the gym wasn't a *huge* fucking mistake that he suddenly wanted to make again. Or the fact that as he stood across the hall from her bedroom doorway, listening to her as she got herself off, that he considered breaking her door down because *he* wanted to be the one doing that.

Guilt.

Lust.

It warred inside him.

He was so fucked.

Not that it mattered.

He was determined to do nothing—say nothing.

It was better this way.

"You think so?" Ginevra asked, coming to stand in front of him. "I didn't know if this was going to be appropriate for whatever—"

"It's perfect, and so are you."

Her stare lifted then to meet his, and he didn't quite know what to make of what he found there. Confusion, mostly, but desire, too. That was his fault—he pulled her in only to push her away, and she probably felt like a fucking ping pong ball, now.

He'd been wrong.

Ginevra was not a mess.

He was.

"Thank you," she whispered.

Corrado had to *physically* hold himself back from reaching out to touch her. Because if he did that, there was no telling what might happen next. He couldn't trust himself around this woman, and as it was, he had already crossed a big line.

Jumped it, really.

"And you look quite handsome," she said, her hand coming up to flatten the edge of the lapel on his suit. "Your vest and tie matches my dress ... was that planned?"

"Probably. I had it sent up by the same woman who picked out your dress."

Ginevra made an appreciative noise. "Just how much money do you have, Corrado?"

He laughed, grateful for the change in topic. "Me, specifically? Or my *Guzzi* money?"

"Is there a difference?"

Corrado smirked. "A little, yeah."

"Which has more?"

"The Guzzi side of me. Saying the Guzzi family is *vastly* wealthy does not even come close to describing how much money we have." Corrado tipped his head toward the door, saying, "Come on, then, and we'll get going."

Corrado couldn't help but put his hand to her lower back, all the while becoming painfully aware of the criss-crossed opened back of the dress she wore at the same time. Doing his best to control the darker urges climbing through his body, he directed them out of the penthouse, and toward the bank of elevators at the end of the hall.

Ginevra said nothing as the elevator dropped lower. He figured he should probably give her a heads up about what to expect for the night, or rather ... the rules he needed for her to follow so that she was safe, and so was her identity.

"If anyone asks, you give your nickname or first name," he said, "but absolutely not your surname, do you understand?"

Ginevra nodded. "Sure."

"Say you come from New Jersey, they won't know the difference. We're old friends. That's all you need to say. I will handle my family, if they ask, and I'm sure they will. Nosy bast—"

"Be nice."

His gaze cut to her.

She winked.

Corrado chuckled. "You say that *now*."

"Actually, I say it because I think you must have an amazing family that they're willing to throw you a birthday party when you're … how old are you again?"

"I turned twenty-three twelve days ago."

Ginevra nibbled on her bottom lip.

Corrado's cock *felt* that.

Fuck.

Tonight was going to be hell.

Absolute hell.

He could see it already. Stuck between his fucking guilt, and the constant want he felt for this woman who had no clue what he had done here. Even as he conversed with her, or spent day in and day out with her, his mind was on constant loop of thoughts revolving around Alessio.

Back and forth.

Ginny.

Les.

One he missed desperately, and knew something wasn't right because Alessio hadn't called in days. And the other, he was desperate to know, and who he thought Alessio should know, too, but the way this had happened would be enough to end it before *that* could begin. Corrado was most sure of that.

More nails in the coffin.

Corrado didn't ask for this.

None of it.

Back and forth he went again.

It never ended.

Christ.

"Anyway," Ginevra said, oblivious to the battle in his mind and heart, "I think they must love you a lot, and your brothers, if they're willing to throw you a party at this age. And not just *any* party … look at us, this feels like an affair."

As she said that, the elevator came to a stop, and opened up to the front lobby of the building. Parked right in front, in full view of the windows, was the white Maserati he'd had taken out of the Toronto storage unit where he kept it when he wasn't in the city visiting.

"And that's ours, I bet," she said beside him.

Corrado sighed. "It is."

"Like I said, a whole *affair*."

He really wished she would stop using that word.

But not for a reason she would know.

Corrado helped Ginevra step out of the Maserati, and her eyes widened at the sight in front of them. Parked at the very end of the long, winding drive that led up to the three-level, two-wing monster that was the Guzzi Mansion, they had a way to go yet before they properly *arrived*.

Not that it mattered.

She could see now.

The wealth was on full display.

"Is this your—"

"Childhood home, yes," he said. "It sits on several acres of private land, and the mansion itself could house a good hundred people or more … living wise. It has a pool, ballroom, three dining rooms, a library that, in all honesty, is bigger than most public ones, and well, that's just scratching the surface."

"Who is the reader?"

Surprising him again.

Those damn *questions*.

Corrado almost said Alessio before he caught himself, and realized she meant in his *family*. Although, Alessio was his family, too. "My mother. And you should know, this place … this night, despite being for my brothers' and my birthdays, and all of the rest of it, is my father's doing. Like the library, and the tiled rose design at the bottom of the pool. Anything my mother wants, my father gives her. She is the queen here, and expect that she'll be treated as such. If she wanted to sit on a throne during the party, trust that one will be provided for her to do that."

Ginevra smiled slyly.

He didn't miss it.

"What?"

"I was just thinking you don't sound at all bitter about that fact. Your mother being spoiled, and loved, I mean."

"I'm not. It's all I ever knew."

Knowing the cobblestone driveway might be a little tricky for Ginevra in her stiletto heels, he wrapped an arm tightly around her side, and pulled her close to him. He didn't miss the shiver that raced through her body, but he did his very best to suppress his own reaction to it. It wasn't like he needed to walk the rest of this very long driveway with a hard-on.

Right?

Apparently, he did.

Fucking hell.

"Oh, wow," Ginevra said softly, her gaze drifting over the pots of roses that lined the middle of the driveway about midway, leading the rest of the way to the mansion. Twinkle lights colored the grass on either side, and hanging from the maple trees were rows of silk and chiffon that matched the white roses and lights. "This is something else."

"I am sure the inside will be just as ... excessive," he settled on saying with a laugh. "And all for a birthday party, too."

"Hey, it's something different than balloons and streamers."

Right.

Except the balloons were roses.

And the streamers were made of silk and chiffon.

Right.

"It's the Guzzi way," he murmured. "And you'll fit right in looking like you do tonight."

Ginevra glanced up at him, those brown eyes of hers reminding him of an ocean. Expansive, dark, and deep. Oh, so dangerous, but pretty, too.

Just pretty enough to drown him.

He swore the music filtering out of the mansion, and the low tones of chattering people as they neared the grand, marble entrance faded away. There were far too many things about this woman that continued to draw him in, and ensnare him in her web of *trouble*. And then there were parts of him that recognized things in her that didn't fit him at all.

Things that fit someone else in his life far better. Except she didn't know that, and neither did the man who needed to know what was happening here.

This was a mess.

How many times had he said that now?

It didn't make it less true.

Corrado cleared his throat, needing to break their connection.

Because they couldn't have that at all.

That *connection.*

Not *now*.

Not ever.

"Let's have a good time, hmm?" he asked, turning back to face the mansion.

Ginevra glanced down at the ground. "Sure, Corrado."

CHAPTER 24
CORRADO

The *most* crucial thing to know about Corrado's mother?

Nothing and no one would ever be as important to Cara Rossi as her five sons, and husband. By most standards, one could absolutely consider her a *mama bear*. And yet, on the flip side of that same coin, she was also fiercely protective of her sons' freedom and happiness. She, like his father, Gian, had made every effort to ensure their sons thought for themselves. That they understood the right choice was sometimes the hard one. They gave them protection and privilege, but also space to grow, and figure out who *they* wanted to be.

Never once had Corrado felt pushed to be one thing by his parents. He knew, safely, that his brothers felt the same way, even if they had clearly chosen a path more like his father's. But his mother?

Cara was the voice of reason.

The *loudest* voice, too.

She made it her first priority to know that her sons were happy, even if she didn't pry for the details as to why. Maybe that was why, when Corrado called his mother's name across the hall, her soft smile stayed permanently affixed in place as she laid eyes on the *woman* at Corrado's side, and his arm tucked around Ginevra's waist.

She didn't act surprised.

Not *concerned*.

Cara simply smiled wider, and opened her arms to

Corrado like it had been far too long since she had seen her third oldest son. He let go of Ginevra to hug his mother. She took him into her embrace—lest she find trouble somewhere she *shouldn't* be because someone pried too much, and she slipped up.

Behind his mother, Corrado found the hoard of his brothers waiting, and their father standing behind the Guzzi sons. Chris stood next to Marcus, and beside the oldest, the youngest at only twenty, Bene and Beni smirked at one another like they were sharing some kind of secret. The second set of Guzzi twins very well could be doing exactly that. Those two shared a bond with each other like even Chris and Corrado didn't have.

Sometimes, it could be unsettling.

He was used to it now, though.

Cara leaned back, her hand still pressing against Corrado's cheek, and he took that chance to pull Ginevra close again. *God*, he loved his ma. There was just something about her that felt like home in a way nothing else could. "Happy birthday, my boy."

Corrado smiled. "Little old to be a *boy*, Ma."

"Not to be *my* boy."

He knew better than to argue.

She would always win.

Another lesson from his father.

"And who is this?" Cara asked, her smile turning on Ginevra in an instant. For the first time, Corrado loosened his hold on Ginevra, but not by much. Just enough to allow her to lean away from his side and take his mother's hands that she offered. His mother looked back to him, asking, "A friend?"

Nice.

That was smooth of his ma.

Cara wouldn't outright ask about his personal business—

she never did. He was sure his mother assumed things, and put two and two together when she could about him and Alessio, but she never verbally confirmed it. It probably helped that his mother was a therapist, and always had a knack for knowing—or being able to pry—all her sons secrets from them, sometimes without their help at all. He figured seeing him without Alessio at his side *would* be a surprise.

Hell, it was a shock to him, too.

"Yeah, Ma," Corrado said, "Ginevra is a friend."

Cara still smiled, unfazed. "*Ciao.*"

Ginevra's gaze darted to him, a silent question there, and he nodded. "*Ciao.* You have a beautiful home."

"A bit much at first, don't you think?"

To her benefit, Ginny didn't miss a beat.

"Not at all."

Cara shrugged. "I always thought it overwhelmed you a little coming up on it for the first time."

The first time …

Corrado shot his mother a look, but she studiously ignored it. If that was his mother's sly way of saying Ginevra had never been here before, well, he heard it loud and clear.

"Actually, I thought it should be in a magazine."

His mother laughed. "Oh, it's been printed a few times. Not magazines, though. More the newspapers. Usually, from reporters trying to catch us coming in, or out."

"*Cara.*"

All it took was the dark call of his mother's name by his father, and Cara rolled her eyes upward like she thought it was ridiculous. Ginevra pressed her lips together, probably in an effort to keep from smiling. Corrado found he had to do the same when his mother muttered, "Yes, Gian, don't talk about *that* … I know, I know."

Gian made a soft noise, and then turned to take a small

flute of champagne from a server as she passed, but otherwise, he said nothing.

Corrado chuckled, knowing he should probably change the subject. "The place looks great, Ma."

"It better," she replied. "But back to this beautiful woman ... Ginevra, you said?"

And that, in a nutshell, was his mother.

Ginevra gave him a wink. "That's me."

He could plainly see that twinkle in his mother's eye—that *curiosity*. "I think you and I should spend some time together tonight, and—"

"Oh, Cara, there's the director for the hospital," Gian said, coming up to slip his arm around his wife's waist, directing her in an entirely different direction as he did so. At the same time, his father passed Corrado a look that said, *we will have words later*. He didn't doubt it. "We need to discuss that donation with him, yes?"

Cara made a face. "*Fine*." Then, turning back to Ginevra, his mother grinned. "I will find you later, okay?"

"You got it, Cara."

And to Corrado, his mother added, "Make sure you dance with her—I taught you well, use it."

Well ...

Gian gave Ginevra a warm smile over his shoulder. "It was very nice to meet you, Ginny. I'm sure we'll be seeing more of you."

Corrado blinked, but his mother and father were already gone. Next to him, Ginevra's brow furrowed. Clearly, she hadn't missed his father's slip, either. *Ginny*, he called her. Like he knew exactly who she was, because she *had not* told them her nickname yet.

He passed a glance to his twin, wondering ... he'd given Chris a few details, about the same he gave to Alessio, about what he was doing in Toronto at the moment. The only added thing his brother knew was the fact that Ginevra was a *woman*, and that was simply because he had brought Corrado clothes for her to wear those first couple of days.

Chris tipped his glass of whiskey up to take a drink, seeing the question in his brother's gaze. A simple nod gave Corrado all the answer he needed. Yes, his brother had shared what he knew with his father. No doubt, Gian had then made some calls to connect the rest of the dots with the information he had.

Great.

"Where the fuck is Les—"

"Ginny, do you want to dance?" Corrado asked, turning his back to his twin, and his other brothers before Bene could finish that question.

She smirked up at him. "What, don't want to introduce me to the rest of the Guzzi bunch?"

"We're a *hoard*, really. And no, I am sure you'll get more than your fill of my brothers before the end of the night. I had to live with them for eighteen years, trust me when I say it won't kill you to lose two extra minutes with them."

She hit his chest, but he was already walking them away. A quick glance over his shoulder let him know Chris was taking care of *that* situation. A sharp shake of his head to the rest of their brothers quieted them all, and yet, every one of them turned to watch Corrado and Ginevra walk away.

Like they just knew, too.

Corrado had secrets.

One too many to name.

It kind of felt like his family probably knew some.

"What is *this*?"

Ginevra walked further into the hall of paintings, and

spread her arms wide as she did a little circle. Corrado stuffed his hands in his slacks pockets as he watched her joyful moment. That, and he liked the way that dress draped over her body, and glimmered when she moved.

"This," he said, "is the hall of Guzzis."

Stopping under one particular piece of art in the hallway, she leaned a bit over the red rope to get a closer look at the name under the piece. The man in the painting, surrounded by his wife, and children when they were just toddlers, stared straight ahead like he owned the world.

At the time, it probably felt like he had.

"Frederic Guzzi and family."

"My grandfather."

Not that Corrado had ever seen much of the man growing up. He didn't approve of some of the things that brought Gian and Cara together, and so, the rest of them suffered for it. A part of him always thought that was quite selfish, but he didn't think Ginevra needed to know that family dirt just yet.

"Do you have one?"

Corrado let out a laugh. "Not quite—we have a portrait, or two, as a whole." He pointed at the end of the hallway where a painting featuring his mother, surrounded by all her boys in a forest as she sat on what looked like a throne, was on prominent display. "There's one."

"Oh, wow."

"But no, I don't have one of *just* me."

"Why not?"

"Our family's tradition has always been family portraits, or those featuring the head of the house, usually the male. My father made my mother an exception to that rule, though."

Like everything else between his mother and father.

"Ah," Ginevra said, grinning back at him, "so you aren't

the head of *your* household yet since you don't have one, right?"

"Exactly, and I'm unmarried, without children … so no portrait, either."

"Corrado, there you are."

He spun to the side fast, finding his father watching him from a separate entry into the large hall of portraits. Next to Gian, stood Chris, Marcus, and two other men who rarely left his father's side. His consigliere, and underboss for the Guzzi Cosa Nostra.

"I wanted a word, if you had a minute," Gian said, gesturing at the hallway.

Corrado opened his mouth to refuse—Ginevra, after all —and he didn't feel like getting the twenty-one questions from his father that were sure to come once Gian had him alone. Not that it mattered, apparently, because his father wasn't going to give him a choice.

Perfect.

"Chris will entertain Ginevra, I understand they've met before," Gian said quickly.

Corrado kept his face passive. "*Met* is stretching it. They've seen each other from afar."

"What, you don't trust your twin with the woman?"

He gave his father a scowl. "That's unfair."

"The low shots usually get me what I want, you know."

Of course.

"Corrado?"

Behind him, he found Ginevra smiling. "I'll be okay for a while. Go with your dad."

"You sure?"

"Yeah. Besides, Chris can probably tell me more about these paintings, right?"

Chris laughed next to their father. "I certainly can."

"Good. See? Everything's great."

So it seemed.

Ginevra gave him a wink over her shoulder when Chris stepped into the hallway, and took her arm in his before they both turned to look at another painting. Dismissed from *their* conversation, he was left with his waiting father, oldest brother Marcus, and the other two men.

"My office, then?" Gian asked.

"I guess so," Corrado replied.

Corrado's father stopped pretending to be *polite* the very second the office door closed, leaving him, his dad, and Marcus within. Standing just outside were Gian's other two men who had not been invited in.

Something Corrado was sure they were unaccustomed to, considering what he knew.

"I will give you two minutes," Gian said, rounding his desk and pulling out the large leather chair to sit in, "to give me every pertinent detail about that woman, and your business with her, Corrado."

He smirked. "Or, you could just save me the time, and tell me what you know."

Gian made a face. "That's less fun, though."

"But quicker, and I would—"

"Like to get back to her, I imagine," his father murmured, steepling his fingers over his desk. Corrado opened his mouth to deny that statement, and the *connotation* behind it, but Gian was quick to add, "You know, I watched you for a while ... the two of you. I could explain your hand constantly reaching for her, or staying on her, when I also know that you are supposed to be hiding the young woman from her family. Except ... you know she's safe here, and two feet of space won't really make *much* of a difference, would it?"

Corrado swallowed back his denial.

What would be the point?

"So," Gian continued, "the only explanation why you keep touching or reaching for her is because you *want to*. And then if I move onto the way you watch her ... the way you stare when you think people aren't looking, and I am left wondering something here."

"Or you could mind your business," Corrado replied.

His father shook his head. "I can't ... not when I'm concerned."

"About what? The fact I have a woman with me, and I seem interested in her?"

"No," Gian replied just as fast and still calm, "the fact that someone else isn't with you ... your brother mentioned, at the time he met Ginevra, you said Alessio didn't know she was with you, and I have to wonder if he does now."

Corrado stiffened.

Gian raised a brow in response. "What, son?"

"What would that matter to you—if Alessio knew or not?"

A flicker of confusion drifted over his father's features before Gian was back to that same, unbothered demeanor as before. "Because I wonder if something happened with Alessio, Corrado. Has something changed there, and you've not told me?"

A lot happened, then.

Or rather, Corrado realized a lot of things.

This moment that he'd wondered and worried about for most of his life was actually happening. His father might not be directly saying it, but he wasn't dancing around it purposely, either. Gian was *outright* asking about Alessio, and Corrado's relationship.

Because he knew.

And that was something else he realized, then.

His father knew.

His mother probably did, too.

All his brothers.

Of course, he knew that. And yet, a part of him had still thought, after all this time, that his family were fine and comfortable in their place of not asking. Because if they didn't ask him, then he would never have to tell.

Not because they didn't love or accept him *exactly* as he was, but because this was how he chose to live his life. Not offering his personal life out like it was meant for their consumption.

"Corrado?"

He blinked, coming out of his thoughts with a bang. "I have not told Alessio about her, no."

Gian let out a slow exhale. "I know you two ... have a different kind of agreement about your relationship and other people, specifically women. I'm not sure if she falls under that, and guessing by your behavior right now, I don't think—"

"How do you know that at all?"

"I asked."

Corrado's jaw ached from clenching so hard. "Asked who?"

"Alessio."

Huh.

"And not *me?*"

And why hadn't Alessio told him that?

When had that even happened?

In the corner of the room, pouring himself a glass of scotch, Marcus cleared his throat, but otherwise, paid the conversation no mind. His oldest brother was good for that

—more like their father than the rest of them combined, honestly.

Marcus was fit for his position as the Guzzi heir.

Undoubtedly.

"Corrado," Gian said, drawing his attention back in, "I just want to make sure you're happy, son, and that everything is okay. Don't think this was me trying to cause a problem, or … something like that. It wasn't. I just worry about you. More than I do the others, sometimes."

"I know I need to tell him," Corrado managed to say. "I just don't know how. It's not just *her* … it's more than what's on the surface of it, Papa."

Gian frowned. "All right. I'm sorry."

Corrado wished his throat wasn't so tight when he asked, "How long did you know?"

"About what—that you liked boys, too, or that you and Alessio were living and sleeping together?"

Well …

"Both."

Gian nodded. "From the time you were fifteen for when I knew you liked boys, too. As for Alessio … I was told about the kiss in The League's gym shortly after it happened. Otherwise, I assumed on that based on the obvious fact you were clearly in a relationship with him."

Huh.

"How did you know since I was fifteen?"

"Cameras caught you kissing the boy from your school. I had the footage deleted, and your mother and I simply decided we wouldn't pressure you in any way. We knew about the women you'd dated before that. And so, when, or *if*, you wanted to tell us that you were bisexual, then that was when you would tell us. It wasn't for us to decide when it was your time to tell *your* truth, Corrado."

"I always thought—" He stopped abruptly, unwilling to

say the words. It was the look his father gave him, willing him to speak, that allowed him to do it. "I thought you didn't ask because ... I thought you didn't *want* to know."

Gian rested back in the chair.

Across the room, Marcus set his glass down.

"Because of the traditions?"

The traditions.

Such a simple way to describe the culture of mafioso that his family was so deeply engrained in.

"Essentially," Corrado replied.

Gian let out a noise, dark and dismissive. "I almost burned the city down once for a woman ... could you imagine what I would do to it for a child that woman *gave* to me, Corrado? Because that is what I would do for any of you —the way God made you never mattered one way or another. This *life,* this legacy, and this name ... it means nothing compared to what you, your brothers, and your mother mean to me. It gave me nothing compared to what she sacrificed and gave to me."

"I should have told you."

He should have done and said a lot of things.

Not all to the people in this room, or house, either. But to Alessio, also, who still hadn't called. The man with the piece of his heart that Corrado left in Vegas probably thinking they were chasing a dead fucking end together.

Because how long had they been doing this together?

How long had Alessio put up with this shit?

How much more would he take?

Except *now* ... now it was more complicated because Corrado had feelings in the game for a woman he had no business feeling *anything* for, and all this without having done nothing more than *kiss* her.

He'd punched those nails in.

That coffin was closing.

Corrado had no one to blame but himself.

"I should get back to Ginevra." he said quietly.

Gian tipped his head to the side, clearly hearing the pain in Corrado's words. "Son—"

"I have to get back."

"Okay."

Gian let him go.

It was his wrongs that chased him out of the office, though.

CHAPTER 25
GINEVRA

"So, what's that like?" Ginevra asked her companion as he directed them back out to the party. "Having another face in the world that looks just like yours?"

Chris chuckled, his hand patting the top of her hand tucked into the crook of his arm. "Depends on which one of us you ask, I think."

Her gaze darted to the other side of the dining room that was currently being used as a gathering area for the many guests. The long table had been used to set up another row of white roses, while silk and chiffon hung from the large, crystal chandelier overhead. People milled about, chatting and laughing as music filtered in from the next room.

It wasn't the décor or the people that caught her attention, but Cara Rossi. And the two boys sitting next to her, and leaning close like they were sharing a secret. The *other* set of twins. Because apparently, there were two sets in this family.

"There *are* a lot of twins in your family to ask, I suppose," she said.

Chris grinned. "And each one of us has a different experience about it. My mother is also a twin."

"Really?"

"Identical, too. Her twin died when she was … well, probably about your age."

Ginevra's smile slipped away. "That must have been terrible."

"She doesn't talk about it, so I assume so. Lea, that was her name." Chris turned his gaze on her, and grinned, saying, "But I'm not supposed to be making you sad, right? And I think my mother would like to sit with you for a few more minutes. You know, *without* Corrado stepping in on every question or deflecting."

"He's so moody."

Part of her liked that, though.

The other part squinted at him a lot.

It was a work in progress.

"Mmm," Chris agreed, "and I bet he's worse right now, too. He usually is when he doesn't have his extension around to keep him entertained."

"What?"

Ginevra peered up at Chris, but he didn't answer her question. She didn't exactly have time to press him for more, either. Cara caught sight of them coming her way, and with a wide smile, she waved them over.

"Be good," she heard Cara tell the younger pair of twins. Although, they didn't look any older or younger than Ginevra, to be honest. It was only once Chris had pulled up a chair for Ginevra to take, and sit beside Cara, that the older woman passed a look to the men on the other side of her. "Ginevra, you didn't get to meet these two properly earlier— Benedetto, and Benito, or Bene, and Beni, as they prefer."

The young men grinned, playful and mischievous. Their gazes drifted to each other, before coming back to her just as fast. Like actual mirrors of themselves, it was almost comical. *Instantly*, Ginevra knew two things about the twins. One, they were probably a hell of a lot of fun to be around. And two, she bet they were absolutely *trouble*.

They just had that air about them.

"Why do the nicknames sound a bit different from how their full names are said?" Ginevra asked.

Cara laughed. "You ask strange questions, don't you?"

Ginevra shrugged. "Corrado says I surprise him with them. I think he likes it."

"He always did like *different* things," Bene said.

"Careful," Chris murmured, his gaze cutting to the twin on the right. "Be very careful there."

"I didn't mean it like a bad thing, I was just saying—"

"Shut up," Beni told his twin.

"*Fine.*"

Cara, still looking at Ginevra as though the conversation beside them hadn't just happened, smiled a bit. "My husband is French and Italian. Their full names are obviously the Italian side, but the nicknames ... we've always said them more with a French flair. That's all."

"I like that," Ginevra replied. "It's interesting. Unique."

"It's about the only thing that sets them apart from one another."

Cara wasn't exactly lying. Passing the twins a second look was like staring into a reflection of them—they sat side by side, their hands in the same position on their laps, their suits matching down to the cufflinks on their wrists, and even their smiles crooked up at the edges on the same side.

They didn't seem aware Ginevra was watching them, since they were too busy staring at something on the other side of the room, but it was ... fascinating. She wondered if they purposely behaved like mirrors of the other, or if this was just something they did from the time they were born.

Twins were like that, right?

Except, Corrado and Chris weren't. Ginevra had noticed that about the men from the first night she saw them standing next to one another. Finding their differences had been easy to her, but this was not the same. At all.

Chris laughed under his breath, gaining her attention. The shrug he offered to her said that *he* had been watching her, and probably knew exactly what was running through her mind. He nodded like he was saying, *yeah, I know, right?*

She understood what he meant earlier now when he said every twin probably had a different opinion about what it was like to have someone else in the world share your face. No doubt, the two next to her had a different perspective than their older twin brothers.

"Now, do you have any siblings?" Cara asked suddenly, drawing Ginevra back to the present.

"Uh …" Corrado wasn't there for her to ask if that was okay, so she deferred to Chris thinking he probably knew the truth about why she was there. He nodded once, and then turned to grab a drink from a passing server. "I do—two sisters."

Well, *three*, if she counted Siena, now.

And she was not mentioning her brothers.

"Are you the oldest?"

"I am."

"Ah," Cara said, smiling, "and your mother must love that. Having all girls around her, I mean. People always think I must lack female attention with all this testosterone around me." Just as quickly, the woman winked, her perfectly applied makeup not showing a bit of her age, and her loose chignon making her striking red hair seem like a deeper maroon under the lights in the room. "Like having all boys somehow made me into one of them, too. Don't I look like that's a problem?"

Ginevra laughed.

Still, in her heart … it hurt.

Cara hadn't known it, but mentioning her mother was still a sore spot for Ginevra. She had moments where she didn't think about her mother at all and passing time in her days where her sisters slipped her mind, too. And then, all at once, it came rushing back like a wrecking ball to devastate her again.

It happened every single time.

"*But*," Cara drawled, grinning slyly, "soon they will all be married, and then I am sure I will have *lots* of women in this house. Won't I, boys?"

Grumbles came from the twins.

Chris altogether avoided his mother's stare.

Cara looked at Ginevra and rolled her eyes. "They don't like to talk about that."

"I can tell."

"That doesn't make it less true, though."

Yeah, she liked Cara a lot.

She felt like a mother.

Ginevra *really* needed that right now.

"There you are."

Ginevra turned to find Corrado coming down the steps of the porch of the east wing of the mansion. He smiled, but it didn't reach his eyes. And it was there, in his gaze, that she found the darkness. Something was wrong, even if he was more than willing to pretend like everything was perfectly fine.

"Chris was showing me the back. It's beautiful out here."

"It is," Corrado said, nodding to his twin. "Thanks, man."

"Sure." At her side, Chris patted a hand against her upper back. "This is where I say goodnight, but it was great to properly meet you, and not … you know, peeking around a corner at me."

She didn't even try to hide her snickers. "Yeah, I suppose."

"Have a good night, you two."

Corrado didn't say goodbye to his twin, nor did he turn to watch Chris walk away from them. In fact, he didn't take his gaze off Ginevra, and with every step Chris took away from them, she became more and more aware that they were alone. Sure, they were alone *most* of the time, but for some reason, it felt different.

"Are you about ready to go?" he asked.

Ginevra's brow dipped. "They haven't cut the cake, yet."

"I'm not in the mood for it tonight."

"It's not really about *you*, is it? Seems like this was more for your mother and father, Corrado, and since they threw the party for you and your brothers, the least you could do is make an effort to please them and stay."

His jaw stiffened at that.

Ginevra arched a brow to dare him to deny it. "Well?"

"Ginny—"

"Something is wrong. I can see it in your face. What is it? It's not … New York, right?"

Corrado cleared his throat. "Not even close."

"Then, what—"

She didn't get to finish her sentence before Corrado closed the distance between them entirely. All at once, the space she had to breathe was gone when his lips crashed down on hers. The soft curves of her body fit perfectly into the fold of his as he leaned over her, a hand falling to her lower back to keep her from falling to the ground entirely. As his lips worked against hers, his tongue seeking the heat of her mouth, she fisted her fingers into the lapels of his suit jacket, needing him closer.

The kiss felt like *heaven*.

And just like sin, too.

How could a *kiss* make her entire body wake up like fireworks had been set off inside her bloodstream? Because that's what it did.

It felt like a hello.

And a goodbye.

All in one.

Corrado's lips slowed against hers, then, kissing her softly once, twice, and then a third time to her lower lip, whispering, "I had to do that one more time."

Ginevra blinked up at him, feeling entirely too high. *Right then*, she would have asked him to take her anywhere. *Somewhere*. As long as there was a bed, or a useable flat surface, she would have been up for it.

Except it was the look in his eyes that kept her quiet. That *pain*—the storm she found warring in his gaze—stopped her from saying anything at all.

Because a part of her knew, then.

She just *knew*.

His heart was not *all in* with her. Maybe that was why he'd constantly kept a distance, even though he *clearly* wanted to get closer. There was a piece of him somewhere else. Maybe she had known it from the start, or perhaps she pieced together the pieces overtime.

What did it matter?

She knew now.

She felt it *now*.

"I'm selfish," he murmured, "so I had to do it one more time, Ginny, before I can't anymore."

Her lower lip trembled.

"There's someone else, isn't there?" she asked.

"There is. It's not as simple as it seems, and we've always been different and open in our relationship. *This* wouldn't have been a big deal except I fucked up and started feeling shit about you that I had no business feeling. At that point, I should have done the right thing, but I didn't and here I am."

Corrado dragged a hand down his jaw, shaking his head at the same time. "So yes, there is someone else. And I love them, but I haven't been good to them, either. They deserve far better than what I gave—I need to give that to them, now." Corrado didn't look away from her as he said, "I'm sorry."

All the air in Ginevra's lungs came out in a painful exhale. She felt his hold loosen on her, but he didn't step back. Not yet.

It was the buzz of a phone in his pocket that made him put distance between the two of them. It wasn't much, just a couple of inches, but he wasn't holding her anymore, and she could stare up at the black, inky Canadian sky dotted with the brightest stars.

For the moment, she was grateful.

She needed that space.

Corrado made a noise, and she looked his way. He was still staring down at his phone, but she caught the name on the contact and what the message said before he turned the device off entirely.

Les, the contact said. And simply, *I'm in the city—we need to talk, now.*

Who was that?

Corrado's head snapped up, his gaze landing on her. "I think ... would it be okay if I had Chris take you back to the penthouse? I have something to handle right now."

Ginevra nodded. "Yeah, sure."

What else could she say?

Chris was quick to help Ginevra out of the silver Mercedes,

and into the building while the rain continued to pour down from the dark sky overhead. At some point during the drive back to the city, the sky had opened, and began to cry.

It felt appropriate.

The sky was breaking open.

Ginevra, too.

Despite how fast Chris moved to get them inside the safety of the building, it didn't matter. Her loose waves were soaked, and so was the silk dress. Likely ruined, now.

Yeah, *so* appropriate.

Like her in that moment.

"I can walk you upstairs, if you'd like," Chris said, making sure to keep his gaze on *only* Ginevra's face, and not the dress that would have to now be peeled from her body. "My job was to get you back safely, after all."

She shook her head.

No.

Right now, all she wanted was to be alone. She highly doubted Chris would understand why, as he wasn't privy to the things that happened between her and Corrado. She really didn't want to explain, either.

Why humiliate herself further?

"If you wouldn't mind, I'd like to take the elevator up alone." Ginevra flipped her hand over, showing the keys in her palm. "He gave me the keys, so I can get in."

"Okay."

"Thanks, Chris."

He flashed her a kind smile. "Don't mention it, Ginevra."

"Well, I'll …" She nodded at the bank of elevators across the brightly lit lobby decorated in soft, neutral tones. "… get going, then. I didn't get to see your mom or dad before we left, but you'll tell them I loved meeting them, won't you? They were great."

And considering that she now knew there was someone

else in Corrado's life, that his parents and the rest of his family probably knew about, she was only now realizing just how welcoming they had been, all things considered.

More kind than they needed to be, honestly.

"Of course."

"Thank you."

Ginevra headed for the elevator, head down, but Chris's voice behind her made her steps hesitate.

"I know things might seem bad right now," he said, "but it's always been complicated with them, Ginevra. They act like it's always been just them, and in their private moments, I'm sure it was. But they made this mess together, and so now they have to clean it up, too. It just so happened that you were the one who got caught in the middle. Give them a chance to figure it out—you might have been *exactly* what the two of them were looking for without even knowing it, but they won't know if no one tries."

Her brow furrowed, and she looked back over her shoulder. "I don't know what that means."

Chris nodded. "I know, but you will. Try to have a good night."

Right.

Once she was hidden by the closing elevator doors, Ginevra tipped her head down, and dragged in an aching breath. She didn't want to cry—she wasn't *that* girl. And besides, she had no business being heartbroken over a man who had never been hers to begin with and was clearly involved with someone else.

Simple as that.

It didn't help.

She still wanted to cry.

Ginevra wiped away the one tear that escaped the corner of her eye as the elevator came to a stop on the highest floor. It opened to the hallway leading to the penthouse. She took another quick, deep breath; she had her weak moment in private, and now it was done.

Right?

Yep.

She decided.

Soon—*surely*—she would be back home in New York with her sisters. Back where she belonged, and far away from a complicated man, and whatever mess he had dragged her into here. That's what would happen.

Ginevra unlocked the penthouse and opened the door to the dark entry. She couldn't remember if Corrado had turned off the lights when they left, or not. Probably, though. Kicking off the heels and pulling down the wet straps of the dress around her arms, she tried to remember where the light switch was for the damn entry.

Then, the lights came on.

All at once.

She spun around fast, letting go of the straps of her dress as she froze in place at the sight of a stranger leaning against the wall at the very end of the hallway. A *man*, actually. His shaggy, dark hair hung over his eyes, and yet even through the dark strands, she could still see the stormy blue eyeing her from the side.

His lips, the lower fuller than the top, stayed affixed in a grim line as he chewed on something in his mouth—gum, maybe? Her gaze traveled over the golden hoops in his nose, his steel cut jaw line, and the few days' worth of facial hair covering his cheeks and throat. Even under the leather jacket he wore, and the black jeans that molded to his thighs and ass, she could plainly see he was fit by the way the material of his white T-shirt stretched across the bands of muscle that made up his chest.

He leaned against the wall like he didn't have a care in the world, his black, scuffed combat boots hooked one over the other, despite the fact she could clearly see the tension wrapping his body. Like he was forcing himself to stay right there, and not come any closer.

My God.

He was *devastating*.

That was the first and only word to come to her mind.

Devastating.

A lot like Corrado, really. That first look at him had made her silent, and took away her breath, too. This was no different.

Except she didn't *know* this man, and why in the hell was he here?

"Who are you?" she asked, her voice faint.

The man smiled.

Just a *ghost* of one, though.

He lifted his head a bit, giving her a better view of the planes that made up his handsome face, and the war that raged in his stare. "Alessio Sorrento—I like Les, though."

Les.

That text …

"But it ain't about me, is it?" Alessio asked, his voice a deep bass that came off both edgy and dark. "Lately, it's been all about *you*, Ginevra."

How did he know her name?

She wondered …

No one had said either way—man or woman, they didn't *say* who the other person was for Corrado. She hadn't assumed, but a part of her just figured it was a woman because that was the default. Not that she cared either way who someone loved or fucked behind closed doors. That was their business, and as long as people were happy, what did it matter?

But *now*, staring at this man, and the way he looked at

her like he was both curious, but he wished she would drop dead on the fucking spot, too, made her think …

This was him.

This man was Corrado's … person. They were a *them* before Ginevra ever came into the picture, clearly. Those shoes with different sizes on the rack when she first arrived at the penthouse; the different style jackets, like they belonged to entirely different personalities; the offhanded remarks Corrado made without realizing it—*and we use it*, he'd said —and then ignored when she questioned him; or even his hesitations when he nearly slipped up like telling her the master bedroom was his, but he'd almost said something different.

She knew now.

It meant these two men had been a thing for a while. She was in the middle. He came *before* her. She understood what she had missed.

It hurt worse because of it.

"Yeah, it's been all about you, huh?" Alessio smirked, adding lower, "And I'm here to find out why that is."

CHAPTER 26
ALESSIO

Above all things, at the end of the day when the sun went down, and he no longer had to pretend like he gave a shit, Alessio was still an asshole. Oh, he had people he cared about —those he *loved*, sure. He usually cared to make an attempt with those people not to be an asshole, but most others were fair game.

And even those he cared for, if he were being honest, weren't special exceptions to the rules when it came right down to it. When things began to feel like they were falling apart around Alessio, or like his life was spiraling out of control ... that asshole side of him liked to make an appearance.

It became *worse*.

Like now.

The fact that he was an asshole was the entire reason why he happened to be standing at the end of that hallway in their penthouse in Toronto. It was every single fucking reason why he had come here to do this tonight.

Near the front door, the pretty thing he'd likely scared the wits out of—*whoops*—made a sound that drew his gaze to her again. And *shit*, she was pretty. Disregarding the rest of this shit that pissed him off about her, and her presence here, Ginevra was a beautiful thing.

He wasn't *at all* surprised she managed to catch Corrado's eye. He always did have a taste for pretty, delicate looking things when it came to women. Ones that looked innocent because he enjoyed finding all the parts of them that were far from it.

Ginevra was certainly *that*.

Pretty, that was.

Okay, he might have been being an asshole again. Pretty was a bit … *nice*. If he were being honest, he would say that he understood entirely why she caught Corrado's eye because Alessio couldn't stop his gaze from drinking her in from where he stood ten feet away, either.

Like the way that silk gray dress, wet from the rain pouring down outside, had molded itself to her body. Silk was *un-fucking-forgiving* against a body. Instead of accentuating beauty, it highlighted every single goddamn flaw it could, but especially when it was *that* tight. Not on her, though.

Because he couldn't find a flaw.

He couldn't find something to dislike in the shape of her hips, or the length of her legs, her skin golden with a sheen from the rain, but olive-toned, too. Her breasts, emphasized by the beige lace of the bra cups peeking out from the low-cut front of the dress, lifted and fell quickly with her breaths, which only drew his gaze higher. To the delicate column of her throat, tense with her nerves, and making that diamond choker glitter as it caught the light.

And her face.

Her face.

Small featured, wide eyes, stained-red lips, and *beautiful*.

Yeah, it was no fucking wonder to him why this woman had caught his lover's eye. Because frankly, it took very little effort for her to make Alessio pay attention to the way she looked, too. Although, physical beauty was one thing.

Anyone could be beautiful.

Lots of people were.

What was it about her that made Ginevra different?

That was his question.

He'd thought, maybe stupidly, that he would come here and find out *why* Corrado had been so willing to lie to Alessio for nothing more than a woman—if he wanted a woman, there were thousands of them all around him, he could go *find one.*

What was it about this woman?

Why lie for this woman?

And that just pissed him off.

A lot more.

"Where is Corrado?" Ginevra asked.

Her voice was musical, really. Soft, and light. Like a melody floating through the air to reach his spot down the hall. He could hear the nerves working in her tone, too, and yet, she still managed to sound polite.

Why was she being polite?

If she knew who *he* was—did she even know?—then she would have no reason to be nice. It made him wonder if Alessio wasn't the only person Corrado had been lying to lately. It wouldn't be such a stretch, all things considered.

"Well?" Ginevra demanded.

Okay, there went her politeness.

Alessio, who hadn't moved from his spot against the wall since she opened the penthouse door, tipped his head up a bit. He'd not *really* met her stare since she found him standing there. Oh, he looked her way, and she looked his. He took his time to check out what made up the woman that his lover seemed determined to hide from him, and he hadn't missed the way she looked him over, either.

Still …

He hadn't met her gaze.

Not until now.

Through the longer strands of his shaggy hair, he met

Ginevra's stare head-on, unfazed and calm on the outside. He wanted her to see *that*—needed her to think that despite her presence here, he was fine.

Even if he was anything but.

He felt like a war, really.

She wouldn't know it.

Ginevra stilled in place, her milk chocolate-colored eyes widening. *No*, she didn't know her presence put him on edge, but he absolutely could see what his company did to her. Not that the beautiful woman wanted him to know, he thought, because she was quick to clench one hand tightly around the clutch she held, and her other formed a fist at her side. That trembling in her shoulders stopped, and she tipped her chin up.

Staring right back at him.

Standing tall.

As beautiful as ever.

God.

Any other fucking time—*any other fucking woman*—and he would have really appreciated that spirit. That determination he found in her gaze, hell yeah, he would have liked it, and urged her on to show him more.

He loved when people surprised him.

Not this woman, though.

Not right now.

"Are you going to answer me, or not?" Ginevra asked.

Fine.

But he was having fun here, that's all.

She didn't have to know that, right?

"Oh, I tricked him," Alessio said, grinning.

He tipped his head to the side a bit to watch her from that angle. He kept finding new things about her to stare at depending on the angle, and the direction at which he watched. Like now, he could see the way the side of her smooth, creamy throat worked as she chewed on her words, and held them back.

Come on, girl, say what you wanna say to me, I fucking dare you.

She had to know who he was.

Had to.

He just felt it in his bones.

Good.

Because he wanted her to.

She'd came into this place after him; she came here when he'd already been here. His thing—his *person*—was not for her. And he wasn't going to hand it over; he would not give Corrado to anyone. They would have to take him from Alessio first.

"I tricked him," Alessio said again, shrugging one leather-covered shoulder. "See, I knew he wouldn't give me five minutes alone with you when, up until now, he seemed determined to keep you from me, for whatever reason."

"I thought he was with *you* tonight." Ginevra's fingers drummed against the side of her clutch, and she glanced away from him. All those nerves—he saw it all and took them for what they were. "I saw the message you sent—that was you, right?"

"That's how I tricked him."

He laughed.

Ginevra simply stared.

Alessio rolled his eyes, getting bored now. "See, if I got him away from *you* ... then I wouldn't have to worry about him being over my shoulder when I came up here to find what I was looking for."

But, oh, he certainly planned to have a conversation with Corrado, and *very* soon. He suspected the man was realizing, if he hadn't already, that Alessio was not, in fact, at a bar two blocks away from this penthouse that he and

Corrado frequented together to play pool when they were in the city.

It wouldn't take much for Corrado to put two and two together—it always made four, after all. He'd be on his way back to this penthouse soon, if he wasn't already, and then Alessio would move into the second thing he came here for.

Dealing with Corrado.

Letting him know he *knew*.

Simple, really.

"And did you?" Ginevra asked softly.

There was something about her lips that kept drawing his gaze in. The bottom lip was a bit fuller than the bottom, making her look as though her mouth was set into a sweet pout. Stained red from whatever lipstick she had been wearing earlier in the evening, the color took away the innocence her mouth might held and made him think of *dangerous* things.

Like how one might smudge what remained of the stain, or how it got that way to begin with. Was it the rain? Her tongue wiping at the line of her lips? *Corrado,* even? Had he kissed it off her—*licked* it off her?

All things Alessio didn't need to wonder.

Yet, he still did.

"Well, *did you*?" Ginevra asked.

"Did I, what?"

"Find what you were looking for here."

How simple that question felt.

The answer was far from easy, though.

Because *no*.

No, he had not found what he was looking for. Some crazy part of him thought he would come here, lay eyes on this woman, and just *know* what it was about her that had Corrado willing to hide her. Whatever it was about her that made his lover prepared to throw away the trust that Alessio gave to no one.

He still didn't know.

It pissed him off.

Pushing away from the wall, Alessio moved down the hallway faster than Ginevra could react to his oncoming form. She took a step back, though, but it was too late because he'd already come close enough to her that his proximity alone allowed him two things.

To see the darker brown flecks in the lighter tawny irises of her eyes. To see the splattering of freckles on the edges of her cheeks, closer to her hairline. To back her against the wall as she stared up at him.

And to feel the warmth of her body.

He was entirely *too* close.

Alessio still didn't back up.

"No," he said simply, "I haven't found it yet."

"Sorry to waste your time, then."

Alessio arched a brow, his teeth grinding against the piece of mint gum that had, for the most part, kept him calm over the last hour while he waited. "It's fine, no worries."

"Really? Because I don't think it is, Alessio. Fine, I mean."

Her voice?

Still musical.

Not that it mattered.

"Oh, it's definitely *not* fine," he replied, "but I won't be leaving until it is."

Ginevra swallowed audibly, and that tremor danced over the line of her smooth shoulders again. Still damp from the rain, and naked now, as she'd pulled the straps of the silk dress down over her arms when she thought she was alone … he noticed entirely too much about this woman.

But he blamed Corrado for that, too.

This *obsession*.

He just wanted to know why.

Why *her*.

Why?

Alessio took a step away from Ginevra when he heard the knob on the penthouse door begin to turn. He glanced to the side, a grin curving his lips as it opened, and the man of the hour finally arrived.

Corrado looked to him first when he stepped inside, and then he checked on Ginevra, too. He didn't seem surprised to find Alessio in the penthouse, but more like he expected it. No one was better acquainted with the asshole in Alessio than Corrado, frankly.

Quietly, Corrado said, "We should talk, yeah?"

Alessio winked. "You think?"

"Les—"

"Yeah, let's fucking *talk*, Corrado."

Time to really get this show started, then.

CHAPTER 27
CORRADO

"Where do you want to—"

"The office," Alessio said, taking two steps backward.

Further from Ginevra.

Corrado wasn't really worried on that. Alessio wasn't the type to get violent when he was feeling some kind of way. At least, not to *women*. Men, on the other hand, were an entirely different story.

Fair game, as Alessio would say.

"The office, then," Corrado said.

He tried to keep his tone calm, but it was harder than he thought it would be. Mostly because he'd figured out quickly that Alessio had fucked him over tonight, and that wasn't like him at all. The second he stepped into the penthouse and saw Alessio stepping back from Ginevra like he'd had her backed against the wall, well ... Corrado simply wanted to put some space between the two.

Make Alessio *think*.

Corrado needed a second, too.

"Yeah," Alessio muttered, shooting Corrado a look.

Just like that, the other man turned in the hallway, and walked away without as much as a look over his shoulder. Not that it made a difference. He could just *tell* ... Alessio wasn't happy, but honestly, neither was Corrado. This could have been done a hundred different ways, but he didn't have to come in like this, either. The tension was still far too thick in their air; Corrado could practically taste it, for fuck's sake.

Once Alessio rounded the corner at the end of the hallway, Corrado looked to Ginevra, but she stared at the floor between them. Like it was far more interesting than him, and maybe in that moment, it absolutely was to her.

Who was he to say?

Still, he needed to check …

"Are you okay?" he asked.

Ginevra nodded, her fingers tightening on the clutch in her grip. "Yeah, Corrado."

"You're sure?"

Her chin tipped up, and through her lashes, he saw the anger and pain staring back at him. It really showed through in the frown that marred her pretty lips, and the tightening in her jaw. *Jesus.* The girl was good at hiding it—no doubt about it, and he wouldn't deny her that truth. But fuck him, if it still didn't cut him deep to see that leveling on him.

He deserved it, though.

Corrado knew that.

All the hell that was about to come his way from two entirely different people … yeah, he earned every bit of it. He wasn't so stupid or selfish that he didn't recognize the fact Ginevra and Alessio were both due their thoughts about what he had done to them. And so, he planned to let them do whatever they needed so that he understood their feelings on it all.

Didn't he owe them that?

At least?

Corrado thought so.

"That's *him*, isn't it?" Ginevra asked, her voice barely breaking a murmur. She wouldn't look at him entirely, but she still watched him through her lashes. It was enough for Corrado. "The other person, I mean."

He nodded. "It is. And I know you don't want to hear it right now, but I'm so—"

"You're right, I don't want to hear it."

"All right." He gestured at the hallway, knowing Alessio was likely already waiting for him in the office. "I have to take care of that, but you're ... it's been a long night, Ginny. You should relax."

She scoffed at his back when he passed. Corrado didn't acknowledge it.

Then, behind him, she said, "He's ..."

He hesitated in his next step. "What?"

"He's overwhelming," she whispered.

Corrado shot her a look over his shoulder and laughed bleakly. "I know."

Because where was the lie?

Alessio had always been overwhelming.

In every sense of the word.

Corrado found Alessio sitting on the edge of the desk, using the arm of a guest's chair to rest his foot on as he sliced through the top of a letter with his favorite pocket knife. He said nothing as Corrado stepped into the office and closed the door just enough that there was a crack to see out into the hallway.

Mostly because he wanted to watch for Ginevra.

All the while, Alessio said nothing. He pulled the bill out of the envelope that he opened, looked it over, and then tossed it aside. Just as quickly, he picked up another from the pile, clicked his tongue as he slid the knife under the paper, and opened it, too.

"That's what you want to do right now?"

"Why not?" Alessio asked, reading over the paper in his

hands. "It's not like *you* care to look at the bills—they fucking sit in a pile."

Well, he wasn't *wrong* …

Corrado simply preferred to let Alessio do those types of things because he found it mundane and fucking boring.

"The maid handles that here," Corrado said. "Because someone needs to keep up on it when we're not around, Les."

"Right, right."

As fast as the bill had been in Alessio's hand, it too was tossed to the desk. Discarded, and forgotten in a blink when his gaze turned on Corrado standing in front of the door.

And there it is.

That fury.

The *sting* of it.

A war raged in Alessio's eyes, and Corrado didn't look away. He couldn't. Alessio was still owed that, after all, and Corrado would let him have it even if every second of it hurt him, too. That's what one did when they hurt someone they loved, or so he thought.

Not that he figured Alessio wanted to hear that right now.

"We're going to talk now, right?" Alessio asked. "*Talk*, Corrado, which is something we probably should have done, oh, what … about a month ago, or so?"

He straightened a bit, stuffing his hands into his pockets at the same time. "I—"

"No, no, no," the other man murmured quickly, stepping down from the desk in one fluid movement, like his entire body was made of water, and he moved like it, too. "No, I don't want to hear you *talk*, unless you're going to say something I want to hear."

Corrado eyed that knife in Alessio's hand. "You going to put that away, or …?"

That was a low blow.

Even Corrado knew it.

Alessio's jaw twitched, and he flipped the blade around in his palm without even looking at the weapon. "Fuck you. Like I would *ever*—"

"I didn't say you would. I asked if you were going to put it away."

Without a word, Alessio snapped the switchblade closed, and pocketed the weapon. He didn't acknowledge he did it other than to raise his brow at Corrado like he was saying, *better?*

"I made a trip to New York, yeah," Alessio said, taking one step closer to Corrado, but coming no further than that, "worried about *you*—because that's what I fucking do, Corrado. I worry about you. I think about *you*."

He sucked in a heavy breath but kept quiet. It wasn't like he needed to be told to shut his fucking mouth right now. He could tell what Alessio wanted, which was to get shit off his chest, and *then* maybe he'd be willing to let Corrado talk.

But who knew for sure?

"And what do you do, huh?" Alessio asked.

"I fucked up."

"*Right.*" Alessio glanced away, staring out the one bay window in the office that currently overlooked a darkening sky and a city that was still awake. "Do you wanna know why I picked this room?"

"Because you always liked it."

"Not even close."

"Then, why?"

"Because there's only one goddamn room in this penthouse that you'll sleep in, and if you're *fucking* her, that's where you're doing it, Corrado."

He didn't reply.

Alessio's gaze cut back to him fast. "You won't even deny it, then?"

"Would you believe me if I did?"

"What—"

"I haven't slept with her," Corrado interjected fast. *That*, he wanted clear. "Yeah, I crossed a line. Yeah, I broke those fucking rules. And *yeah*, I got too close, and I didn't let you know from the start like I should have, but I didn't fuck her."

Alessio made a noise under his breath.

Dark.

And oh, so painful.

It cut Corrado deep. That one sound could have been a knife driving into his chest because he *felt* that. He felt that betrayal swimming in Alessio's mind, and heart. Felt it like nothing else, but it was done now.

He couldn't change it now.

"But you want to," Alessio said. "You've *wanted* to."

"Les—"

"Fuck you, don't give me bullshit, Corrado. Not right now. You give me the truth you should have given me a month ago, or you say *nothing*."

If one was unlucky enough to see a snake right before it struck, they would know the serpent liked to coil its body tightly, saving all its energy, and letting the power of its muscles do the work before it attacked. And that was Alessio in that moment—coiled, prepping, *almost* ready to come at him, and barely holding back.

"Why not?" Alessio asked, his head turned just a bit so he could watch Corrado from the side. "You wanted to fuck her—still do, I bet—so why not do it? Just do it, right?"

He wanted to speak.

Wanted to tell Alessio exactly why.

His throat tightened, though, making the words hard to get out. To his companion, it only made it seem like Corrado was holding back, something that had always hit a raw nerve with Alessio when it came to them.

"Why the fuck not, huh?" Alessio demanded, blue eyes blazing. "Because the rest didn't matter—you didn't care to tell me anything else, so why not just *do it*."

"Because I couldn't."

"That's a coward's answer."

"It's the truth," Corrado murmured, "and I know I should have told you, but it wasn't that simple, Les. I fucked up, *yes*, but it wasn't as easy as you're thinking. I didn't purposely decide to do this, or do it to you, okay, I—"

In a blink, Alessio closed the distance between them. Another person, no doubt, would have backed up at the sight of Alessio coming at them looking like he did right then. Dressed in black, leather and combat boots, his expression darkened from his rage.

But not Corrado.

No.

He stayed right where he was, letting Alessio get as close as he fucking could, until their chests touched, and they were eye-to-eye. Stormy blue irises could have nailed him to the floor, but he still wouldn't have moved.

"No?" Alessio asked, leaning in closer until their mouths were a breath apart. "*No*, Corrado? You didn't purposely do this, huh? You didn't *purposely* decide not to tell me that you were watching a woman, that you had something going on here I should have known about because that had *always* been our way? You really wanna say you didn't do that knowing what you were doing?"

Alessio pointed a finger at him, but didn't touch Corrado with it, and lost all his sense of decorum at the same goddamn time. His next words came *loud*, and sharp, because he clearly wanted Corrado to hear and feel every single one of them.

"I knew shit was up, and I went looking for it, Corrado.

And I'm so fucking glad I found it before you could tell me, right, because I don't think you would have."

"I was going to tell you."

"When, tonight? A little late, yeah?"

Corrado shook his head as Alessio took a step back. "If you'd just let me talk—"

"I'm *sick* of hearing you talk," Alessio returned, "because you don't say anything new, and you certainly don't tell me what I want to hear anymore. You've been saying the same shit to me for the last five years, so why would this be any different?"

"Stop it," Corrado said lowly, his fists clenching at his sides. "It's one thing to be pissed about this, but it's another to act like this has been something that's happened time and time again. Because it's *not*. It's not, Les. And I didn't mean for it to happen this time. She wasn't supposed to *be* anything. She was just a fucking job!"

"A *job*, right. That's fucking rich." Alessio let out a laugh, bitter and aching, and moved closer to Corrado again. This time, Alessio coming forward forced him back a bit until his side hit the edge of the opened door and made the crack wider so that both of them were almost standing in the doorway. "If you had wanted to fuck her, all you had to do was tell me. It's the one and only thing I've always asked from this, but you couldn't even give me that. I shouldn't be surprised."

"And what in the hell does that mean?"

Alessio shrugged. "At the end of the day, I'll always be the second choice. To everything else, I come second, and you just made sure to really let me know here."

No.

If it were possible for a heart to split in two from nothing more than someone's words and their pain, then that's what Corrado's did. He wished Alessio could see himself through

Corrado's eyes. He wasn't so good at this thing they had, and he screwed up, but that didn't change what they were at the end of the day.

It didn't change what he felt.

Alessio couldn't be his second choice when he had already been his first.

"That's untrue," Corrado said, refusing to back down on that. *Ever*. "Don't say that, because you know it's not true, Les."

"I know you made it clear here. With *her*, yeah, you made it look like fucking crystal to me, Corrado. I see it far too well."

"You don't know any—"

"I know enough!"

"You won't let me *talk*!"

"I told you why that is. I don't care to hear what you have to say." Alessio took one step back from him, but it still wasn't enough. A part of Corrado wanted the room to breathe, but another part of him wanted this man as close as he could get him. That heartache was still there, bright and clear, and vicious. Ready to *hurt*. "I came here looking for something tonight, but I haven't found it. I don't know if I will, or if I even want to anymore."

Corrado let out a shaky exhale. "Don't say that; you don't mean that."

Alessio rushed forward, pressed against him, and stared him down *again*. Teeth clenched, body coiled, and emotions ready to go to war.

Corrado didn't move an inch. "If all you wanted to do was *fuck her*, then you could have told me, but that's the thing, isn't it? That's not all you want from her—that's not all you want to do with her. And that's why you didn't tell me about her, Corrado. Just *say it*."

"I won't deny that, but it's more than that, too."

A nod answered him back, but Alessio wasn't hearing him. He was too fucking mad, and ready to strike out because of it. That was the thing about him—once he reached his point of no return, it was over. He couldn't be reached.

Corrado simply had to weather the storm.

And what a fucking *hurricane* Alessio could be.

Violent, destructive, and raw. Unforgiving, willing to devastate, and unrelenting as he tore whatever was in his way apart piece by fucking piece. Even if it meant tearing apart the thing that he loved while he did it. Anyone caught in his path when he was like this would be lucky to survive, and if they did, they certainly wouldn't come out of it the same as they went into it.

Corrado was not an exception to that rule, but he *earned* this. Alessio was due this. So, he let him have it. Corrado let him do what he needed. Even if it killed him by the time his lover was done.

It wasn't about Ginevra, really. It wasn't that Corrado found a woman he was attracted to, or felt something for. It was the betrayal in it—the trust Alessio never gave to anyone, but that he willingly handed to Corrado.

It was *that*, and not the rest, even if Alessio used everything else as a backdrop to spell it out for Corrado. He'd always been good at reading between the lines, and he didn't need help now to see it written like black ink on white paper. Alessio was the paper. His eyes, his words, and his anguish became the ink.

"I'm so glad you found *something* in someone else," Alessio murmured, that betrayal coating every word and each breath he took, "because God fucking knows you never found what you wanted in me."

Fuck him for saying that.

It wasn't even close to being true.

Corrado had *everything* he wanted in Alessio—he'd found things he never knew he needed in the man looking like he was ready to burn him to the ground right where he stood. And he loved him more for it, too.

That's what made this hurt worse.

Because he couldn't explain why this happened at all. He would never be able to explain Ginevra, the things he felt for her, or why it happened at all … not when he already had what he wanted and needed from Alessio.

Not that it mattered.

Corrado had crossed Alessio's one line.

It was already too late.

"So, is that what you need to do, then?" Alessio asked, dragging Corrado from his thoughts as lightening streaked across the sky in the window behind him. "You want to fuck her, Corrado? Then *fuck her*. Have her."

CHAPTER 28
GINEVRA

"You want to fuck her, Corrado? Then *fuck her*. Have her." Alessio's bitter laughter filtered down the hall to Ginevra's spot where she leaned with her shoulders against the wall while she stared down to the dimly lit office. She could see them in the doorway, standing too close, both seeming ready to strike out at one another. "That's our deal, right? I just have to know about it, and now I do. So, you want her, now I know, and you can have her."

"Les, it's not like—"

"Not *what*, like I think it is?" Even if Ginevra were able to see more of Alessio's face in the shadows of the office, she bet he would be sporting a sneer. It couldn't be missed in his tone. "It's exactly like what I think it is, and you can't deny it."

"I don't want to deny it, but that doesn't change *us*, either."

"Us?" Alessio scoffed. "*Us?*"

"That's what I said, wasn't it?"

"What is that?"

Ginevra lifted her gaze again to watch the scene playing out down the hall. She had no business standing there, and it certainly wasn't her place to watch this whole thing play out like she was a fly on the wall.

And still, she couldn't move.

She was compelled to stay.

The two men stood toe-to-toe in the doorway of the office, their bodies angled toward one another like one was waiting for the other to strike, but neither knew which one would do it first. She didn't even think they realized their fight had been this loud, or that it had almost moved entirely out into the hallway.

"What is *what?*" Corrado snapped.

"Us—what is that, huh? Because you haven't known, or you sure as shit didn't wanna say before, so let's not pretend like you do now."

"Low blow, Les. That's a low fucking blow, even for you. You're mad, so you're saying shit you don't mean because that's how you deal. And I get that, but that's low. You're pissed—so *fine.* I crossed a line—*yeah.* None of those things are untrue, but it doesn't change what this has always been to me."

"But all of them mean one fucking thing for me, Corrado."

"Stop saying that."

"What, you don't like having your bullshit thrown at your feet for you to unpack?"

"That's not it at all. It doesn't matter how many times you say it, it won't make it true."

"Then, what? Go on, tell me. I'll wait. *Surprise me* for once, please. I've had five damn years doing this with you, so what's one more night, right?"

"*Stop it.* This doesn't prove shit about us, or some complex you've had about what we've been for the last five fucking years," Corrado said, his tone roughening enough to make Ginevra startle against the wall. She looked down their way just in time to see Corrado step forward fast enough to force Alessio back a step, making the man press against the doorjamb. "It doesn't change the fact that I love—"

Corrado didn't get to finish his sentence before the

inevitable happened. She'd been watching it from the time they came into her view—the way both of them seemed like one was going to strike out at the other. Only, Alessio didn't strike out the way Ginevra thought he would.

This all felt *violent*.

Anger overflowing.

Pain spilling out in words.

And yet, Alessio struck out at Corrado with affection. If one could call the kiss that he leveled on Corrado as *affectionate*. Ginevra didn't know if she would, not considering the force of the kiss pushed Corrado back until he was the one with his spine against the doorjamb, and a hand was at his throat.

She heard Corrado hitting the wall, saw the way Alessio's lips dragged against his, fingers curling into a suit jacket, and another fisting into leather. Somehow, though she didn't think there was any room left between them, the men moved closer. Their kiss wasn't soft or *easy*. Certainly not slow, or sweet.

Vicious, maybe.

Bruising, definitely.

And oh, so painful.

Painful, she thought, because one of them seemed to be fighting to leave something behind while the other was refusing to let go.

Ginevra sucked in a sharp breath, her heart aching as a whisper of heat shot through her body at the same time. It would be impossible for someone to see that sight, those beautifully haunted men showing love in their hurt, and not feel something for it. She simply didn't think she *should* feel something for it.

This was not the time for that. God knew, she had her own reasons to be mad here, and that was enough to make her want to slip out of the hallway and leave those two to their … *mess.*

Because fuck, she could see it was a mess. Somehow, she'd been put in the middle.

But still …

She couldn't look away.

This wasn't for her to see. Their moment—their *fight.* None of it was for her, even if it had been brought on because of her. She didn't have any business being privy to something that felt *far* bigger than her.

Because wasn't that much obvious?

It wasn't *just* her.

Alessio pulled away first, his face still darkened by the shadows, but that didn't stop Ginevra from noticing the way his jaw trembled when murmured, "*Don't,* Corrado."

Corrado dragged in a ragged breath. "Les—"

"Don't you fucking *dare* say that to me," he interjected, swift and harsh, his voice straining with every word. "Not right now, not after everything and all this time … don't you dare do that to me. You never wanted to do it before, so you don't get to do it tonight. You don't get to use it *now.* You don't get the right to use those words when you did *this,* too."

"I'm not trying to say it to use it like a weapon—"

"You *are* because you know what it means."

Corrado released a rough sound that echoed down the quiet hallway. "Let me explain, please."

"Except you can't, can you?"

"Or you don't really want me to, Les."

Alessio nodded. "Don't do that, either."

"If you're going to throw my shit at me, then at least look at your own."

"Fuck you, Corrado."

As fast as Alessio had moved to corner Corrado, he

stepped away, moving into the hallway with his back facing Ginevra. Although, she didn't think he knew she was there. She *should* move—now would be the right time to do exactly that—but she couldn't. Her feet might as well have been cemented to the floor.

Stupid, foolish girl.

"Just … stay," Corrado said, "calm down, and then maybe we can talk without *this*. It doesn't have to be like this."

"Nah, I wouldn't want to intrude, you know?"

Alessio said that, and the same time, tipped his head to the side. Ginevra stilled against the wall, her eyes growing wide when the man pointedly looked her way. He'd known the whole time she was standing there, it seemed.

He didn't appear bothered by it.

Corrado sighed, his stare following Alessio's path until it landed on her. Still, he said nothing, and he didn't move when Alessio turned around, and headed down the hallway. He met her gaze, and held it even as he came closer, and didn't drop it as he passed.

"You really found a mess here, girl, huh?" Alessio asked her.

Ginevra looked away.

He wasn't wrong.

Silence echoed in the penthouse long after the slamming of the front door reached the far hallway. The hardwood floor suddenly became a hell of a lot more interesting to her, because it was easier than watching Corrado drag the pad of his thumb over his bottom lip.

Like he was still feeling that kiss.

Too many things warred in her mind, and her heart. All the things she'd clearly missed, and others that still didn't make sense. Oh, she had questions that needed and deserved an answer, sure, but some of them probably weren't her place to ask.

She'd been lied to.

She'd been hurt, too.

And still, all she could think to ask in that moment was, "You didn't think you should tell me about him?"

A hoarse sound left Corrado, but she continued her perusal of the floor. It was still easier than looking at him when she wasn't even sure how she felt right then.

"You should have told me," she whispered. "Maybe then, this wouldn't have happened."

He laughed, then.

Hard, loud, and *bitter*.

God, so dark.

Like someone ripped it out of him.

Ginevra looked up to find him staring at her in that way again. So intense, and pensive.

"You think that would have changed what happened here tonight?" he asked, shaking his head as he turned to go back into the office. Over his shoulder, he added, "In case you didn't figure it out, *this* was a long time coming. This was years in the making—you just happened to help it along."

"You still could have—"

"I should have done a lot of things, Ginevra. I don't need someone else to point it out to me, and I certainly don't expect you to understand me, or him, or this."

Ouch.

That hurt.

"Or is it because I'm just a job to you, Corrado?"

His next step into the office hesitated, his shoulders tensing before they visibly dropped, the same way his head dipped down, too.

Did that hurt him?

Good.

He should know how she felt, too.

She didn't give him the chance to respond before her feet finally decided to start working again, and she slipped down the hall out of sight.

There, she could hurt.

And he wouldn't see.

CHAPTER 29
CORRADO

"And how long has it been since you had contact with him?"

Corrado's molars ached from how hard he continued clenching his jaw through this entire fucking conversation. How Cree was even able to understand half of what Corrado said to him was a goddamn mystery.

Better Cree than Dare, though.

Dare would tell Corrado he was a fucking asshole, didn't deserve Alessio—he wouldn't be wrong—and then he'd likely refuse to help him, or try to pull information on Les's possible whereabouts. All the while, he'd make sure Corrado understood every single bit of this was his fault, and again, he wouldn't be *wrong* ... but it wouldn't solve the problem of finding Alessio.

"Corrado?" Cree asked.

"A week," he said quietly, pacing the length of the office as he spoke, passing rows of books and the large window, and then coming back again. "It's been a week since he showed up here, and then he left. He won't pick up calls, doesn't answer texts ... I just want to make sure he's good, you know? I know Dare has access to his tracker, but I didn't think I should call him."

Cree released a sardonic laugh. "*No*, I promise you, that would have been a very bad thing to do. For you, not for Les."

Right.

He didn't need to be told.

Dare didn't have children, and as far as Corrado always understood, Alessio filled that place for the man. He protected Alessio far more than anyone realized, and not for one second did Corrado think that his relationship or love for Les would make a difference to Dare at the end of the day.

"I can't go into the tracker data without alerting Dare," Cree said, "and I'm going to assume you don't want me to do that."

"I just … I don't know if he's okay."

Because this worried Corrado, not that he had any fucking business worrying about Alessio at all. If the man wanted to fuck off somewhere, then he was due that. If he needed to take time away and figure out this shit, then it wasn't Corrado's place to deny him that.

And he *wasn't*.

But he didn't think that was it, either. He figured Alessio was doing this *to* him because that's what he did when he couldn't deal with shit. After all, this wasn't the first time Alessio had gone off the radar when things caught up to him. Usually, he made sure at least *someone* knew where he was, or what he was doing, but not all the time. Sometimes, he hid away purposely, made sure *no one* could find him, if possible, and when he was good and ready, then he would come back.

Only when he was ready.

Corrado didn't know if this was the same, though. That's what bothered him the most. That's where his concern came into play because how in the fuck was he supposed to fix this between them if he didn't even know whether or not Alessio was going to come *back?*

"Maybe …" Cree trailed off.

"What?"

"Alessio always seems *one* way to everyone else looking at

him," Cree murmured, "but you know in his mind, he's different. He's always been that way. There are very few things he holds close, Corrado, but if someone tried to hurt those things, well ..."

"He would slaughter a city for them."

"Exactly."

"But someone didn't hurt *me*, Cree, I hurt—"

"Him," Cree interjected. "I figured that much out. And so, what we're learning now about Alessio, because I don't think he's ever had to handle this before, is that when the thing he loves hurts him, well, he does the opposite."

"What does that mean?"

"He wants to slaughter *you*."

Corrado stiffened, coming to a stop in front of the window. The late July sky was cloudy, and dreary. A mix of wetness, and heat had made a fog sit around the tops of the buildings surrounding his. It felt appropriate for his life right now.

Confusing.

Suffocating.

Messy.

Horrible.

"But he can't hurt things he loves, because he has so few of those, and he knows what it's like to be hurt by the things that are supposed to love him," Cree continued on like Corrado was actively conversing back with him. "Go back to his parents, his abandonment ... it's really not hard to put it together, Corrado."

"Well, it is for *me*."

"Yes, because despite what you may think, and what everyone else likes to say about you and Alessio being shadows—or extensions—of the other, you are both actually *very* different people. Two people who lived entirely different lives and see things like love and loyalty and bonds in varying ways."

"So, what you're trying to tell me is that—"

"He's staying away because he doesn't want to hurt you right now, and if he's too close … he might do just that. He can't trust himself, so he needs some time. All you can do is give it to him Corrado."

"Huh."

Didn't that mean this wasn't done, then?

It wasn't *over?*

Corrado thought so because Alessio wasn't the type to play games. If he was done, and he wanted this to be finished between them, then he would have made that clear. He wouldn't have disappeared for an entire week like this, he simply would have *said.*

He just hadn't come back yet.

Eventually, he would.

Corrado still didn't like it, though, because it put him on edge. He didn't know if Alessio was okay—probably not, in some ways—and he couldn't stand this heavy feeling pressing down on his chest that only seemed to grow day after day.

Cree cleared his throat. "I pulled the aliases I could and did a quick check. Nothing came up on any of the ones he uses, so he must be using one I don't know about. I know you only want to be assured he's okay, but I won't check his tracker. For one, because of Dare, and it's best he stays out of this until the two of you figure out this … problem for yourselves. And for two, because Alessio is allowed his privacy, even if I was willing to deal with Dare when I checked the tracker. Which I'm *not*," he added in a grunt about Dare, continuing on with, "But allow Alessio his privacy, Corrado."

"Yeah, okay."

"You don't sound like it is."

Because it wasn't.

He was fucking *breaking apart at the seams*.

Corrado wasn't good at this. He didn't do *this*. And if this shit was what heartache was, well, fuck that, he didn't like it at all. It felt like his entire world had come to a stop, and yet, all he needed to do was look outside the office window to see … no, in fact, everyone else's world was still turning.

But his?

His was at a standstill, gone somewhere out there, away from him, and it was all his fault. He had no one to blame for this but himself.

"And," Cree added, bringing Corrado back to the conversation at hand, "if I understand the situation properly … the young woman is also still with you, yes?"

"It's … not like I have a choice."

For one, because Ginevra still couldn't go back to New York. And for two, because if Corrado were being honest, he had unfinished business with her at the end of the day. The feelings he had for Ginevra did not negate or change the way he felt for Alessio. But that worked both ways, too. The thing he had with Les, and the last five years they spent together, didn't change or negate the situation he found himself in with Ginevra, either.

"Don't be defensive," Cree said, "what happens behind your closed doors is not my business, which has *always* been our stance."

Our, he said.

Meaning Dare, too.

That was about as much as Cree gave regarding his relationship with Dare.

"I meant," the man continued, "that at the same time, did you consider Alessio might be also giving you what you want by staying away?"

"Excuse me?"

"The woman, Corrado."

"What—"

"While protecting you from him, he may also be giving you the chance to figure *that* out where he isn't imposing or making it more complicated. You were clearly in a situation with her before he came into the picture, and by stepping back, he's allowing you to continue it whichever way you want."

"I'm not sure that fucking her after all of this is going to make him come back, if that's—"

Cree made a harsh noise under his breath. "Never understood the appeal of vaginas myself, really."

Yep.

Great.

This conversation was just perfect, now.

"Could you not?" Corrado asked, pinching the bridge of his nose. "Make your point, or just hang up the phone."

"Oh, I'm going to do that soon, too."

Yeah, he figured.

"The point is," Cree added quickly, "sex is like every other physical thing for Alessio. Eating, sleeping, fighting, or working ... it's something he does because he either has to, he likes it, or it fills a need he has. He only gets emotional with sex when there are emotions attached to it—like with *you*. For her, he feels nothing. And he feels nothing about the fact you may or may not be having sex with her—that isn't his problem, is it?"

Cree wasn't wrong.

"No, I don't think that's his problem. More ... that I kept her presence and my interest from him. He asks for loyalty, that's all."

"Because *loyalty* is what is most important to Alessio, and to him, faithfulness doesn't fall into that category when that's not what he asked for, right? When sex is just *sex* to him ... then, you having sex with a woman is just that to him as well. He's complicated, Corrado, in ways you are not, although that may not be a bad thing."

"You know, it's almost disturbing how you understand people the way you do," Corrado muttered. "And with very little information to go on, too."

"Is it, though? I always thought it was like a gift."

"No, it's disturbing. Definitely fucking disturbing."

"To be fair, I have known Alessio since he was ten, and I have *a lot* to go on in order to make sense of his mess." Cree made a dismissive sniff. "And it being disturbing to you doesn't change the fact that I'm right here, and you know it."

"Well …"

"Hmm?"

"She's complicated to me, too," Corrado murmured. "Like him, but in different ways."

"I bet. That sounds like something you should figure out. If Alessio doesn't call me before he comes back to you, then you're to let me know he's safe. If he's gone for more than a couple of weeks beyond this, I want to know so I can make the choice to bring up the tracker data on his chip implant and let Dare decide what he wants to do."

"All right."

"Also."

"Yeah?"

"Stop fucking this up, Corrado. Despite how it used to be amusing to watch you stumble over your feelings and bury your issues so deep that even you can't find them, it's no longer funny. It's time you figured your bullshit out, and fix it. *All of it.*"

He blinked.

And Cree hung up the phone.

Fuck.

His frustration at *everything*—this week, Alessio, feeling like he was walking on eggshells, the conversation with Cree

—spilled over as he stared at the blank screen of the phone in his hand. Before he could think better of it, he whipped the phone to the side. It smacked the arm of the chaise in front of the large window, causing the back and battery to pop out of place, and fall onto the floor in three pieces.

Good.

Better that than him breaking it entirely.

Because that's what he wanted to do.

A quiet noise at the opposite side of the office had him spinning on the spot. There, he found Ginevra standing with a book in her hands, watching him. A million and one emotions raged through him at the sight of her there.

Annoyance.

Concern.

Amusement.

Indifference.

Lust.

Anger.

He didn't know how to deal with it all, but he went to the easiest to handle first, which just happened to be his annoyance. This girl had a bad habit of *spying*. Being places she shouldn't and standing there for way too long to listen. Like last week while she watched him with Alessio in this same fucking office.

"What are you doing?" he snapped.

Ginevra's brow knotted, and she glanced down before lifting the book. "I just … wanted to get another book, that's all. I thought it would be rude to interrupt."

"So, instead you eavesdrop?"

"It's not like you were being *quiet*. I could hear you all the way down in my room, thanks."

Corrado sucked in a shaky breath, willing his nerves to calm. He was snappy because of the shit happening around him, and sure, Ginevra didn't help in a lot of ways, but it wasn't *her* fault, either. She didn't choose to be here, but rather, she had been thrown right in the fucking middle of it.

This whole blow out between Alessio and him had been years in the making, always one step away from it happening. They hung on together by a thread because of literally everything else in their life except Ginevra.

Sure, she was a catalyst.

She pushed them over the edge.

And it still wasn't her fault ...

She didn't ask for this, but here she was. It also wasn't lost on him that there was an almost poetic irony to the fact Corrado had realized all the things he'd done wrong in his relationship, what he wanted with Alessio, and that he was ready to fix it ... at the same time he was looking this woman in the face, and feeling *something* he couldn't explain for her.

He wouldn't say he was in love with her.

But it was something.

The only other time he had felt that for anyone was Alessio, and so, he didn't know how to correlate this *thing* he felt to anything else.

Koi no yokan, he knew.

Except ... it only made this harder.

More difficult.

Compli-fucking-cated.

Ginevra hadn't asked for this.

Neither did Alessio.

Corrado didn't know what to do.

"I'm sorry," he murmured, "I'm just in a mood lately, is all. It's not your fault, and I shouldn't be short with you, Ginny."

She didn't smile.

She only shrugged.

"Doesn't even faze me now," she replied, "I think it makes sense, actually."

"I'm sorry?"

"Your *moods*. I thought it was just you before I knew about … him. But now I think it's really you *without* him."

Corrado's throat tightened, a lump forming there.

Why?

Because she was right.

Entirely.

What made it worse was the pain he could plainly see staring back from this woman as she stood just a few feet away from him, hugging that book close to her chest, and refusing to meet his gaze. Her stance, the aura she was giving off, it all screamed *one* thing.

She felt unwanted.

Discarded.

Secondary.

It only left him more torn.

"Do you think he'll come back?" she asked suddenly.

Corrado sighed and tipped his head to the side. "Eventually. It's a messy thing … me and him, I mean. We're not normal. Nothing about our relationship has ever been that, you know? We've had an open bedroom for years where women were concerned, but this was different. Things were different this time, and I can't expect you to understand it."

Ginevra nodded. "That's what you meant by loyalty, right? You weren't *unfaithful*. You were disloyal."

He stiffened, realizing just how much she had heard in his conversation with Cree.

She didn't give him the chance to reply before she added just as fast, "But you're right, Corrado, I don't understand because you never thought to tell me. You didn't give me the chance to *try* to understand. Instead, I get to be the person in the middle—the one *ruining* something for someone else. I get it, though, it's not about me for you, right? I'm not the one you want."

Instead of coming into the office to drop off her book, and get a new one, she set it on the stand next to the door. All the while, Corrado's heart *raged* because this woman didn't understand.

She didn't know anything at all.

Not about him.

Or Les.

And certainly not how he felt for *her*.

She deserved to know.

CHAPTER 30
GINEVRA

"You're wrong," Corrado said behind her. "You are *entirely* wrong, but I don't know how to explain this to you because it barely makes sense to me."

The last thing she needed to do was stand there and let that man justify his shitty actions to people he claimed to care about. And yet, something deep inside her soul came to wrap around her heart tightly, keeping her still in the doorway, even if her back was still turned to Corrado.

"Try, then," she whispered.

"Ginevra—"

"Try, Corrado. That's all you have to do. *Try* to explain it to me. You owe me that much, at least. I think you owe someone else a lot more, but he's not here, so for now … we can deal with this. Me and you. Try."

"There's never been a *you*, Ginny."

The crown molding on the hallway took her attention as she considered his words. "I don't understand what that means."

"Exactly, and neither do *we*. But there has never been a you—oh, there's been women, yeah. Women he and I shared, or women we found separately, but there has never been a *you*. Someone like you who I felt something for, someone I was interested in beyond taking to bed. The more I tried to ignore it, because I *did* try, the worse it became."

Corrado sighed loudly. "And that makes this complicated thing *more* fucking complicated than it already is with Alessio and I. That's not your fault. You didn't make us complicated or create this mess. We did it. The bigger problem is I don't think this can be simplified down to who I want here, and that's what you want me to give you. Isn't it?"

Twisting her hands together, she wanted to say no. It would be a lie, though, and Ginevra wasn't a liar. So, because she couldn't say no, she chose to say nothing at all. It was just easier, and God knew there was enough about this situation that was hard.

Her heart felt like ashes.

It'd been burning down all week.

In her chest, a constant inferno raged on, searing her from the inside out. She didn't know how to deal with it because it wasn't only *her* pain that was the cause of it. Instead, it was him, too. Corrado, and the things she saw him dealing with.

His struggle.

How he didn't sleep.

Constantly watching his phone.

Running himself dead on the treadmill at night.

Day after day, and night after night. It never ended. He struggled all the time because he was without something he needed and wanted, and she didn't want to see him in pain. That hurt *her*. She shouldn't feel like that at all, though, because he didn't deserve that.

Right?

She should have been pissed that instead of him wanting her, he was obsessing over someone who wasn't even there. She shouldn't want to give him anything—not her time, her attention, or even *this* here.

Except ... Corrado was right.

This was complicated.

Emotions were a tricky thing.

"It can't be simplified down to who I want," Corrado repeated, his voice a hell of a lot closer to her than it had been before, "because that's not the problem in the first place. I know exactly what I want here, but it's the rest that makes it a mess for everyone else."

She turned around slowly only to find he had come to stand right behind her in the doorway of the office. He was entirely too close to her, really, as she could feel the head of his body drifting to hers and smell that musky scent that he seemed to prefer. It only served to muddle up her mind and emotions more, but she chose to ignore it.

She was doing that a lot lately.

"But *why*?"

Corrado frowned. "Why, what?"

"Why can't it be that simple? Pick the person you want."

"And you want me to pick you."

Ginevra blinked. "I didn't say—"

"You don't have to. It's in everything you do. Everything you say, and the things you don't say. I see it in your eyes, and in your silence. But you're *good*, you know. In your heart, you're far too good. Better than me, that's for certain. Because in there," he said, pointing a finger at the spot over her chest where her heart was beating far too fast, "… in there, Ginny, you don't want to be selfish, so you say nothing, and you do nothing. That's who you are, but I can't say the same."

"Or," she countered, "it's because I think love is—"

"Love?" Corrado scoffed, grinning a little too sardonically for her liking. "Let me tell you what I know about *love,* yeah? I met a man once, and I knew from the start he was going to change everything for me."

Her eyes burned, but she refused to blink. Then, the tears that were starting to threaten her calm façade would fall, and he would know just how much this hurt. She didn't want to do that—didn't want to give him that.

"And he did," Corrado continued, "he changed everything. That's what I learned about love, but I wouldn't tell him that. I kept that for me, and it hurt him. And then I met *you.*"

Air pulled painfully through her lungs, but still, she stayed quiet.

What choice did she have?

Corrado stepped forward, closing the inch or two between them until the soft cotton of her sleepwear dragged against his slacks and button-down shirt with every breath she took. "So, here you are," he murmured, his head tilting down a bit as she stared up at him, "and I got *that* feeling again—that same fucking feeling like nothing was ever going to be the same because of you, but this time, I just ignored it altogether. Because that's what I do, Ginny. I ignore, I pretend … I just *don't.*"

"Corrado—"

"I take too much, I want too much, and I demand *too much* from people who only want to love me. And that's what you're standing here asking me to give to you. Do you understand that? You're asking for me—this *mess* who is selfish and ruins the people who love him—to give those same things to you."

Corrado shook his head, saying softly, "So, when you ask why I can't choose who I want … it's because I don't deserve what I already have, and I'm sorry that you seem to think you're the person who doesn't deserve me. You're wrong, and I'm so fucking sorry for *that.* I'm sorry for this, and nothing I do or say is ever going to make this better, but you should know that before anything else. I'm *sorry*. I'll say it every single day. Every hour on the fucking hour. It won't change a thing, though. It won't change it because I won't give you what you want. I can't … not the way you want me to."

"But …"

"Hmm?"

Ginevra stared hard at him, trying to find that lie. *Anything* to tell her that he was saying things he thought she wanted to hear, and not the truth. Instead, all she found was a stark, harsh reality staring back at her.

He wasn't lying.

It broke her heart more.

"I think the choice should be easy for you," she said softly.

Corrado laughed dryly, tipping his head away from hers as he asked, "And why is that?"

Wasn't it obvious?

"You don't love me—you love him."

She could see it in Corrado's eyes before the words even left his mouth that he wouldn't deny what she said—because it was the truth. And like her, this man seemed to make every effort not to lie when he could.

"But I could," he murmured.

Her heart stopped.

She swore it did.

"Pardon?"

"Love you," he clarified, "I could, and the longer you're near, the stronger it's going to be for me. This happened to me already—I did this once, I know how it ends, Ginevra."

Ginevra laughed, but it was far too faint. Hidden in her chest, that traitorous heart of hers pounded like it was going to explode. She liked what he said *too much*. And the way he was looking at her again?

Intense, and *knowing*.

Like he was so sure.

And daring her to challenge him.

She'd felt that, too. From the second she stepped into his vehicle in front of that church, she thought ... *everything was going to be different.* Maybe then, she'd assumed it was because of her sisters, and everything that was happening around her. The chaos, and the unknown waiting for her.

But was it?

Or was it him?

"You can't know that about love," she said, her words slipping out on a breath. "You *can't*, Corrado."

"Why not? I knew it about him, so why would you be any different? My life wasn't right before him, and then it was ... but now it's tilted again, confusing—wrong *again*. I keep thinking it's because of you, because nothing else changed except here you are, and I don't know what to do."

"I'm sorry."

Corrado gave her a look, a sad smile curving his lips up at the edges. "Why on earth are you apologizing to me?"

"Because love shouldn't be that complicated or painful. It should be everything but those things."

"It could be," he agrees. "I want it to be."

"And you want him," she whispered.

"I do."

"And me. You want me, too."

Corrado's agonized stare landed on her again, causing her heart to clench from the truth she found waiting there. "Don't you know?"

"I thought I did, but I think that I don't know anything at all."

"Yeah," he muttered, chuckling darkly, "I have a way of doing that to things I care about. Fucking up, I mean."

"Don't say that, Corrado."

It hurt her heart more.

For herself.

For him.

For a man who wasn't even here.

It all hurt.

"But haven't I?" he asked, his hand coming up so he could tuck the loose strands of her hair behind her ear with the softest touch. That was all it took, just his skin grazing against hers, and heat shot through her every single one of her nerves, making her air catch hard in her chest, and her heart skip beats all over again. "Haven't I made this mess?"

God.

This wasn't fair at all.

He didn't play fair.

The bigger problem was that she didn't think Corrado was trying to play games at all.

"I told you once before," Corrado said, his head drifting lower until his lips nearly touched hers with his next words, "I ruin beautiful things. I won't be the one who pushes you away, Ginevra, so if you want to save what is left of your heart, you need to be the one to do it for me."

If heartbreak was a picture, it would be his face.

Handsome.

Devastatingly so, really.

And tortured.

It killed her.

"You have to do it," he said again, "do you hear me?"

She did.

But …

"I can't," Ginevra breathed.

She couldn't say the words loudly.

Not yet.

They meant she was going to hurt worse. This would have to be enough.

Corrado didn't move an inch.

That was okay.

Ginevra didn't need him to move when he was this close —not when all she wanted to do was kiss him, *have him* … take him for herself. Even if that meant, all too soon, she was going to have to give him to someone else.

So, she did just that.

CHAPTER 31
CORRADO

Corrado was a selfish fuck.

How many times had he said that about himself already?

Too many.

Thing was, it didn't make it any less true. Because that's exactly what he was.

Selfish. Greedy. Immoral.

He wasn't all those things at once, sure. Or, he tried not to be. And yet, when Ginevra's lips found his in that office doorway, the same way Alessio's had done a week earlier, he realized he could, in fact, be all those things.

Selfish. And greedy.

So fucking *immoral.*

Because all he could think in those seconds was how goddamn *sinful* Ginevra's kiss felt, and how Alessio's had bruised beautifully, too. He felt her softness and felt Alessio's roughness. The memory warred in his mind, dragging him closer to a place he had tried so hard to stay away from. A place that, once there, he wouldn't be coming back.

He couldn't stop.

Ginevra seemed all too willing to let him do what he wanted, too, and so he did just that. Each kiss he landed to her lips, her jaw, and throat pushed them back a step. His hands were harsh, and demanding, yanking at her clothes and pulling them from her body as they moved down the hallway.

Those tainted emotions of his …

Those ruining hands of his …

She only asked for more.

He couldn't get enough.

Corrado didn't remember when they hit the bedroom, but he'd stripped her of her clothes except for the cotton panties hiding the last bit of her from him. His gaze dragged down her olive-toned skin, taking in collarbones he wanted to bite, and tits that heaved with every breath she took.

Her trembling fingers reached for him, undoing the buttons on his shirt, and working at his slacks as he reached for her. He let her feel the weight of his fingertips driving down her chest before he tweaked her nipples into hard peaks.

"Won't you fuck me?"

Corrado's stare snapped up, slamming into hers. "After."

"After what?"

God.

Who had this woman before him?

Did she not know that the best of sex happened when one *knew* a body they were touching? Didn't she know how good it would be when he learned all those spots and the things she needed to make her gasp, or moan, or *scream*?

"I have to learn," he murmured.

Ginevra smiled shyly. "What do you have to *learn*?"

"All of it, Ginny. All of you."

And he did, after she'd helped him from his clothes, and as her fingers closed around his hard cock to stroke him softly as he learned her body. He used his mouth on her shoulders, at the delicate column of her neck, and along her jaw line. And then his teeth and tongue followed the same path, drinking in every noise that slipped from her lips and the way her fingers would tighten or slow on his length when he found something she liked.

His hands worked, too.

Slipping under the waistband of her panties as his mouth sought hers to taste when he found the wetness between her thighs. *Fuck.* She was slick at the slit of her pussy, and hot to the touch. Silky, and needy, too.

"*Mmm*," Ginevra breathed against his cheek.

Corrado grinned.

She liked that.

Slow touches, his fingers sliding against her slit, but not entering her pussy. He let the side of his fingers come high enough to drag against her clit, too, taking in how her hips jerked, and a higher sound fell from her lips.

"What do you want, huh?"

"To come."

"Yeah?"

"So bad," she mumbled, turning her face against his so her mouth shuddered along the seam of his own. "*So fucking bad.*"

He'd have done it with his hands.

Fingers working her pussy.

Sure.

But he wanted a taste.

Hadn't he earned that?

Corrado thought so.

He dragged Ginevra's panties down with one yank of his hand against the gusset. Her soft gasp came high above him, because he was already down on his knees, and burying his face at the crevice of her thighs as he pushed her legs wider. He got that taste of her—heady and *tart.* Hot, too, as her arousal coated his tongue when he dragged it through her slit.

"What are you doing—*God.*"

All that noise.

He loved that noise.

His thumb worked at her clit as his tongue lapped at every drop her pussy gave him. There was nothing quite like the taste of a woman when she was ready to crash into an orgasm ... just like there was nothing that compared to the taste of man when he found his.

All it took was his tongue replacing his thumb at her clit for a beat or two before he sucked hard on the throbbing nub ... and she *flew*.

Wetness slicked her further.

Heat pulsed against his tongue.

But it was the sound of her crying his name into the dark bedroom that had his control snapping. He couldn't stand fast enough ... couldn't get her to that bed quickly enough to satisfy the need coursing through him.

And then she was.

On her back, thighs spread.

He found the condom he needed in the drawer beside the bed, tore it open, and slid latex down his cock as he climbed between her thighs. She was already reaching for him, one arm snaking around his back, and the other along his neck. Her fingers threaded into his hair as their lips crashed together again.

She didn't submit to his kiss, now.

She demanded more from it.

Corrado needed that, too.

If he had a vice, that was it.

His hand worked between their bodies until the head of his cock found her slit. He only flexed his hips forward enough that she'd get the tip of him, but not much else. He had to let her know he was there—feel her tense and clench around him before he took the rest of her, too.

Or rather, she took him.

All nine inches.

"Please," she gasped against his lips. "Please, *now*."

That did it.

His hips snapped forward, and he was buried deep in the next breath. His hand splayed wide to her side, holding tight and pulling her back into every pull and thrust of his body. She couldn't get enough, and he loved it.

All her *yeses*.

All those *pleases*.

Every single *oh*.

He drank them up.

Swallowed them whole.

Devoured them like he was starved.

"Fucking take me, baby," he said throatily in her ear, as their bodies moved faster. "God, you fucking love that, don't you?"

"*Yeah.*"

Her whisper was barely there at all. So fucking high, like she was *right there* all over again, and ready to shatter around him. He wouldn't mind picking up those pieces, though.

"Give me it, then. *Fucking give me it, Ginevra.* Give it to me again, baby."

Her heart tipped back as his mouth climbed her throat, his tongue striking out to taste every fucking inch of her that he could. He felt like he waited too long for this, and at the same time, he was so fucking weak for giving in.

Still, he wasn't stopping.

He was taking all he could.

Every bit she gave.

He was *keeping it*.

"Almost," she whined, eyes flying wide to nail into him as he pounded into her. "*Almost, Corrado.*"

Oh, fuck.

There was something in her voice, and her stare. Something in the way she moved against him seeking to get herself off like she knew what she fucking wanted, and she didn't care if she used him to get it, really lit him on fire. It made him want to get off as she moaned and panted against him for more.

The salt on her skin skimmed his lips with every word, each fucking breath. Her thighs held him tight, her back moving against the soft sheets with his own rhythm as her fingernails dug into his sides to find purchase. She was *wild*, then, hair fanning through his fingers and spilling to the bed. Her lips found the stubble on his throat, and then her teeth found his jaw. All those noises of hers muffled against the trembling of his overheated skin.

And yet, he could still hear what she said.

Felt it in his bones.

"Please, please, *please.*"

His hand on her trim waist glided over smooth, damp skin that shivered from his touch until his thumb grazed her clit between their tightly grinding bodies. He swiped at her clit once, then twice, pressing harder the third to really make her scream.

And that's when she came.

It was a beautiful sight.

He leaned back a bit just to watch it all unravel for her, too. The way her pussy was stretched full of him, her arousal soaking his cock as it slid out of her before slamming back in to feel those inner muscles of hers clenching around him. How her body trembled against the bed, her hands falling from his sides to fist into the sheets.

The muscles in her throat flexed and tensed with the shout of his name that fell from pinked, quivering lips.

And what a sound that was.

All throaty.

Broken.

High.

As fast as he'd come up to watch that sight, and sear it

into his memories so it wasn't one he would soon forget, he fell back into her. His arm locked around her back, and his other found steadiness against her vibrating thigh. He worked his body harder against hers, soaking in every second of her orgasm as he came closer and closer to his own.

"Come," he heard her mumbled. "Fucking *come*."

It sounded so *needy*.

So desperate.

He just wanted to give it to her.

Soon, the thrusts of his came to a still with one final flex of his hips as he spilled into latex while he panted against Ginevra's heartbeat thrumming fast like a hummingbird's wings at her throat. He couldn't make sense of anything— couldn't *speak* beyond the dark cusses that fought their way past his lips.

"Fuck, fuck ... *fuck*."

It was blinding.

That release?

Everything he needed.

And it changed everything.

Of that, he was most sure.

Ginevra dragged in lungful after lungful of air as she stared at the ceiling, and he stared at her profile. "Oh, my God."

"Stay in my bed tonight," was all he could think to say. "Sleep here with me. *Be here with me.*"

Because if he couldn't have one, then he needed the other.

She blinked. "Okay."

Corrado stared out the window of the office as he fixed the phone in his hands simply by touch alone. He didn't look down to check what pieces he was snapping back together. The battery, and the back. Holding the phone, he pressed the button on the side until he felt it vibrate against his palm.

Turned on.

He swore it was muscle memory that allowed him to swipe his thumb across the screen, pulling up the messenger app, and hitting the most frequent contact at the top. *Alessio.*

He was too busy watching his reflection in the window of the office because he thought part of him didn't recognize the man staring back in the glare of the city below. The shape of his body, and the way his undone pants rested low on his hips were all the same.

The face?

Identical.

But in his eyes, something was different.

He didn't know what to do with that.

Corrado glanced away from the reflection, not wanting to indulge those thoughts more than he already had, he peeked over his shoulder at the dark doorway of the office. Just down the hallway, sleeping in his bed, was a woman who, a month and a day ago, had meant less than nothing to him and his life.

He'd never known she existed.

But now that he did?

Corrado knew nothing would be the same.

He'd done this once.

Except it couldn't be as simple as it once was where there was now a *before,* and an *after.* A time when Alessio and Corrado were them before Ginevra, and this … what they had become after her. What came next would be now, but he didn't know what that was, or what it would look like for them.

The phone still in his hand waiting for him to just do what he had to do, his thumb danced across the screen, keying in a message he knew would be received, but that he couldn't predict the impact when it was delivered. He poured over the four words, taking them in until the black letters began to bleed together. And yet, even had he hesitated to send the text, he never once considered *not* sending it.

It was just a matter of *doing it*.

He sent the message.

As the phone beeped, and the tiny *delivered* popped up under the message, Corrado let out a breath he hadn't known he was holding. He waited longer, still staring at the screen for maybe fifteen seconds before the *delivered* message turned into a *seen* one.

I slept with her, he'd written.

Alessio needed to know, whether that was what he wanted or was waiting for ... whether he was planned on staying away another week or coming back right this minute. It didn't matter, this wasn't about *that*, it was about the truth.

The loyalty.

The thing Corrado had already broken and failed to give Les. He didn't think the message would fix what he'd done—not by a long shot, really. Still, it was a step forward. A reminder that, he knew what he had done.

He was so fucking sorry.

It was all he could offer Alessio because he no longer knew what to do; he didn't think there was any right or wrong way to move forward here, and he couldn't decide alone. There were now two other people he'd dragged into this mess that had to make their choices, too.

The text was one.

The rest was in God's hands.

Or rather, Alessio's.

Corrado lifted his stare, and watched the lights of the city below dance as he thought, *well, what happens now?*

BETHANY-KRIS

Bethany-Kris is a Canadian author, lover of much, and mother to four young sons, two cats, and three dogs. A small town in Eastern Canada where she was born and raised is where she has always called home. With her boys under her feet, a snuggling cat, barking dogs, and a spouse calling over his shoulder, she is nearly always writing something ... when she can find the time.

Find Bethany-Kris at her:
www.bethanykris.com

Sign up to Bethany-Kris's New Release Newsletter here:
eepurl.com/bf9lzD

BOOKS BY BETHANY-KRIS

The Guzzi Legacy

Corrado

Alessio

Chris

Beni

Bene

Marcus

Renzo + Lucia

Privilege

Harbor

Contempt

Andino + Haven

Duty

Vow

John + Siena

Loyalty

Disgrace

Cross + Catherine

Always

Revere

Unruly

The Companion

Naz & Roz

Guzzi Duet

Unraveled, Book One

Entangled, Book Two

DeLuca Duet

Waste of Worth: Part One

Worth of Waste: Part Two

Donati Bloodlines

Thin Lies

Thin Lines

Thin Lives

Behind the Bloodlines

The Complete Trilogy

Filthy Marcellos

Antony

Lucian

Giovanni

Dante

Legacy

A Very Marcello Christmas

The Complete Collection

Seasons of Betrayal

Where the Sun Hides

Where the Snow Falls

Where the Wind Whispers

Seasons: The Complete Seasons of Betrayal Series

Gun Moll Trilogy

Gun Moll

Gangster Moll

Madame Moll

The Chicago War

Deathless & Divided

Reckless & Ruined

Scarless & Sacred

Breathless & Bloodstained

The Complete Series

Maldives & Mistletoe

The Russian Guns

The Arrangement

The Life

The Score

Demyan & Ana

Shattered

The Jersey Vignettes

Standalone Titles

Dirty Pool

Effortless

Inflict

Cozen

Captivated

Dishonored

Find more on Bethany-Kris's website at www.bethanykris.com.